Sanctuary

More From Darkhouse Books:

SANCTUARY

A Collection of Poetry and Prose

Edited by Susannah Carlson and Peter Bradbury

DARKHOUSE BOOKS

Niles, California

"God! Help me survive amid this mortal love"
(Russian grafitti on the cover photo)

TABLE OF CONTENTS

Introduction
by Susannah Carlson, Editor

WHEN WE STARTED this project eight months ago, we had no way of knowing how bad things would get or how timely the final product would be. The idea of sanctuary has become a flashpoint. Empathy and kindness seem, on the surface, to have taken a backseat to hatred, nationalism, and fear. Yet, while some spew hatred, still more speak out on behalf of kindness. Such scenarios are playing out around the world, as war and economic and environmental pressures have driven people from their homes, seeking sanctuary and too often being turned away or worse.

The fifty pieces you find here were gleaned from over 700 submissions. They explore the concept of sanctuary from angles direct and oblique, political and comical, religious and secular.

Some approach the sanctuary itself, the structure or the institution. Nancy Cook's two stories, *Illuminations and Illusions* and *The Afterlife,* were written during a residency in a 19th century insane asylum, the stories pulled from old newspapers and brought to life in her deft prose. Several pieces deal with shelters, both animal and human. Leslie Muzingo's story, *Heroes on the Ceiling,* and Joyce Kryzak's essay, *In the Whispering Breezes,* explore the experience of adults and children at battered women's shelters, while Jennifer Stuart's story, *House for Girls,* introduces us to youthful victims of human trafficking, and Gayla Mills's essay, *Becoming Human,* brings us inside an animal shelter and the heart of one who works there.

Other authors approached sanctuary from the point of view of those who seek it: refugees and escapees of both the innocent and the criminal kind, sometimes blurring the lines between. Michelle S. Myers's essay, *Communion on the Road,* relates her experience escorting "barely documented" Central American asylum seekers to submit their applications, and Jennifer Stuart's story, *The Other Side,* gives us a moment in the life of one such refugee on the first steps of her journey to America. Caroline Taylor's story *Creature of Habit,* Charlotte Platt's, *Claim Sanctuary,* and John M. Floyd's, *The Blue Delta,* tell the stories of fugitives whose quest for sanctuary have very different ends, while Jesse Falzoi's story, *With Every Thought,* tells of a bittersweet experience housing a Syrian family before they move on to their new lives.

Several pieces are harder to pin down, but the concept is still there. Gina Grande's flash piece, *Drag,* explores the safety to be found in physical self-transformation, while Scott Archer Jones's story, *Contentment,* introduces us to an aging hedonist who seeks comfort in the hand of a friend, and Sage Kalmus's story, *The First Lo'ihian,* places one young man's sanctuary 50,000 years in his future, on an island that today is just beginning to be born. Ed McCourt's essay, *What We Leave on the Curb,* finds solace in the face of death, in the rebirth of a bicycle, while a physician-priest seeks sanctuary in the bottle in Nick Bouchard's story, *Father Pearson's Last Day.*

It's a cold and disquieting world out there. I hope you find some comfort in these pages and will offer the same to any strangers who show up at your checkpoints or wash up on your shore.

—S.C., June 2018
Sunnyvale, California

Introduction

by Peter Bradbury, Poetry Editor

THE NEED FOR SANCTUARY has increased dramatically in recent years. As a concept it crosses the barriers of religion and politics. Once, sanctuary resided in a specific place: a church or temple, a safe house, a country, or somewhere put aside for threatened or abused animals. The word originated in medieval Europe when, under the laws of the Church, fugitives were immune from capture in certain holy places (Latin *sanctuarium* = holy place). But over time the meaning has become more metaphorical and more general. The fugitive has become the refugee. The idea of sanctuary has become the idea of escape to safety or into solitude. With it comes peace, perhaps freedom. It was in the late 1800s that the word came to describe a place of refuge for non-human animals, particularly wild animals, and the term 'animal sanctuary' now slips off the tongue with ease.

For much of its history the United States has included sanctuary as part of its shared destiny. It became home for people escaping the persecution and violence, the economic inequalities, of anywhere else in the world:

> ... Give me your tired, your poor,
> Your huddled masses yearning to breathe free,
> The wretched refuse of your teeming shore.
> Send these, the homeless, tempest-tost to me,
> I lift my lamp beside the golden door!

America was home to the homeless. But history shows that the brave aspiration of Emma Lazarus' sonnet, enshrined on a plaque at the foot of the Statue of Liberty, has eroded. We have entered one of the bloodiest periods in history, and it has become apparent that there is no place on Earth, no country, no building that is safe. In America, those who came to these shores hungry and alien and somehow made it, now wish to shut and lock the gates.

The poems in this anthology reflect the erosion of physical sanctuary, the cruel ways in which hope can be dashed by reality. In *Binate*, Gabriella T. Rieger writes about the apartheid that has emerged in Jerusalem. Atar Hadari *(A Knife in the Hand)* writes with the anger of Ariel Sharon's mother when she realized what Israel was doing to her European aspirations. The poets whose work appears in this anthology—and there were hundreds of submissions—have found distinctive, often subtle ways to approach sanctuary. Their work is highly personal while being at the same time universally true. With few exceptions they write about sanctuary as, at a fundamental level, a place in the mind. Or not even a place. Sometimes a feeling, perhaps a thought, an escape. A retreat. And where they see the end of sanctuary, the scent of threat and danger, they seek solace, that dream of beauty at the least beautiful of times.

For Emily Vizzo, sanctuary is resolution, when the breakable finally breaks; for Kathleen McClung, it's an imagined place in the world, a girl pitching a baseball game; for Aileen Bassis, it's the inner vibration that guides a pigeon to her home. And for Laura Foley, it's music, in this case the sound of a piano played by her son.

Where sanctuary is still located in space, it is connected to memory, and it is fleeting. In Alice Morris' poem *After My Mother Has Been Attacked…* ancestral grounds are connected to the idea of home, a place from which she has been dispossessed and to which she might return. In *Ritual* Bernardine (Dine) Watson asks, "Who knew… that my broken heart would one day seek its healing / in the places I knew first and best"? And in Gabriella T. Rieger's *Solastalgia* it is continuity in a changing landscape: "The Italian restaurant on La Salle is still there. And with it, / the angles of your frame through my camera lens."

Above all, in these poems, sanctuary is something we make ourselves. In Jory Mickelson's *Sanctuary with Internment Camp and Shrinking Glacier* a wildlife refuge shares space with an internment camp from WWII, and what unites them is the woman's camera, returned at last: her ability to make images and memory. Aileen Bassis finds sanctuary in the ability to draw her own reality, to create home through mind and body.

Of course, poetry itself—well, writing really—is sanctuary. In a world where the surface shifts and the right to be human is something we have to fight for, with no guarantee of success, words and images are a reality we can create and live in, and through them we have the possibility of finding truth. The poems in this anthology all bring a depth and breadth of thought and feeling to our search for truth— sanctuary itself—and to our search for a place, a memory, a state of mind where we feel free and safe.

It is itself a relief, a haven, to consider how the versatility of the creative spirit can shape what otherwise is no more than dream.

—P. B., June 2018
San Francisco, California

Foundling

by Charlotte M. Porter

WE ARIZONA SHEEP FARMERS are people of few words. We travel dirt roads, passages of habit, not county planning. Many lack names or numbers, even on maps. Yet, we know the way home, the pitfalls and seasonal hazards. Raising sheep can resign a person to fate. The large loom of life and death weaves days in a run-on pattern. But something larger is always out there—dog packs, poisoned water, poachers. Unexplained loss toughens sheep herders, but also makes us soft. Nothing is sweeter than the bleat of a newborn lamb in lands we hymnbook hopefuls call grange. We welcome arrival as a new center of the world.

With grazing rights west of the Four Corners, me and Toff keep our herds on a hanky of the Kaibab National Forest rubbing up against the Navajo Nation. Out here, forest is a strange word—a federal term with much fine print. Stony hunks of fossil wood scatter a petrified forest across the desert floor. Lick them, and you feel the grain and sniff the ancient odor. As for real forests, bare tops of wooded mountains poke above the tree line. The valleys at lower elevations are rough runs of juniper, interrupted by balds and scruffy plants on nobody's radar. That's the vegetation our sheep eat.

Some years ago, Toff, a childless man in his middle years, walked in the door of our cabin with a bundle wrapped in his coat. I thought he was carrying an early lamb, an orphan for me to care for. We always keep ewe's milk on hand for this purpose.

No, cradled in Toff's arms was an infant.

Here, Tippi, he said. You find out.

Taking the bundle, I realized he hadn't inspected the privates the way he did with lambs. A girl, I announced.

The dog found her, Toff said, Jip did, near the fifth stop-gap. Wearing nothing more than a diaper, wudda froze to death. I mighta run her over.

I nodded, not needing his excuses to cradle this child.

We hunkered in for the late winter snows that grey these parts and smudge in the desert shadows. Baby Babette grew hardy on ewe's milk. Word gets around even in the outlands, and people were amazed a couple our age had a big fat healthy baby, but they minded their own beeswax.

Let 'em guess, said Toff, and we laughed, softly rocking Babette to sleep.

Come spring, roads to the two branches of 64 cleared, and Toff got busy checking on lambs and ear tags. Weekends, we sheared the bushiest wethers.

The child was slow to sit up, but she had great lungs. Our cabin sounded like a dovecot. Babette would hold my finger and coo louder than a flock of pigeons. That fall, later than most, she was crawling. Toff refitted a sheep sling as make-do car seat, and Babette rode around with us in the truck. Her face brightened during these dusty trips to the gas station and convenience store. Tourist books talk up the Painted Desert, but one gas sign shows more color than our region boasts in a year. Not to mention the billboards with spiffy hair, good teeth, and salon tans—not the sunbaked surfaces Toff and I called skin.

TV shrinker Doctor Phil deserves our story, Toff joked. With talking points on the benefits of sheep's milk and *baa*.

Who would the doctor bring in as foundling expert, I wondered, a gumshoe or PBS scholar blowing lyric plots about shepherds? Yes, poor as we were, we watched highbrow programs about olden times.

Sitting in the porch swing one summer morning, Toff and I nursed our coffee cups and watched a speeding dually on the road below.

Raising Cain, all that dust, like there's not enough, I said, running my finger along the railing.

Driving like that, must be somebody new to these parts, said Toff.

He was always the pensive one, the thinker.

The dust snake came in closer and closer and stopped out front. We have serious dogs—all sheep keepers do—but they did not bark at the man who climbed out of the spiffy lavender F-350 pickup truck. No, they fawned at his feet. The man snapped his fingers, and fierce Jip went silly as a stunt dog and rolled over.

Toff, puzzled, stood up. Sensing trouble, I took the coffeepot inside, checked on Babette, and returned to the porch.

The man looked slick as lanolin in his new jeans, pressed plaid shirt, and TV kerchief. He smiled my way and tipped his white cowboy hat like he was casting us magic sparkles—pearls to swine. Then, he leaned in and cocked his head. Inside, Babette was cooing full flock.

Top of the morning, folks! I'm Beau Versailles, he said, and I've made this special trip to audition Dove Girl. You see, I own Palace Traveling Circus, the only big top from the Great Salt Lake to the mighty Río Grande. My, my, what a range that child has, a unique talent, money in the bank.

Toff and I were dumbstruck.

Coo, coo, coo, Babette belted from within.

We had so few possessions, the cabin created an echo chamber. *Ooco, ooco, cocococo, wowoo.*

Brava, said circus man. Superb that last coo, the ground dove, *Columbina passerina,* a blow-in from the Sonora. And, yes, the tender *cohoo* of the Inca dove, *Scardafella inca,* a tropical delight at visitor centers in our National Parks.

Babette was on an international roll. *Coo coo cooooo…cuck-curoo roo.*

Ah, the spotted Asiatic *Streptopelia chinensis* and ringed turtledove, related *S. risoria,* caged bird of Jacobian literary fame, not to mention

Mia Angelou.

No, I blurted, I want something better for her than circus and poesy.

Do you? Beau Versailles replied. As a kid, I dreamed of becoming an ornithologist, but no money for college. Now, like you, I live with animals. But I make good moolah.

Do you, mister? Good luck and good bye, said Toff, hands on hips.

And that was that.

We both turned heel, stomped across the porch into the cabin, and shut the door. Through the front window, we watched the dogs roll over in a row. We couldn't believe our eyes. Beau Versailles paused on the running board of his fancy truck. With a little broom, he was whisking dust off the hood, now blazing lilac as desert verbena.

He's giving us bumpkins a moment to reconsider, said Toff, clearing his throat.

Pwee ah pwee ah grrk grrk

Song of the whiskey jack, I said.

Can't be, Toff said, wrong time of year for those thieving jays.

Must be circus man whistling for a mate.

More like a drink, one for the road, replied Toff.

We laughed and raised two tin cups of cold coffee.

Babette could now manage a few syllables, *curio,* as in Curious George, the TV cartoon monkey. Or, maybe as a rhyme with Cheerios, her favorite cold cereal. From a *National Geographic* special about doves, she picked up *passerine*—as in flocks passing over. The word made me think of the Bible.

Circus man apparently groused at the nearest motor court, a run-down motel on the outskirts of Flagstaff, and our obscure dovecot received more visitors. A couple of weeks later, we were on the porch combing wool. In the distance, a vehicle, little more than a speck, was fast approaching.

No dust, Toff said. Must be the Law.

I held my breath, fearful for the foundling.

Sure enough. At the junction with our roadway, big colored lights began to spin to the siren's wail. The dogs packed up, raised the hair on their backs, and howled. Toff took a deep breath and hitched up his pants.

How to hide Babette? I asked. She's noisy.

No point. Signs of her everywhere, said Toff, gesturing toward the child's TV perch on the couch.

The telltale fanny dent was too small even for our sorry butts, and I'd darned funny faces on Toff's old socks, turning the lot of them into curio Curious George. How to explain a pile of monkey socks as mended footwear for a grown man?

I put down my comb, shook wool balls from my apron, and went inside. I'd already mopped the floors and tidied up the bedroom and play mat. I checked on Babette and closed the bedroom door partway. Two figures in uniform and hip holsters approached the porch.

Sir, said the male cop, I'm Sergeant Cooper and this here is Lieutenant Riddle from Children's Services. We're serving you with **AZ Rev Stat 36.335.**

So?

Title 36.335, Arizona Revised Statute, Finding: Foundling. Failure to file, said the big ginger-haired male officer, and he, showed Toff a form. The missus here needs to witness, he added, pointing to me. *¿Usted comprende?* Understand?

I nodded.

Under a paragraph of fine print were a list of questions. We did our best to answer. Using a black ballpoint pen, Lt. Riddle filled in the form with the child's estimated age and approximate race.

Approximate?

Anyone could see Toff was disgusted by the race question. As for *location found,* he replied, Beats me, officer. Ask the dog.

He took the pen signed his name and P. O. box. I signed the witness line. About the date, I asked in slow clear English, then or now?

Don't matter. *No importante.* Leave blank for the agency.

I nodded, and looked over my shoulder. Babette began to cry, and she-cop made fast tracks for the bedroom.

Lt. Riddle had a pleasant face with raven-black hair pulled back under her wide-brimmed hat. Navajo, I figured. Our flocks shared range with those of the Dine—no problem. Sometimes, they had one

5

of our sheep. Other times, we had one of theirs.

Ahéhee', hello, she said, and the child stopped fussing.

Dropping to her knees, the lieutenant walked her fingers up her uniform shirt and began to sing, *Itsy bitsy spider went up the water spout.* Babette gurgled. The lieutenant had a pretty voice. *Down came the rain and washed the spider out.*

I joined in with my finger spider. Babette beamed and walked her itsy bitsy spider up the spout again.

Look at those big-boy cheeks, Lt. Riddle said. Nothing like sheep's milk to bring out good color.

Babette cooed. The lieutenant laughed, and said, My brothers and I grew up with *tsídii,* all kinds of wild birds, the *coo ooh* of the gray dove and the cranky *who cooks for you* of the scrub dove. But the big city beggars, that waddle pigeon and prissy round-tail, they do fine downtown, but not out here.

She was trying to put me at ease. She could see the baby had love, but we both knew the child needed more than a safe bed, sheep's milk, and pile of sock monkeys. I shrugged, and the two cops left without verifying the child's sex or name.

Listen, I said to Toff. Rain.

Wrong time of year, he replied.

Blame Riddle Woman, I said. First Spider, the Navajo superhero, I thought, walking my fingers across Toff's arm.

My mother called a basket a riddle, Toff said, gently cupping my spider in his two warm hands.

About ten days later, Toff was out front, changing the oil on the truck. Tippi, he called to me, come look.

The main road was a cloud of dust.

New to these parts, Toff said, shaking his head, wiping his grimy hands.

A Cadillac pulled in the driveway, drove up to the cabin, reversed and parked. I thought the novelty tag was out of state, Nevada, maybe, but hard to tell with all that dust. The dapper driver opened the door for his passenger, a blonde dish. The two of them in dark designer sunglasses were right out of an ad—she, slim in sundress and flimsy sandals, he, cocky in a fancy suit and slick hair.

They frowned and, high-stepping, waved their hands at the dust.

This is the child's mother, the driver announced in a loud voice, as if Toff were deaf.

Says who? said Toff, blocking the front door.

Hey, pal, what kind of guy snatches a baby?

Leave. Now.

No, said the young man, arms across his chest in righteous indignation. My client, a young mom, stopped by the road...

Which road? I blurted. Why?

She placed her baby on a knoll and went into the bush, *err*, ma'am, to use the restroom.

Toff fired back. You telling me she drove out all this way to pee in the bitterbrush?

The man flared his nostrils. Mister, when she came back, her baby was gone, carried off.

Sorry to hear that, said Toff, and bunched up his lips with concern.

Such a sweet little boy, chirped the woman, sensing an in.

Why sure, assured Toff, turning to me. Tippi, hon, go on in, and let's give this pretty lady her baby.

Toff continued, we aren't asking for money, no, just a good life for the child.

You bet, said the lawyer, reaching in his briefcase, handing Toff a brick of bank notes.

On cue, I hastily dressed Babette in a blue tee-shirt and shorts and chopped off her baby braids at the scalp.

The mother was shocked to see the size of the lost boy. The child cooed, and, on cue, the woman cried. Smudged mascara left two dark wet lines on her makeup.

Warrior lawyer wasted no time loading mother and child into the Cadillac. They sped away, as they had arrived, in a cloud of dust.

How could you Toff?

My turn to cry as he placed the cash brick in the kitchen cupboard.

Come on, Tippi, set a spell on the porch swing, he said, taking my hand. Trust me.

I sobbed. Toff fixed his stare on the dust headed northwest.

Twenty minutes passed. The blur stopped, then started up.

Relieving themselves, Toff said sarcastically. Leaping from the swing, he grabbed the truck keys, whistled for the dog, and sped off with Jip.

After a long hour, Toff returned with Babette wrapped in his sweatshirt. The child, dirty and thirsty, was missing her shorts.

The dog found her, Toff explained. They dumped her and left her crawling—a little boy turned girl retard of *approximate* race with a plug-ugly haircut.

He tugged my braid, and we both laughed.

That's a difference between Toff and me. I worry. He figures. No one bothered us about **Title 36.335** or the money, and we found a church-run daycare for children with special needs. Babette got on well, shared the toys, learned more words, and saved her birdcalls for home. She still slept in the box with faithful old Jip by her side. We didn't mind. We were content.

Nights are quiet in the desert. Little jumping mice hop and scurry and the lonesome coyote howls, but after a long day, Toff and I crash like logs. One night, we woke to an awful ruckus. Jip was standing by the window and barking. Birds were scratching at the glass, landing on the metal roof by thousands, pecking at the juniper soffits. Then, they were gone.

Silence. Eerie silence. Dread.

Jip whined.

I clutched Toff's arm. We both knew Babette had left us, passed over in the commotion.

Once in a while, Toff stands on the porch and coos like a mourning dove.

Keeping in voice, he explains.

Meaning keeping a stiff upper lip. He also keeps the best pup of the litter housebroke. Just in case.

Thing is, Toff says, old Jip, now, she's too cripple to track. But the sun won't rise if that dog don't sniff about the bedroom.

Searching for the foundling, I think. Well, in our heart of hearts, who isn't?

Contentment

by Scott Archer Jones

I, JOSEPH, am king of all I survey. The steam roils off the water and into the dry crisp air over the village, anointing my subjects like incense. I loll back, silver hair streaming from my temples. They always say that I look like Leonard Bernstein. The principal difference is that I am tone deaf, and he is dead.

It's been a perfect day for me, so far. My contentment stretches out before me. I turned sixty-eight last week and the proper number of people paid obeisance—this I remembered at the moment of awakening. The market opened up in New York, rendering life even easier. I arose at seven and shaved away all my body hair, taking due care with the razor. I then drove here to the gym.

After the tanning bed, I visited with Becky of the Black Tights and attended a spin class, followed by the easy version of water aerobics. Now, here in the hot tub float three of my friends and a ravishing stranger. I recline in the hot water, sense the morning's strain of body maintenance melt into liquid magic and into camaraderie, flawed as it is. We all paid the price, spent our hour or more panting and heaving. In that shaky, ragged feeling from the workouts, we'd retreated from the fitness center to our hot tub outside. To my regret, our stranger rises up, water cascading from her hair and body, and in the twenty-degree weather, flip-flops for the door. She's quite young, about forty-five, and I undergo that stirring I call the Viagra Aftershock. I've felt it several times this morning.

Across from me sits my old friend, Carl. Besides being the best orthodontist in Taos, he is the original comb-over man. I've stared at that comb-over for twenty-five years. Now though, it has parted from his scalp and flies away as a crumpled up wing, out over his left ear, angling off toward the Taos Mountain that looms above us. The Viagra and my hypertension medicine make a potent mix, and they have improved my fantasy life—the drugs help me see his thoughts.

A cartoon text balloon forms over Carl's head. It reads, 'Just this once.'

Carl's voice comes through the steam. "Let's troop over to the Plaza Café after we shower. I want a five-thousand-calorie salad and a pinot grigio." The bubble flashes 'Bacon, cheese—lots of cheese.'

I count nods of assent all around. I announce, "And so it shall be."

Beside me, my Egyptian beauty Noha stirs, irritated by my patronizing tone. Her thought balloon reads, 'Really, Joseph. Shut up.' She perches upon my right hand as I drape my arm around behind her. Her delicious bottom presses up against my palm. She is a full and charming woman, with beautiful skin and black hair, long and luxurious. Her eyes are huge and brown. I feel her weight shift as she leans forward and her thigh presses into mine. Noha is our cougar. We hear of all of her encounters, real and imagined, with the young men that she—well—hunts.

"Philip was my trainer this morning. We did lunges on the half ball. Each time, as I moved from the floor onto the ball, you know," and she glances over at me and flares her eyes. They are enchanting eyes, like fireworks. "He'd steady me on each lunge. At first, he gripped my waist, but then he moved to my knee, to keep me from drifting.

At least, he started at my knee. By the end, his hands had moved up my leg—just below, nearly there. I became all flushed. He's so strong."

I say, "Noha, they are always strong, or you wouldn't be interested." She squirms just that little bit and my loins tingle. I have had that ample plump dessert—and I would go back for more.

"Yes, Joseph. You're not jealous of youth, are you?" Her bubble indicates, 'Time for another face lift, my friend.'

"Unlikely, sweetheart. They have stamina, but I have guile. They have a certain charm—not to mention supple and unwrinkled skin. But I have a true appreciation and understanding of women."

Mara, the fourth friend in the hot tub, interrupts us, once again, about her mother. She and Carl are burdened by family, unlike Noha and I. Instead of flying free, they drag their aged parents along behind.

Mara is Irish-fair, and as we say, beat-all-to-hell. Even for seventy, she would be rough and hard—and she's sixty. She had plaited her hair, really iron gray but dyed to its original red, up onto her head, but it has begun to fall in the steam. The balloon over her reads 'I'm twisted off!' She leans over to Noha and touches her knee under the bubbling water. I believe Mara must have been a lesbian, before she gave up sex for bitterness.

"Noha," she says. I watch the bubble spell out, 'My angel.' Mara pauses, a claim for our attention. "Your mother and dad are dead, aren't they?"

"Yes, Mara. You know I flew home to Egypt two years ago, when my mother passed on."

"That's right. Lucky you."

Noha shakes her head, a furrow chasing sadness across her forehead. "Mara, that's cruel. I loved my mother. I miss her every day."

Mara's thought balloon reads, 'Typical.' She snorts, an ugly sound of mockery. "Be glad you got out when you were young. I remember the old joke about life begins when you're forty sleeping with twenty."

We all chuckle for her, but she doesn't want a laugh—she wants a tirade. "I always thought life began when your parents died."

"But Mara," I say. "Your mom lives in a home in Kansas. Surely, she can't be ruining your life from there?"

"She expects a call most every day. And I have to visit, every couple of months."

Carl's bubble displays, 'My turn! My turn!' Carl stutters when he's in a hurry. "My mo mo mom lives over in Arroyo Seco, and it's a lot of work, taking care of the details she can't handle anymore. Wh Wh Who would have believed I'd be babysitting when I turned sixty-three?"

Mara's bubble reads, 'Who gives a shit, Carl.' She ratchets back up. "Mom will live to a hundred and ten. She looks like it already."

Noha tries to defuse the so-unpleasant rant, "It's only natural, Mara. They took care of us. So, we take care of them."

"No, it's unnatural. Old people should croak in their late seventies, not hang on-and-on ruining our glory times. All those drugs and treatments, they drag it all out. It's just pathetic, that's what it is, a horror." Mara's cartoon bubble shows, 'I could kill the old bitch.'

I think, who wouldn't hold on to the last bitter second? A bed you're dying in is better than the casket on the other side. I say, "Mara, it's not that much of your time. You have a great life here with us and I don't think you miss much. With a butched-up body like yours, you'll outlast us all, much less your mother. Don't worry so much about it."

She says with raised eyebrows, "Why thank you, Joseph. That makes me feel all better." The balloon reads, 'Screw you, you old lecher.'

"You'll see, darling," says our delectable Noha. "This weekend will be our usual round, as Joseph says, of parties and laughter. I promise you at least a good meal and lots of wine." I see her bubble waver up over her head, half-formed, murmuring, 'A long afternoon with my trainer. A private workout.'

Carl heaves himself up by grasping my hand and jerking. Water cascades from his meager shoulders and off his pendulous belly. His balloon reads, 'You'll be dead in a month.' My mouth drops. He shakes his head over me, dripping down into my iconic face.

He sloshes to the tub edge, grabs his towel. "Mara, I promise you a drink right now. Come with me to the Café and we'll eat spinach salad with fried cheese croutons, with sliced egg and hot bacon dressing. We can even split an order of truffle fries. That and a margarita will hold the Living Dead at bay."

I stand, turn for my towel. The wind at twenty degrees cuts

through me. I shiver like the damned.

It starts slow, a perception of fullness, a distension of the belly. I get so the wine doesn't work—I experience nausea after, and sugary desserts give me intense diarrhea. My back hurts. She hovers across from me, my doctor. She wears a new perfume—its high-dollar scent wafting toward me. But I don't care. Not today. "Okay, Joan, I can take it. Is it a brain tumor?" My ancient joke.

She flashes me that beautiful smile, the one so nice to wake up to. "Joseph, you wouldn't be peeking down my lab coat and blouse if it were a brain tumor. However, it's definitely something. I don't like your weight loss—I know you think you worked off those love handles by yourself, but your legs and arms look, well, spindly to me. Far too thin." A cartoon forms over her head, 'You look like shit.'

"Then I shall return to lifting weights and guzzling growth inducers, dear. I shall bulk up enough to please you."

She ducks her head to the paperwork. "And your blood work isn't right. You're hyperglycemic, with some ketone buildup in your urine. I'd swear you were diabetic if you had any history of smoking and obesity. Then there's that back pain."

"Admit it, Joannie. You're puzzled. A beautiful mind in a beautiful body, but once again I baffle you."

She chuckles, but she does it for show. "I'll write you a referral. I want you to see an old classmate of mine in Santa Fe—he's the best. He'll order the workup, and we'll find out what we're dealing with. I'll call ahead—I want you in quick." Her bubble pops up, 'Cancer. It's always cancer.'

I am bloody cold lying here in this hospital bed. Off and on for two weeks they have scanned me, probed my orifices, inquired about the health of my sphincters. They have whittled all of my dignity away. Now they have thrust a hollow sword into my back, through my intestine, and into a mass the CAT scan detected and the MRI paints like a bird's nest in violet hues. I have a foreign body lodged within me, a frightening plague of my own cells.

Mara sits beside me. She has driven down from Taos, a two-hour journey, by herself. She actually appears to care. At least she has all the right behaviors. My cartoon bubbles have failed me, so I don't know what she really thinks. Probably ruined by the extra drugs.

She hitches forward in her chair. Now I will have to suffer through the explanations. "How big's the mass, Joseph?" She appears distraught—amusing.

"Oh, the size of an orange. Perhaps a grapefruit by today. Of course, it is not a simple round thing. Rather messy, tangled up with my pancreas. And gut."

Her eyebrows arch and her pupils dilate. "Pancreas!" The bitch already knows, from Noha, but we must pretend.

"Yes, Mara, we all know about pancreatic cancer. That's why they thrust that huge, painful needle into me." I hold up my hands, eighteen inches apart. "A monster."

Ridiculous, playing the role, she nods. "Biopsy. You're taking it okay."

I know different. I am a little man inside my godlike head, screaming away. My smart phone delivered the web-page news days ago. Only a one-in-four chance to live a year. I summon a smile—it feels plastic on my face. I work harder, try for sincerity. "I am less worried than you think. I've always had luck on my side."

She leans forward to take my hand. "I'm sure it'll all work out. How long before they get the results?" Her red hair floats forward across my arm. Ghostly.

Her kindness makes me want to smash at her, and I would too, if I were not so tired. At least with unkind words. "It's about a week. But they will peer at it through the microscope before it goes off to the lab. That should tell them something."

"And then you'll know."

I try on the condescending grin. Silly woman. "Oh, no. They won't tell me. If they were wrong and it's not malignant, they would have to explain later. And I would sue for mental anguish."

"Surely not. They'll tell you."

My turn to pat her hand. I know the conventions. "I have become a cog in the machine, Mara." The little screaming man is louder now—I think he wants out.

She slips her hand out from under mine. "So, it's a week. Do you stay here?"

"Oh, God no, not here. But I have a room at the Residence Inn. The drive back and forth to Taos, it's too much."

She frowns. Her lips have those vertical trench-marks of a woman who doesn't care what she looks like. "Joseph, you should have told us. We could drive you."

"Hah. You think that I drive myself? No, Carl chauffeurs me. But speaking of back and forth…"

"Yes, sweetie?"

"They'll check me out in a couple of hours. Can you give me a lift to the hotel? Drive me back to my modest suite, tuck me into bed for the night?"

I watch her grin, the first genuine thing today. "Why, I believe you are trying to get me in the sack, you old fart."

I can feel the burning in my eyes. Tears want to form. I hate it when she is right. I ache for a woman's coddling, even a burned-out grizzled lesbo's. At least a distraction.

No chemo, no radiation, no surgery. Oh, to be Mara's parent, lying in a Kansas nursing home, waiting for my centennial so many years away! Instead I lie in this unimagined terrain—hospice. A morphine-infused wait for the cancer to explode out of my abdomen and vomit across the room. A wait for blood to cascade out of my rectum and float me off the sheets and onto the floor. I hear a skritching in my ears, like dog's claws on the linoleum. It is my anger.

Her head eases round the door, hesitant. Noha is still the most beautiful woman I have ever taken to bed. But now, when I see her, I see what I will lose.

"Are you awake?"

She, among all, still deserves a smile from me. "Come in, come in. You'll relieve this continuous tedium."

She leans across the bed, touches her lips to my forehead. I had imagined they would be hot, like her blood, but they are cool and dry. She asks, "Why are you all the way down here in Albuquerque?"

"No one at home, Noha, no one to shuffle my bedpans or stick

15

morphine patches on me. Carl took my cats over to his mother, and the house sits empty."

"Can I watch the place for you, water plants?"

I nod. "That would be lovely, dear. Or better yet, throw them all in the trunk and take them to your place. You can have them."

She tosses both hands up in protest. "Oh, but you'll be coming home."

"Noha, you saw the sign on the building. I'll not be coming home."

Her face collapses like a melting milk chocolate. She didn't have to confront the imminence of death as long as it went unsaid. I have spoiled it.

She dabs at her eyes with a pink Kleenex. "How are they treating you here?"

I see no need to swamp her with complaints about the service, service that cannot matter compared to my Big Event. "They're quite kind. Sit beside me, beloved."

Not in the chair. She perches on the edge of the bed, bundles my hand up in both of hers. She presses her tush up against my side and my glance flickers there before proceeding up past her breasts. She gazes down into my face. "We've had happier times, Joseph."

I clear my throat. "This morning I was thinking about our trip to Florida, five years ago."

She has the sweetest smile. "All that lovely sand and the sun."

I chuckle, for her benefit. "You didn't want to spoil your complexion. Instead you lay under the cabana."

"And you burned bright pink, racing around in the sun."

"But the pain of sunburn did not inhibit my performance."

Now her face flares pink beneath that luscious Egyptian chocolate. "Just at dusk, lying together, the sides of the cabana hanging down to give us privacy."

I remember that the fabric fluttered like wings as the evening breeze drifted in from the ocean, showing me flashes of the hotel, of the beach, of the lights at dusk. As I poised above her. "Dearest Noha."

She is pleased by the memory. She smiles, her full lips open slightly to show white teeth gleaming. "Yes, Joseph. It was so lovely."

"Noha, would you do me a favor? The smallest of favors?"

"What is it, Joseph?"

"Perhaps, one last time. Could you…"

Her eyes open as wide as they can. She stares at me from head to toe. My hair, no doubt sticky and matted, the beard stubble-gray across my cheeks. The gown wrinkled, and perhaps odiferous. Crumpled sheets. The squalor of sickness.

I gaze up into her face. "No, not the full shebang. Just a little manipulation. For old times sakes."

Her forehead crinkles, then clears in a beautiful smoothness. She hops down, whirls to the door, and locks it. Back by my side, she fishes the sheets down, raises the gown. "No catheter? Thank God."

"I should allow a man to thrust a tube up my penis? Not until the very last, my dear."

Using the lotion on the overbed table, she straightens me, rubs in the lubrication, begins her motions. "How wicked you are, Joseph."

I stare at her, the part in her hair, her head dropped, concentrating on me, on this thing we share again. "That is so very nice. It's like we are teenagers in the back of a car."

She raises her face, a grin appearing at the corner of her mouth. "I grew up in Egypt. Father had a chauffeur and we dared not use the backseat."

"Oh, oh, ah." My body contracts, three times. I curl up in the final shudder, and she hesitates, then strokes me a few times more. She catches all of it in her other hand—it pools up and looks like lemon curd. Nothing. I feel nothing, though my body performed the oldest dance. I have ejaculated without an orgasm.

She kisses my forehead again, fishes a tissue out of the box, and wipes her palm. "You scandalous old man. Promise me you won't do this with anyone but me."

"I promise." My voice gags in my throat. I promise to let it go, cast it away from me, not to think about it.

"I can't wait to tell Mara. Or perhaps it should be our secret." She reaches up, strokes my face with the hand that brought me to my sticky end.

I want, I need a moment by myself. "Noha, love. Can you fetch me a cup of ice? My mouth is so dry these days. The nurse's station on the hall will tell you where."

She is so pleased, her face soft and adoring. Some domestic task, after having done the dirty. Taking a Styrofoam cup, she unlocks the door, slips out like a courtesan leaving the chambers of the king.

I stare about the room. Institutional, florescent light eradicating all shadow. A giant TV hung from the ceiling, a black, vacant slab. The side table and the overbed table filled with bedsore ointments, tissues, a box of alcohol swabs, bedpan and urinal, moisturizing wicks for cracked lips, abandoned Styrofoam cups. A litany of objects, my final possessions.

It's been a perfect day for me, so far. My contentment stretches out before me. Unlike Mara, I am not dragged down by paternal constraint. Unlike Carl, no gluttony gnaws at me. Unlike Noha, the need for sexual congress has disappeared. The air conditioning blows down upon me. I feel a cold wind.

Illuminations and Illusions

by Nancy Cook

Fergus Falls News, April, 1903
Local Man Attacks Catholic Rectory, Is Taken to Insane Asylum

      Axel F. became violently insane Monday evening and created quite a disturbance on the Catholic Church premises, breaking the transom door and smashing the storm door of Reverend FW's residence. His hallucination was that he had some cattle in the church and that during the day he had purchased some chains and locks, imagining that he was going to chain up his stock.

      There is a strong current that he was enamored of a young lady of the Catholic faith and that their discussions relating to religious matters tended to mentally unbalance him.

FATHER WESTON WOKE to sounds of chopping and smashing. In his dream, he'd been flying, then suddenly and inexplicably he'd become the victim of an attempted robbery. In horror, as his eyes popped open, Weston saw first his little book of inspirations, clutched in his

19

fingers as if being protected from a robbery that was still and actually in progress. Next he noted the dark outline of the crucifix on the wall near the foot of the bed. Instinctively he crossed himself. Then, just as instinctively, he hastened out of bed because the loud banging persisted, and it was no dream. Someone was trying to break into the rectory.

By the time Father Weston had covered his nightshirt with a cassock and reached the top of the staircase, the clamor had stopped. Below, at the unlit end of the foyer, the front door stood wide open, the upper transom in battered disarray. Mrs. Morganthau, the housekeeper, crouched inside the doorframe, holding a rolling pin aloft. She looked, Father Weston thought, eerily seductive. He could not think what to say or do.

Mrs. Morganthau turned to him.

"It's the dairyman, Axel Falk. He's running toward the church, Father."

"The church?"

"Yes, Father."

"But the man is a Protestant, is he not? A Lutheran." There was trepidation in his voice.

"I don't believe he's armed, Father. But should I go for help?"

"Yes, Mrs. Morganthau, yes," said the priest, recovering from his initial shock. He could surmise from the housekeeper's expression that his comment about the man being a Protestant was foolish. On the other hand, he could not think his fears misplaced. The butchered transom was surely evidence of a violent disposition.

"And knock at the Holmstroms, if you would, Mrs. Morganthau. Tell the brothers I may require their assistance."

Father Weston approached the church with caution. It was Diocesan policy that the doors remain unlocked at all times, so that sinners and lost souls might find a sanctuary whenever the need arose. Weston did not think it the wisest practice, not in this wild, uncivilized place of uneducated Swedish and Norwegian farmers and rough German Protestants. They were not thieves, these people, but they were at times too free with their spooning, and he suspected improper uses of the church at night.

"Yah! Yah! Git now! I'll tan yer hides and with my own hands! Move yer arses! Yah Yah!"

From outside the door, Father Weston could hear Axel Falk's loud rant. At first he thought another man must be in there with Axel, the two men caught up in an argument. Weston heard only one voice, though, leading him to wonder whether Axel's rage might be directed at God. Since the bellowing sounded more like that of a man in the fields than one in discourse with another human or with God, none of this added up to a comfortable conclusion.

Now Axel lowered his tone just a little. "Where for the love of Daisy did I lay those irons?" he mumbled before raising his voice again. "Lock you up I will! These chains will stop you from running."

Father Weston was unnerved by the man's raw hostility, yet his mind remained stuck on the hunch that unbelievers might be using the church for sexual diversions. Chains and Daisy Imhoff, arses and hides, the images were fleeting and unsettling.

"Is he herding his cows in there?" Carl Holmstrom asked. Carl and his two brothers had arrived at the church and had snuck up behind Father Weston without him even noticing.

"His *cows?*" asked Father Weston, now envisioning the Holmstroms' four rather buxom sisters. He had a momentary vision of the sisters huddled in a sixteenth-century barn with the frail and sickly St. Germaine, who'd become a saint by suffering terrible abuse and being forced to sleep with livestock.

"Cattle," said Wilbur Holmstrom. "He thinks he's in the fields."

The Holstrom brothers, Wilbur and Carl, arranged the delusional Axel Falk into a pew with little trouble, while the youngest brother, Curtis, departed for the asylum to request a transport. It was obvious to the Holmstroms that Axel had taken a turn into madness. There was no other explanation for what they'd witnessed. Axel Falk was a literal man, like most of his neighbors, no more capable of conjuring up a herd of cattle from his imagination than of turning straw into gold. Yet there he was, intent on shackling phantom cows with locks and chains he claimed to have purchased in town but did not, in fact, have on hand. What's more, the brothers pointed out, were he not possessed by unnatural spirits, Axel would never have voluntarily entered a Catholic church.

Father Weston, while alarmed by Axel's bizarre behavior, was far from certain that they were dealing with a case of mental illness. In all the confusion, however, and a little awed—even shamed—by the bold action of his burly neighbors, he hadn't been quick enough to formulate and express his opinion before Curtis departed for the hospital. Now, with the older Holmstrom brothers standing by and medics on the way, the specter of actual chains and cattle shunted aside, Weston felt impelled to reclaim some stature.

He'd brought his little book along as a stimulus. But as the mortification had cleared his head, he felt no need to rely on a prop. Not just now. The situation called for a simple injunction.

"Pray with me, Axel," Father Weston implored.

"There's no use in it," said a distressed Axel. "Besides, I got no time for your God."

"There is always time for God."

"But—"

"No buts. The Lord will provide."

The Lord does provide, Weston insisted to himself. Hadn't he been offered this parish far removed from the temptations of city life? A crude place, to be sure, but one with a few compensations. No crowds, for example. Space and opportunity for private reflection. Sky of such a magnitude as to persuade even agnostics of the proximity of heaven. If the older population was too hardened by the environment, there were still plenty of young people who respected words spoken by a man of God, who needed the priest's guidance.

Father Weston started in on the Our Father, a dependable all-Christian standard, but Axel Falk was too distracted to join in. The Holstrom brothers feigned deafness and were no help. So, after he finished reciting the prayer on his own, Weston consulted his little book of inspirations in search of just the right conceit to bring Axel out of his dark mood. The ideal maxim popped out almost immediately: "Jesus is the light. Trust in him." As if on cue, radiance from the rising sun infiltrated the east church windows. The priest was elated. Axel only stared blankly ahead, but, for the moment at least, he was calm. That gave Weston encouragement to go on.

"If you just have faith—"

"Begging your pardon, Father—" Wilbur Holmstrom interjected, and his brother, astonished at the rudeness of the interruption, gave him a swift kick. "Begging your pardon," Wilbur continued in his monotone, ignoring the kick, "but you might like to know that Axel here has suffered a bad blow recently, just this past week, in fact."

"What sort of a blow?" Weston was picturing the sledge hammer lying abandoned on the rectory's front stoop.

"Well, he was enamored of a young lady of the Catholic faith, and you might say that their discussions relating to religious matters mentally unbalanced him."

Father Weston opened his mouth but did not speak. What was the trouble with these simple folk, he wondered. For the third time that month someone was about to blithely dismiss an offer of grace and instead submit to "help" from doctors at the insane asylum on the hill. First there'd been a young merchant of great promise who'd succumbed to drink. And last week it was a woman, new to the area, unmarried and unemployed, whose insanity, according to the papers, could be ascribed to "poverty and worry." But the real problem in all these cases, Weston was certain, was one of licentiousness, which, in his mind, was the equivalent of Godlessness.

"What Wilbur means," said Carl, "is that Axel's young lady left him. That is, he was thinking to be betrothed, but she turned him down."

A castoff. Weston looked at Axel Falk as if for the first time. The little book of inspirations lay open on the priest's lap. He gave it a glance.

"The Lord never gives us more than we can handle, Mr. Falk."

It was good advice for anybody, Catholic or Protestant. Weston thought about the battered transom over at the rectory, and about the troubles he'd had back in Massachusetts. Probably Axel, too, had devils to oppose, to outwit and outrun. That idea gave Weston a certain satisfaction, and without deliberating further on it, he murmured, "God works in mysterious ways."

Axel Falk sized up the priest, disgust in his eyes. The eyes were blue, pale, and though it was cool in the dawn air, two drops of sweat passed over a heart-shaped freckle on the side of Axel's face. A reflection from the stained glass, yellow in color, whisked the young man's cheek. The sight inspired Father Weston to say, "When God closes a door, He opens a window."

Axel closed his blue eyes, his brow furrowed. Father Weston sighed.

❖

Born in Philadelphia, and educated in New England, Father Frederick John Weston had never expected to find himself amidst farmers and lumbermen, stuck in a parish that competed with the Lutheran Church and a state lunatic asylum for souls. But a minor matter and a penitent's indiscretion had induced his superiors to transfer Father Weston to the far reaches of the northern prairie.

Many found the climate here harsh and unforgiving. It was not, however, the climate that Frederick Weston found to be harsh and unforgiving; it was the people. That, he realized, was a cold judgment, coming from a New England man of the cloth. A man who had entered too often into deliberate, skillfully executed sins of immodesty and immoderation. A priest who, arguably, had demanded more severe mortifications than necessary from certain members of his flock as penance for their transgressions. He'd confessed as much. Still, one could say for him, at least, there was a path to redemption, if not love, through the thorny brambles of East Coast Catholic doctrine. Whereas in this wild and open space, sinning was indulged in by the locals like a dive into a sty, the consequences treated as nothing more substantial than icy snowflakes or dry chaff left to blow away on a wind of forgiveness.

Mrs. Morganthau tapped on the priest's shoulder. Without her saying as much, Father Weston understood the asylum transport had arrived. He thought to simply escort young Axel Falk outside to the waiting conveyance, but at the suggestion that they leave the church, Axel grew immediately suspicious.

"What now?" he yelled. "You'd expel me? My faith isn't good enough? My love not worthy? What papist tricks are you playing?"

"No tricks, Axel," Weston said, but he hesitated before saying more. He could not pretend to believe Axel would be helped by hospital professionals.

Mrs. Morganthau picked up Father Weston's reluctance. "Don't you worry yourself, Mr. Falk," she said. "Just rest easy. You look comfortable right where you are. Carl and Wilbur will keep company." She eyed the Holmstrom brothers and they nodded. Axel was mumbling curses, but he sat down.

"Father, why don't you come with me?" said Mrs. Morganthau. "There's some visitors outside you ought to meet."

Weston could hear the Holmstroms speaking in their measured voices as he meekly followed his housekeeper. He could not discern exactly what was being said. Something about crops and a storm expected. Nothing about God or the matters at hand. As if breaking down a rectory door and creating a ruckus over fantasized loose cattle—all somehow set in motion by religious discord—was a passing peccadillo, too trivial to be reckoned with. Dry chaff.

Outside the church, Weston was happy to see Constable Pederson on hand along with the hospital's orderlies. Pederson was a big, soft-hearted man, reputed to have once taken down an ogre who'd been living in the wilds. An exaggeration, of course, but surely the peace officer was capable of handling the likes of Axel Falk. He stood by quietly while Father Weston consulted with the orderlies. The plan, according to one of the men, was to enter the church quietly, and as swiftly as possible, escort Axel to the waiting carriage and thence to the asylum. For a breed so slow in speech, Weston thought, these people certainly made quick decisions.

They all entered the church at once, the two hospital aides, Constable Pederson, Father Weston, Mrs. Morganthau, and Curtis Holmstrom, who'd returned to the scene after fetching the hospital employees. The aides moved with purpose to the pew where Axel sat between Carl and Wilbur while Curtis and Constable Pederson followed a few steps behind. Mrs. Morganthau hung back, wrapping her right arm around Father Weston's left, and using her weight to restrain his forward movement. "Let them do their jobs," she said calmly and quietly.

It didn't take but a moment for Axel to register the presence of other people in the church, and he'd no sooner turned around to look than he jumped from his seat and started to shout. Just as quickly, Carl and Wilbur grabbed one upper arm each and Curtis rushed forward to lay his big hands on Axel's shoulders. The two hospital orderlies whipped out a long drape of white rubbery sheeting which they used to hogtie Axel as if they were all part of some strange branding affair. The peace officer quietly slipped into the shadows, out of Axel's sight.

In spite of himself, Father Weston found the whole thing quite stimulating. "It's ironic, isn't it?" he whispered to Mrs. Morganthau, squeezing the hand that grasped his elbow. "This man, taken down like a bull at a rodeo, when it was he who had illusions of cattle being here in God's house."

Mrs. Morganthau did not reply.

"And there is something about being arrested in such a manner, something so, I don't know..."

He had in mind to say "sexual," or maybe "sensuous," but he would never speak such words out loud.

"Father, you forget yourself," said Mrs. Morganthau, as if the priest had finished his sentence, and she released his arm.

At the carriage, the priest thanked the asylum aides and the Holmstrom brothers. Despite his own jitters, Weston did his best to console Axel, who was securely restrained inside the rig. Wrapped in the straitjacket, Axel was like an alien beast, soon to be cached away in the sterile recesses of a man-made purgatory, disguised as a problem that could be fixed by medical science.

"Everything happens for a reason," Father Weston repeated several times. It was what his superiors had said to him when he'd been exiled to this midwestern outpost. At the time, he'd thought it an outrageous insult, but just now he found it oddly comforting.

As the rig moved off, Constable Pederson sidled up alongside the priest.

"Axel might appreciate you being there, at the asylum, when they try to check him in," he said. When Weston didn't immediately reply, Pederson added, "Seems funny, but sometimes it's the big, strong men need a word of comfort when their hearts get broke."

Father Weston nodded. Pederson was probably right. He didn't mind going over to the mental hospital. High on the hill overlooking farmland and pasture, it was a peaceful place, outdoors at least. The center of the main building rose up like a cathedral bell tower. Balancing on either side of that were two rounded watch towers, which sprouted four-story batwings extending for hundreds of yards behind. Constructed in pale gold and cream and infused with light from a plethora of enormous windows, the place had the aura of a benevolent castle, protected from earthly strife and proclaiming safety like a lighthouse on the rocky coast.

Father Weston asked the Holmstrom brothers to hitch up his wagon, and offered to drop them off at their homestead door. They gladly complied. Having left home before breakfast, their big appetites welcomed the chance to get back by the fastest means available.

En route, remembering what the constable had said, Weston thought to ask after the young woman, the Catholic girl who had refused Axel's proposal of marriage.

"Maudie Borg," said Curtis. "You want for me to tell her about Axel?"

"Borg?"

"Yes, that's right."

"A redhead."

"You could say so, that ginger kind of blonde."

Weston knew well who she was. She made her confession every Saturday. Very devout. Intelligent. Beautiful in a fragile kind of way. Of course she had refused Axel Falk's proposal, the priest thought. Of course she could not be expected to make a match with a man whose illusions, it was easy to see, were so simple. There were many such cases to be found in *The Lives of the Saints*, of women who preferred a relationship with God over relations with men. St. Lucy, for instance, stood her ground when threatened with a life of prostitution if she did not consent to marriage. St. Agatha endured a month in a brothel, and later her breasts were crushed and cut off, yet she remained true to her vow of chastity. There was St. Agnes, of course, and St. Barbara.

Susanna, Margaret, Katherine, Juliana. They all died, were martyred for their purity.

Well, clearly it was God's will that Axel Falk had wandered into Father Weston's remote parish church. It was God's will for the man to lose his reason. And God must have intended for Axel to be handed into the custody of white-coated caretakers. Still, Miss Borg would likely have concerns about any injury she may have caused, might even blame herself for Axel's current situation. Her grief and regret, too, had to be part of God's plan.

Weston thought he might yet come to understand the ways of these neighbors in the wilderness.

"Please don't say anything to her. She's likely to take it hard. I think I know how best to approach her."

The following Sunday, Father Weston delivered a handwritten note into Maudie Borg's hand after services. He'd spent an entire afternoon combing through his little book of inspirations before settling on just the right composition. First he'd been drawn to "God is all wise, we must yield to His will," but feared it was too vigorous a sentiment under the circumstances. Instead he opted for softer phrasing, more appropriate to addressing a young Christian woman who was troubled, yet capable of rising above the literal. "God forgives all," the message began. Next, he'd written, "The Lord helps those who help themselves." Finally, Father Weston had added a favorite sentence on the theme of redemption: "Remember what Jesus told the sinner, 'Truly, I tell you, this day will I see you in paradise.'"

Grandmaster Clint Eastwood's Tour of Holy Places

by Max Sparber

BECAUSE AMERICA did not have any holy places, Reuben decided to declare some.

He quit his job at the Family Dollar store and fasted for thirty days, during which time he made himself a cilice.

He refrained from sexual congress, which wasn't hard for him. He had not enjoyed sexual congress in four years, since an ex took pity at a birthday party for a mutual friend.

At first, he refrained from drinking alcoholic beverages, but that proved too hard, so he reversed his position and consumed alcoholic beverages at a prolific rate. Corona. Bourbon. Tequila. Tequila most of all, and a lot of it.

Sometimes one misunderstands the will of God at first, and then, through tribulation, His will becomes clear. And His will was this: Drink!

Joyce was the first to see Reuben when he emerged from his

preparation, when he was now Grandmaster Clint Eastwood the Six Times World Champion on the Wheels of Steel, Who Would One Day be a Saint.

She saw an emaciated man in a month-long growth of beard, wearing a hair shirt, a sombrero, and nothing else, the bell end of his penis just visible from beneath the shirt, red and inflamed from 30 days of chronic masturbation.

Grandmaster Clint Eastwood presented her with his photocopied manifesto, but only after he had chased her down and cornered her in a strip mall. His manifesto read as follows:

The TIME is on us NOW this is as it was FORETOLD read the books watch the movies we have been TOLD THIS DAY WOULD COME HALLELUJAH and come it has with FLASHES with ROARS with THUNDERCLAPS with TRIALS with TRIBULATIONS with FIRE with DUST with RAINSTORMS THAT DROP STINGING SCORPIONS and so it is that the WILL of the GOD or maybe the GODS is upon us there will be NO SANCTUARY so SINK TO YOUR KNEES HEATHENS FALL TO PROSTRATION AND SEND UP YOUR BEGGINGMOST PRAYERS and YOUR GREATFUL-MOST SUPPLICATIONS as you are among the TRULY BLESSED to live in a time when WONDERS WILL BE REVEALED and MIR-ACLES WILL BE SHOWN and THE HEAVENS THEMSELVES WILL PROCLAIM GLORY GLORY GLORY and then the END COME amen.

When Joyce finished reading the manifesto, Grandmaster Clint Eastwood had already moved on, leaving a trail of fallen photocopies behind him like a path for those who might follow. And Joyce thought, is it possible?

It was.

There was much afoot, and the manifesto was right: There was no sanctuary. The Mississippi River caught fire, burning to cinder every city along its path to the Gulf of Mexico. Bemidji was gone. New Boston was ash. Thebes up in smoke. New Orleans an inferno. And the conflagration even took Des Moines, which is not on the

Mississippi River, but the river was spiteful and burned what it wished.

And so it was that Grandmaster Clint Eastwood declared the Mississippi to be a Holy River.

Los Angeles was beset by wolves. They emerged from unexpected places, bursting forth from poolside cabanas and Jack in the Box restaurants, crawling out from under parked Maseratis and running in packs along the Los Angeles River.

At first, they ate only studio executives whose films had grossed less than $400 million the previous year. Then they ate screenwriters who had not written a successful script in five years. Then they went after reality television show stars. At first, Angelenos applauded the wolves, because who wouldn't, but the animals' hunger proved unstoppable, and soon Los Angeles was a wasteland of bleached bones and wolf scat.

And Grandmaster Clint Eastwood declared the Hollywood Sign a Holy Place.

And plagues fell on Dallas. All roads to the city were blocked with armadillo husks, so many husks, where the hell did all those armadillo husks come from? Trucks tried to batter their way through, but the armadillos had leprosy, and it was an especially virulent form, very fast acting, and the truckers fell apart within moments.

Soon, panicked Texans turned to the only thing that gave them comfort, their barbecues, and cooked the only thing remaining, their neighbors. And so, Dallas devoured itself, cannibal eating cannibal, which, had you asked any local, was how they expected to go anyway.

And Grandmaster Clint Eastwood declared the Good Luck Gas Station to be a Holy Place.

And then God or perhaps gods grew especially angry at New York and sent down their worst plague, the plague of bad sushi. All in the city died but for the one chef responsible, who owned what had previously been a pretty hip sake microbrewery in Chelsea. He went mad and fed himself, bit by raw bit, to his goldfish.

And Grandmaster Clint Eastwood declared the Chelsea Hotel to be a Holy Place.

San Francisco simply slid into the bay, and Grandmaster Clint Eastwood was there, and he said it was holy. Spiders emerged from the hair of every citizen of Baltimore, even those without large hair, and they were all stung and all died. And Grandmaster Clint Eastwood was there, and he said it was holy. Every man, woman, and child in Florida overdosed on cocaine, and the street was filled with feasting alligators, but nobody noticed, as they had problems of their own. Nobody noticed but Grandmaster Clint Eastwood, who kept with him a tablet of yellow, lined paper, and he wrote the name of Miami on it, and marked the manner of its death, and he marked it holy.

And so it was that every American city, every American village, every American hamlet, every American town met its end as Grandmaster Clint Eastwood watched and noted in his book.

When it was done, he walked across the ocean to Tokyo and found a city in the midst of its own apocalypse, involving ancient submarines that washed up on shore and spat out rockabillies on motorcycles.

He walked through the chaos to the Imperial Hotel Tokyo, and he went into the Old Imperial Bar. There, in that room, were other prophets and saints, each in their own sackcloths, each with the bell end of their penises exposed, each with their own distinctive hat, each with a lined yellow tablet. All sat and drank, and they spoke to each other.

I say it was a sea god, said Obayana the Nigerian. I say we now enter the time of Giant Squid and Killer Whales, who will move into our cities and turn them into vast aquariums.

How stupid! declared Dakshesh from Patna. It is surely a monkey god. Who else would enjoy such mischief?

It is none other than the devil himself! cried Quando of Brazil. And we have served him, and we will sit at his feet in hell!

Grandmaster Clint Eastwood cleared his throat. All fell silent. And he rose.

It was none other than the God in each of us, he said. And Grandmaster Clint Eastwood took off his cilice. He stood before them naked, and then tore open his chest. And there, inside him, where his heart should have been, was a tiny god, no larger than a worm, perhaps a tequila worm, looking very much like a tequila worm, and, thinking on it, it was a tequila worm.

And the worm god looked out at them and laughed in a tiny voice, really more of a chuckle, and one pitched so high that it was scarcely audible by human ears, although it caused nearby dogs to emerge from their hiding places and bark.

And the god said: Is this how you thought it would end, you men, you prophets? Is this how you imagined the terminus to the reign of men? We will wash you off the lands and start anew with some stranger beast, perhaps turkeys, and we shall rest in their hearts and watch as they grow great, and then we shall kill them all for our amusement. So it has always been, and so it shall be, until our cruel humor is sated, which it never may be.

All assembled bowed and wept, and they called the Old Imperial Bar in the Imperial Hotel Tokyo to be the holiest place of all.

And so the turkeys considered it, although they knew not who had made this building, or why.

Drawing Home

by Aileen Bassis

Four lines make a square
without window or a door.
No way in and no way

out. Can you call this
home? Draw more. Two
lines meet and slant. A roof

perhaps. Do you remember
when you pressed your thumb
against a splinter

to mark that place
with blood, held a fistful
of dirt from your mother's

garden? Remember wind
against your face. Loud bursts
and air filled with wet

and flakes and flesh.
Have you smelled
metal burning?

Ask me about the touch of insect
legs, the spiral screech of birds,
the color of walls, my broken

cups, cracked bowls. There was
a shore where grey-black water
peeled back like skin

and pale foam glimmered hunger.
Gulls were sharp needles pulling
white thread through a cloth sky.

Find a way back for me. Draw
a map, show me where
to turn right or left.

Draw a door, draw
windows. Look, pigeons
are flying. What vibrates inside
each body to guide them home?

Solastalgia

by Gabriella T. Rieger

"Solastalgia: A condition described by the philosopher Glenn Albrecht as a kind of existential grief for a vanished landscape, be it a swallowed coast, a field turned to desert, or a bygone geological epoch."
—Ross Andersen

"Grandmother Cell: an antiquated theory of cognition that supposed the memory of a person, place, or event was held in a single cell, e.g., the memory of your grandmother."

I thought I left you tucked away in a grandmother cell,
but that too is a myth of cognition.

Remember when we went to hear Franz Wright
at the Jamaica Plain Cemetery-- it was perfect

except for the poetry. Paul's mother died
I wanted to tell you,

but you were too far, our conversations of late too few.
The other day, on the phone, I was more New York than you
could bear.

I wanted to let you fall away, except
who would remember the horizon

of our imperfect excursions,
the contours of our partings,

the visions of tractors and subways-- your voice
is familiar, distant; a destabilizing juxtaposition.

The Italian restaurant on La Salle is still there. And with it,
the angles of your frame through my camera lens.
And saying goodbye to our goodbyes.
And the realization that I had achieved something,

merely by losing you,
because in this abandoned landscape I had lived.

Perfect Game

by Kathleen McClung

A quiet girl leaves on Saturdays before they wake,
delivers bottles of rum drizzle to the dump,
padlock combination leaking from her fingertips.

Alone on the mound, she pitches orange peels
to expectant gulls, as though it's the World Series,
a hushed stadium crowded with wig heads,

belt buckles, legless stools, shards of baby food jars.
All marvel at her changeup, her breaking ball, how she
allows nothing, no hits or walks or errors in the field.

However Deep the Glass
by Emily Vizzo

Your happiness is the glass bubble that fills your mouth.
Experience its roundness as if you exist within a cylinder of light,
because you do. When you trust your happiness, crush it
w/your teeth. Experience the crunch of broken glass as
perfectness. The space inside the bubble can release itself,
floating between your teeth like the solar system. The glass
you love won't cut you, but of course, this is ridiculous,
no one loves glass that much. You invented both your blood
& your happiness. This is where they meet to love each other.
The mouth is a snowglobe where plastic figures play in the
glass powders of your happiness. Your blood warms &
floats your ancient teeth. Walk carefully forever, without
the grace of swallowing. Invisible threads pull the inner
corners of your eyebrows upward. This is the part where
you are overcome w/a longing so strong you hide your face.
Deep in your brain there is a single piano note. The glass
kisses you from the inside. Happiness is when the breakable
finally breaks. Something cold carving you. When you have already
lost everything. When your tongue is a stump, & it loves you.

White Noise and Other Muses

by Ellaraine Lockie

The woman sitting next to me in Starbucks says
I wish I were as dedicated to something
as you to whatever you do here every day
Little does she know I'm eating her alive
Dissecting her and spitting her out on paper
That I'm bulimic about everything
surrounding me in any public place

Here air animates like caffeine
pumped through lungs
The ongoing coffee grind aroma that's over
at home every morning as fast as orgasm

Music a pep pill dispersed by satellite
Set of 60s hits today; *A Hard Day's Night*
and my first boyfriend stares
at my newly swollen breasts
Wanting more than the poem I'll write
about the Catholic Church and hand jobs

He's soon swallowed by a John Cage cacophony
Staccato of espresso machine and blender
Bow of chairs scratching across belly of floor
Whoosh of milk steamer as soft as a chinook
floating a mélange of multi-voices

A sanctuary so oddly tranquil that time stands still
Senses sharpen and I cut into the lace
of sunlight that embroiders my table
Into the man outside talking to himself in a bathrobe
The rough-draft-of-a-woman sitting next to me
That earlier version of myself

Heroes on the Ceiling

by Leslie Muzingo

They arrived at the shelter late on a Sunday afternoon, bringing nothing with them but two suitcases. Clancy couldn't understand why they needed so many clothes. He wanted to bring some toys, but his mother claimed, "There's no room for things like that where we're going." One suitcase was stuffed with papers from the file cabinet. This annoyed him; why did she get to bring her old papers when he couldn't even bring a ball and glove? Even his baby sister, Marie, got to bring that stupid ring to chew on. It wasn't fair.

Before knocking on the shelter door, Clancy's mother grabbed him by the arm and yanked him to her. "You're going to be good, right?"

"Yes!" Clancy said.

"I mean it Clancy. No screwing around." She tightened her grip on his arm.

"I'll be good!"

43

"Because if they throw us out or if your father finds us—"

His arm throbbed. It was the same place she'd grabbed him last week when he'd sassed her. "I'll be good," Clancy whispered.

His mother let loose of his arm. She bent to kiss him, but he turned away. It annoyed him that she always wanted a kiss after she'd hurt him.

They were led into a small office where a smiling woman motioned for them to sit in the chairs in front of her desk. To Clancy, it seemed like the principal's office, except for the smell; at school, it smelled of cleaning stuff while here it smelled like pee. Soon he heard the woman praise his mother for bringing the papers in the suitcase. "You'll be able to get your son registered at the school in this district without any problem," the woman said.

Clancy had to speak up. "But Mom, why can't I go to my school? There's only two weeks left, and I'm supposed to pitch next week!"

The strange woman shook her head before his mother could answer. "I'm sorry, but we don't allow that. If Clancy's father went to his school and wanted to take him, the school couldn't stop him. He's the boy's father, and until your divorce goes through and you're given custody, he has as much right to the children as you do."

"His father never paid Clancy no mind. I doubt he even knows where Clancy goes to school," his mother demurred, moving Marie to her other leg.

The woman shook her head again. "I'm sorry. But no. It's for our safety as well as yours." Clancy quit listening. Instead of Dad bossing his mother, this strange woman was now in charge. Anyway, no one cared what he thought.

He sort of understood why his mother had to come here, but why did it have to be now? Things had been this way ever since Clancy could remember; only recently had it gotten so bad that Mom needed to go to the hospital. In Clancy's opinion, she should've just stayed away from Dad when he'd been drinking. Besides, she was always telling him he had to wait for things, like when he pestered her about Christmas coming, so why couldn't she have waited to leave Dad till he was done with school and softball? Couldn't she have taken it a little bit longer? Why did he have to come with her? Dad never hurt him, not much anyway.

Clancy didn't think it was right, the way they had left—sneaking off like thieves, so Dad wouldn't catch them. Dad would come home soon, expecting dinner, and all he'd find would be an empty house. Clancy felt he should have stayed home with his father. He knew how to follow directions on labels and could cook a little.

It was the height of embarrassment to him to hear his mother tell this stranger with the scratching pen what his father had done. I could tell her things about you, Clancy thought. Not that he'd ever tell—the very idea made him sick. It was one thing to come here for Mom's protection, but quite another to come here for her to tattle. Yet, his mother droned on. Each word she said was another prick behind his eyes; he felt she was taunting him for being a fool, for lying for her all these years. "Mom fell down the stairs," he told the neighbors. "Mom can't come to my conference because she's sick," he told his teacher. As for his own bruises, well, that's what long-sleeve shirts were for.

They were taken into a dormitory where a maze of bunkbeds and dressers were grouped to give each family a cubicle of privacy. Six other families shared the room with them, but Clancy paid them no attention. Climbing up to his bunk, he hid his face because ten was too old to be crying in public. Once his tears dried, he rolled over and gazed upward at the ceiling cracks above his head.

Those cracks became his best friend over the next few weeks. Some days he followed them and found alien lifeforms, while other days he saw Indians lying in wait for pioneers on the Oregon Trail. Each crack was a new discovery, each bump in the plaster became his friend. The peeling paint provided nuances to his fantasies, which depending on the amount of light in the room, could be friendly or menacing. Gazing at the ceiling, Clancy lost himself in the trails and shadows of his mind and discovered the process of thought without thinking. Sometimes his hero had a white horse or a speedy spaceship and sped across the cracks in defense of justice. Sometimes his hero died. Clancy never put himself in the hero role; he just watched the hero do what he would do. It was more real to him that way.

Clancy went to the new school and endured the schoolyard

taunts of "shelter kid" without a murmur. Each day after school Clancy marched straight to his bed the moment he entered the shelter. The other children scurried through the labyrinth of beds like rats in an experiment, but Clancy was deaf to their games. He ate little, ignored his mother, and refused to participate in the shelter's planned activities. Nothing mattered to him but the cracks over his head.

School ended, and more activities were planned for the children, but Clancy still refused to participate. The women attended parenting classes when not looking for work. The classes caused Clancy's mom to come to him in tears, "You think I'm a good mother, don't you Clancy?" She broke down sobbing when he refused to answer.

A shelter worker heard the disturbance and came to investigate. "What's wrong here?" she asked in a too cheery tone.

Clancy's mother dried her eyes. "Nothing," she replied. It was the first time since they'd arrived that Clancy felt happy. He'd thought she'd lost all pride.

The woman wasn't giving up. She sat on the bunk directly underneath Clancy. "Don't you want to talk about it?"

"Oh, no... it's jus ..." his mother's voice trailed off.

Keep your mouth shut, keep your mouth shut, Clancy thought, holding his breath and squeezing his eyes tight as if he were making a wish. He'd spent years perfecting lying to teachers and neighbors; what had he done it for if she was going to talk all the time?

"Yes?" Clancy heard eagerness in the shelter worker's voice, like she was hungry for their troubles.

"I wish Clancy were happier, that's all," his mother said. Clancy's eyes blinked open and he took a breath. He smiled.

The shelter worker then went into a dissertation about the children, how hard it was for them but how, "They are all so very, very special." Satisfied with his mother's performance, Clancy went back to his cracks. His hero was crossing a mighty river when the whispered words, "Sunday is Father's Day, but we don't tell the children," floated up to him as if they were tied to the end of a helium balloon.

Anger, confusion, and betrayal flooded Clancy's hero with a giant wave and destroyed him on the spot. Clancy was in shock; he was also so mad he wanted to hit the wall, but then someone would want to make him talk about it. Father's Day! They were going to let it slip by and act like he and the rest of the kids didn't have fathers. His eyes narrowed. He stared at the cracks, searching for a secret exit. Even after all the lights were extinguished, he stared upwards, thinking.

He approached his mother on Sunday morning when she was busy with his baby sister, who was teething. "Mom, I'm going with the other kids to Sunday School," Clancy said.

"Fine dear. That's fine," his mother replied, preoccupied with the baby.

Clancy stuffed a couple of biscuits in his pocket and grabbed a box of juice before getting on the church bus with the rest of the children. In Sunday school, he chose the seat closest to the door. Waiting till the teacher bowed her head in prayer was difficult, but when everyone's eyes were closed, Clancy made his exit.

Once in the hallway all he had to do was run.

It was as if all those days spent staring at the ceiling were done to conserve his energy for this moment. He couldn't—wouldn't—be the hero, but he could be the white horse or the rocket ship, bursting out the door into the sunshine and speeding down the street.

Once he'd jumped some hedges and ran a few blocks, he felt safe in stopping to get his bearings. It took him several minutes to map it out, but the church bulletin provided the address from where he'd come, and he was a smart boy and knew how the streets in the city worked. Now all he had to do was get back home to Dad. It shouldn't be too hard.

It wasn't. He avoided the busier roads in case someone was looking for him and instead zigzagged through back streets and alleys. Travel made him hungry, but the biscuits and juice box were rationed out to last his entire journey, and he wisely took breaks at appropriate intervals, whether he was tired or not. The sun was an orange ball low in the horizon when he came to the creek. The water was full of trash and leeches, yet Clancy's spirits rose when he saw it because it meant he was almost home.

Finally, he saw his house. Joy immediately became confusion and then sorrow when Clancy realized that there was no car in the driveway. He plopped down in the weeds to think. He had come so far, and now his father wasn't even home. What was he supposed to do?

Then it hit him—of course! Dad was at the bar. He always went there on Sunday. That's how Mom was able to escape so easily.

He was named for the bar on the corner, that's how much his Dad liked going there. It was called "Clancy's Bar and Grill" except it was owned by some guy named Joe and the "C" in "Clancy's" had long ago burned out. The sign was turned on by the time Clancy got there —"lancy's" it said in bright red letters. Clancy went in and there his dad sat, at the end of the bar, looking up at the television over his head.

Clancy crept over to his father and put his hand on the man's arm. "Dad?"

His father turned to look at him. Clancy saw the look on his father's face was the bad look, the one that always meant trouble. "Where's your mother?" his father growled.

"At the shelter," Clancy whispered.

His father grabbed him by the arm. "So, what are you doing here then?" He gave Clancy a shake. "Are you here to spy on me? Or maybe you came to steal my wallet—I bet that bitch is out of cash." He shook Clancy even harder. "Talk boy! What do you want?"

Clancy hadn't cried since that first night in the shelter, but suddenly all that he'd been holding in came pouring out of him. "It's Father's Day," he sobbed. "I wanted to see you. I've missed you—it's Father's Day—that's all."

Scared to look and scared not to, Clancy peered up and saw that his father wasn't even looking at him. He wasn't looking at the television either. Clancy was confused; his father didn't look angry; it looked like maybe he had something in his eye. Before Clancy could think about it further, the drunken man had picked up this son and plopped him on a bar stool.

"Joe!" his father called out. "Bring a coke for my boy! And a steak sandwich while you're at it!" Father and son sat and chatted about nothing in particular; Clancy asked questions about home and his father gave lighthearted responses and drank more beer. His food arrived, and Clancy thought the sandwich was the best he'd ever tasted, until he saw his mom enter the bar accompanied by a police officer —then the food in his mouth turned to dust.

His mother ran to him. "Oh Clancy, I was so worried," was all she could say, over and over again. She pulled him to her and held him so tightly that Clancy couldn't hear all that was said. He heard the policeman say something like, "restraining order" and "run him in" but he didn't know exactly what they were talking about. Clancy felt the tension in his mother's body, and he knew it was up to him to stop something bad. "It was my fault Mom, not Dad's. But I'm so glad you came for me," he whispered in her ear. Although Clancy hadn't voluntarily given his mother any affection in a very long time and never had in public, he gave her a shy kiss. Clancy felt his mother's body relax. It was as if that kiss was a magic key that opened something gentle inside of her. "Please. Just take us out of here," his mother said to the police officer.

She took Clancy by the hand and led him out the door. Clancy squeezed his mother's hand to let her know everything was all right, and she squeezed his in return. Clancy turned to smile a goodbye to his father, but the man had returned to his beer and television. Clancy didn't really blame him. He sort of understood.

That night, lying in his bed, he followed the cracks in the ceiling with a new scenario dancing in his head. He saw himself mount a white charger, and on that mighty steed, jump rivers and climb mountains.

And then he fell asleep.

Getting Away Safe
by Ariadne Wolf

Everybody needs a safe place to get away.

THE STORY, as it was told to me:

Israel is ours. God gave it to us and we earned it by surviving the Holocaust. The Arab people do not wish to give it to us because they are evil, they will harm us. The white people of this country cannot be trusted to protect us because they are racists and it is only the Jewish men who can be relied on to protect us, the Jewish women, from the threat that brown men present.

They are the ones we require protection from. Any sacrifice to earn this safe place is worth it.

To claim otherwise was anathema.

I grew up expecting a knock on my door. My family kept cans of food we did not need in preparation for another genocide, and we had closets and a cellar, and I expected to have to hide in someday.

For years I was grateful for the reliable ugly walls of my synagogue, rising like Jonah's mythical whale to swallow me whole against my will. B'nai Shalom was my succor, and if it asked more from me than I wanted to give, well, perhaps the bargain was worth it. So, I sat in the uncomfortable, high-backed pews, trying not to squirm in the scratchy tights my mother insisted on, trying not to bat my mother's hand away when she yanked my shirt down over my seven-year-old tummy. Trying not to insist on self-determination. What does self-respect compare with survival?

While the endless services in Hebrew, a language I could not read, droned on for three hours—an eternity to a child—I read about our deaths in the backs of *Siddurim*, Jewish prayer books.

Soldiers picked up a child my age by the ankles, and while she was still laughing, they threw her headfirst into a wall and shattered her skull. Soldiers shot another child just for fun, just for a good time. Soldiers stole Anne Frank away and we know her name because she left a journal for us to find. I traced my way to these children through time, and for years I was obsessed with stories from the war.

B'nai Shalom synagogue began in 1948 as Beth Israel synagogue in Pittsburg, California, an outgrowth of military collaborations with San Francisco's Jewish Welfare Board to meet the needs of Jewish military personnel returning from World War Two. The founders accommodated the shifting nexus of the East Bay Jewish population and moved to Walnut Creek in 1964. The first full-time rabbi, Gordon Freeman, is the man I think of as *my* rabbi; darting, joyous, the man who burst through the doors on the holiest of holy days to preach to a group of conservative voters about global warming. A series of male cantors culminated in Cantor Dinkin, with whom I studied Torah for my Bat Mitzvah, and who bragged to the congregation about me wanting to spend an extra ten minutes with him in that way men do when a young teenage girl is awkward, and they think that means she is awkwardly flirting. One more betrayal. One more humiliation.

Spring, 1998. I color the Negev lavender, the color of the sky at dawn. The color of heaven.

My teacher Maya, who is from Israel or who has been to Israel or at any rate *is* Israeli, comes to tell me what a good job I've done. I hug her, because she is the mother I almost had.

Lavender like my grandmother, who has died. Lavender like the bathroom of my other grandmother, who has little money but has a bathroom made all from purple. Purple everything.

Yitzhak Rabin was to be the savior of Israel. A left-wing liberal who preached peace with the Muslim Palestinians, he was shot by one of his own people. Yigal Amir was against the Oslo Accords because he could not see what my family did, what everyone I knew saw—that any peace, even a blood-spattered one, is better than none at all. Rabin died in 1996, and our hopes and prayers went out to him, but we were all in mourning. A world away, a black shade dropped over our sky and we began to talk in hushed tones about what would happen now to the country that was supposed to be our paradise.

This is what I learned from Hebrew school: Israel was originally intended to be a colony of peace, a gathering place for all the world's great religions. That Israel was supposed to be a great communist paradise.

There is no proof of this. There is no way to search for proof of this.

It is a wonderful story. I seize hold.

One day I will go there. To Israel. Where no one will humiliate me again.

1999. The entire Board is composed of white men. The Cantor and the Rabbi are both white men. Children notice these things. Adults know better than to mention them out loud.

I barely speak for years, and there are reasons why. Uri Wilensky of *The Huffington Post* in 2016 wrote that Jews are more often the victims of hate crimes than any other group in the US, according to the FBI. I was welcomed as a white person, so long as I did not bring up that pesky Judaism. So long as I did not give any "real" white people a reason.

I was safe as a Jew and as a woman, so the story goes, so long as I did not mention feeling unsafe. Feeling afraid of the men in my life, white or Jewish, was unacceptable.

Spring, 1999. I lock my properly submissive, efficiently feminine Hebrew School teacher with the lace keepah, Jewish hair covering, permanently bobby-pinned to her scalp, out of our classroom. It is an accident, but as she pounds, it becomes a calling. When I finally unlock the door, she barges in and takes aim at each student in turn, explaining precisely what is wrong with each of us. Attacks verbally, the only way a woman is permitted to attack. I am quaking but defiant.

After, I dart outside to the undeveloped back lot, my hideaway. The entire hillside glows golden, and God is here. God is right here.

Later that day my friend Carly and I discuss in hushed tones the deaths of young Palestinian boys at the hands of Israeli soldiers. Each of us nervy and wide-eyed, scared of something we cannot name.

I cannot stop picturing their weeping mothers. The photographs of ruined homes. All the ruined things.

2013. My father looks sideways at me in the pretty sunlit kitchen composed of pretty, expensive appliances, which neither he nor my mother ever use, for which he spent thousands of dollars from my would-have-been college fund, to please my mother, who is so anxious to belong. He says, "The congregation hired a female rabbi."

Amy Eilberg, in 1985, was the first female rabbi to be ordained in a conservative synagogue. 2013 is better than nothing.

I respond in the affirmative. "How wonderful!"

My father shakes his head. "She's not going to stay. She's from New York. She does not fit in with the culture."

Translation: she is a woman with self-esteem and the Board, which to this day is primarily comprised of white men, wants her out, so out she will go.

2011. I have called Cantor Dinkin, with trembling fingers. I am backlit by a sun, happy to be beyond the dour walls of a theology I can no longer accept.

I picture my cohort. Gabriela from the Palestinian Justice Movement, who patted my back while I sobbed a whole year of my life away. Devin who was sexually assaulted then drank herself to death while no one noticed, including me.

I tell the cantor, "My father raped me."

Silence.

The cantor asks, "What do you want me to do? They're members of my congregation."

I turn off my phone.

Everybody needs a safe place to get away. But away from what?

2017. My father has "forgotten" to reserve an extra room for me at our hotel in Seattle. He twists and whines and convinces my mother it will be fine for us three to share a suite.

I am unmoved. There will be a locked door, or I will flee and leave him to explain the situation to his cousins. Leave him to explain the 'why'.

I get my way. I make myself safe.

2017. My cousin Carol insists, "I have no idea how Trump could get away with saying those things about women!"

Greek music plays gaily all around us. Greek gods and nymphs lounge luxuriously on the wall behind us. The food I denied myself for years of misdirected punishment sits pleasantly on my tongue.

"I understand," I insist right back. "Based on my experiences and those of my friends, the idea someone could get away with that did not come as a shock."

Blatant is my father's shame. My mother's attempt at withering rage. Carol's instant of recognition.

My mother interrupts to say, "if black people had gathered behind Hillary the way they did Obama, Trump would not have been elected."

Gently, I tell her, "It was not their responsibility."

It was not my responsibility, what happened to me. But what happens as a result of me is.

2017. My cousin Caitie and I have rediscovered one another after twenty years of in-between. She sits with her bleach-blonde pixie cut and three-hole piercings next to her hulking, wealthy husband, talking with a flutter in her voice while her anxious hands paint the air. We discuss science fiction until he leaves early.

Her words pour forth like a waterfall, and she says, "I learned after the election what white feminism is."

"Yes," I say. "I learned things about my friends that I wish I had not learned."

Translation: I learned things about my parents I wish I had not learned.

We sit in the grand and grandiose dining room, with its museum exterior and intricate painted objects from dozens of different countries. We fill the space with our words about feminism and racism and who we want to be.

Not once do we say, *but those men of color who are rapists*. Not once do we say, *but those white men, and those Jewish men perceived to be white, who would never rape us*.

Because we do not lie to each other.

John, too thin and balding, wanders by. "What are you girls doing in here?"

We turn beatific smiles toward him and pose, and hold, until he backs away. Slowly, as though we are dangerous. As though we are prepared to pounce.

We turn relieved faces back to each other. We do not acknowledge what we have just done, what we are doing.

That we are rewriting the story.

That we are making ourselves safe.

Distances
by Kurt Newton

CAROLINE LEWIS SAT at the kitchen table, enveloped in her usual early morning headache. Her temples throbbed with each beat of her heart. Two cups of coffee and still no relief.

"Honey? Where's my burgundy tie?" her husband called to her from the bedroom.

"It's where it always is, Ted," she called back, eyes still sealed shut. She could picture him looking in all the wrong places.

A mumble from the other room; the sound of coat hangers being shoved back and forth. "It's not in here." A whine on the word "here" told Caroline that Ted had given up ten minutes before.

God, do I have to do everything?

Her head pounded as she stood up from the kitchen chair. When she opened her eyes, she saw that her three-year-old daughter Allison had scooped out most of her cereal onto the table—all except for the marshmallow hearts, moons, and stars, which she corralled with her spoon into color groups.

"Allison! Stop playing with your cereal. And pick up each and every piece you've laid out there and put it back in your bowl!"

Her daughter shot her a sullen look of defiance. "No." The three-year-old picked up her spoon and threw it across the table. It bounced once and then clattered to the floor.

"Stop it, Allison, I'm warning you..."

Allison was looking for something else to throw.

"Stop it right now."

"Can you help me find it, please?"

"Coming!" Caroline grimaced as twin pistons fired above her eyebrows. She glared at her daughter. "You better have that mess cleaned up before I get back."

As Caroline had suspected, the tie was where it always was.

"It's not *always* there." Ted yanked the tie from the hanger.

"How would you know? You don't put the clothes away."

"It's not always there," he said again, as if repeating the words somehow made them right.

Caroline saw the red in her husband's face and decided to drop the subject. "I need some aspirin."

"Headache?"

God, he was so stupid sometimes.

Caroline headed for the bathroom medicine cabinet. A few minutes later she heard a knock at the kitchen door.

"Auntie Marge, Auntie Marge..."

"Hi, Peanut."

It was Marjorie Wilks, Caroline's best friend. Marjorie had taken the day off from work for their planned all-day shopping/lunch/shopping spree at the Emerald Square Mall.

"We're going to McDonald's."

"We are?"

Caroline shouted from the bathroom. "Be with you in a minute, Marge!" Her head complained with each word.

"No rush, Carol. The mall doesn't open for another hour. Take your time. Remember you have to look nice for all those young, adorable salesmen. Oh, hi, Ted."

"Hi, Marjorie."

"Beautiful day, isn't it, Ted?"

"Go ahead, rub it in. Some of us have to work, you know."

Caroline listened from the bathroom. She looked at herself in the mirror. Why Ted had married her and not Marjorie, she'd never know. Marjorie was the one with the better looks, the better figure, the one whose spirit seemed to soar a little louder, a little higher than her own. Why Ted would still choose to be a devoted husband, when she only seemed to fail as a mother and bruise his ego most of the time, was beyond her.

Ted popped his head in the bathroom doorway. "See ya, Hon. Gotta go. How's the headache?"

"Fine. Have a nice day." Caroline continued to put on her make-up.

"Kiss?"

Caroline kissed him and went back to what she was doing. He lingered in the doorway.

"Don't let Allison get to you, okay? When she gets like that, you just gotta take a step back." He patted the doorjamb as if to seal some kind of agreement. "See ya tonight."

Easy for you to say, she thought. She brushed her hair in quick, firm strokes. In the kitchen she heard Allison's patented whine when Ted told her he had to leave.

"But I want to go with you, Daddy."

"You're going with Mommy."

"Nooo."

"We're going to have lots of fun at the mall," said Marjorie.

"McDonald's, too?"

"I don't see why not."

Caroline's ears burned just to listen to it. Allison never whined when she left the house to go anywhere. In fact, if given the choice, Allison preferred to stay home with her daddy. If not her daddy, then Auntie Marge. Even the babysitter seemed to have a better rapport with her daughter than she did.

The Emerald Square Mall was more like the Emerald City from

the Wizard of Oz. There were pretty, tiled walkways, wonderful white fountains; islands of exotic green plants. Allison was Dorothy; Marjorie, Glinda, the Good Witch of the North; and Caroline—well, the only thing missing from Caroline was the black hat and broomstick. They sat at a small table in the food court. It was lunchtime. Caroline and Marjorie picked at their Taco Grandes and talked about the men in their lives, while Allison sat nearby with a large soda and some cheesy fries.

"So, who is it this time, Marge—Bill, Bob, or Henry?"

"His name is David. David Devereaux. I met him at the office." Marjorie worked as a legal assistant.

"Devereaux. That's French, isn't it?"

"Hmm, I hope so." Marjorie held a suggestive glint in her eye.

"Marjorie, you're terrible!" They both giggled. To Caroline, Marjorie led a glamorous life. She had an exciting job, wore nice clothes, and was free to choose her own whats and whens and with whoms. Caroline thought about her own life. She was a stay-at-home mom who cooked a mean chicken scampi and tended a cute little herb garden. Ted sold life insurance. He calculated the best deals for people so they wouldn't have to worry once they died. Together they had enough insurance to survive any catastrophic illness each could burden the other with. Her whole life was contained in a canvas folder they kept on the top shelf in their bedroom closet—right above the ties Ted never managed to find.

"... a child someday."

"Sorry, Marge, what did you say?"

"Listen to me, I must be rambling. I'm probably boring you to death, right?"

"No, no, my mind just... wandered. What were you talking about?"

"I said if and when the right guy comes along, I wouldn't mind having a child of my own someday, that's all." Marjorie glanced over to where Allison was now playing. "Allison's such a charm. Caroline, you're so lucky."

Caroline looked for her daughter. Allison had drifted off to another table where an elderly couple sat. Allison hung on the back of the old gentleman's chair as he tried to eat. Caroline glared at her. But

Allison only stared back, a grin creeping up the sides of her mouth. It wasn't until Marjorie was ready to go that Allison rejoined them, and when it came time to ask for candy, it was Marjorie who was asked, not Caroline. Never Caroline.

That night, Caroline lay in bed, waiting for Ted to join her. She listened to the low murmur of his voice from across the hall as he read Allison a bedtime story. Finally, as if left with nothing else to do, she fell off to sleep, and quickly slid into a dream where it felt as if she was drifting away.

She was at the beach, wading in the surf. Ted and Allison were there, building a sand castle. She watched them from a distance. They looked so serene, so happy. The sun beamed down, everything was so bright and happy. Caroline wanted to join in that happiness, but instead she felt the water pulling her farther away. She began to panic, frantically waving her arms. Ted and Allison looked up, saw her, but merely waved back, smiling. The water bobbed around her neck, and it was all she could do to keep her head above it. Then she saw Marjorie walking down the sand toward Ted and Allison. The three of them began working on the sand castle together, like one happy family. It was then that Caroline let the water overtake her.

Caroline awoke to the sound of a DJ's voice announcing unbeatable prices on mufflers and brakes. When she opened her eyes, she saw flowery bedroom curtains, smelled lavender-scented sheets, and felt a distinct emptiness in the bed beside her.

Her hand reached up instinctively and shut off the clock radio.

But wait. She and Ted didn't have a clock radio. In fact, she didn't remember ever having flowery curtains like the ones she was now staring at.

She sat up and took in the rest of the room.

There was a tall, white dresser standing next to the window, a white wicker étagère in the corner, a white dressing table with a wide oval mirror facing the foot of the bed. None of it hers. The first blossoms of fear began to bloom inside her chest. Where the hell was she?

Then she realized. She must be at Marjorie's apartment. This was

Marjorie's bed. Those were Marjorie's curtains. The necklaces draped across the ceramic hand on the dressing table were worn by Marjorie. What was she doing here? Did she and Ted have a fight? Funny how she couldn't remember.

She looked at the clock, saw that it was 5:20 am, and felt a sudden necessity to jump out of bed and hop into the shower. She was going to be late for work.

But she was a housewife. There was never any need to hurry—the housework wasn't going anywhere.

What is this? She got out of bed slowly and searched the apartment, calling out Marjorie's name.

She was alone.

Confused, Caroline picked up the phone and dialed her home number. As she waited for either Ted or Allison to pick up, her eyes drifted around the apartment. Everything was different and yet somehow familiar. The pictures on the wall, the books on the bookshelf —she knew she had never seen them before, but they triggered memories. But they couldn't be memories. These were Marjorie's things.

The phone picked up on the fourth ring. A groggy voice answered. "Hello?"

Caroline couldn't believe this was happening. "Marjorie?"

"Carol? What time is it? Is something wrong?"

Caroline's mind reeled. The sofa—she remembered it now. She remembered shopping at five different furniture stores before deciding upon it. But how could this be?

"Carol? Is everything okay?" Marjorie sounded concerned—as she naturally would be if her best friend were to call her at such an early hour in the morning.

"Yeah, I—" *Think fast.* The more Caroline looked around, the more familiar things became. *Think!*

Saturday.

Just like that, it came into her head. There was something about this Saturday.

"I just called to see if we were still on for this Saturday?"

"At 5:30 in the morning? Jeez, Carol. Of course we're still on. My hair looks like squirrels have been nesting in it."

"Okay, great." Caroline paused. Still thinking. She spoke cautiously. Along with the sudden onslaught of memories, she also retained some remembrances of her own; years together with one man occupied a majority of them.

"Is Ted there? I mean... is he there beside you?"

"Yeah. Where else would he be?"

Oh, God! What have I done?

"And Allison?" The question struggled to escape her throat.

"Allison's down the hall, why? Carol, you're starting to worry me."

"I'm sorry, it's nothing. I—" *I just woke up in your bed... your apartment... your life, that's all! We've traded places, for Christ's sake!* "I had this dream that something happened to you guys. I just called to see if you were all right."

"We're all here. Safe and sound."

"That's good." Another pause.

"Good-bye, Carol. I've got to get back to sleep if I can, okay?"

"Huh? Oh, sorry. See you Saturday."

The phone clicked. Caroline's eyes filled with tears.

It was time to get ready for work.

Saturday came sooner than Caroline had expected. God, work was hectic, but it felt good. It also felt as if she were an impostor. She kept expecting her boss, Mr. Thorndike, to suddenly stop what he was doing, stare at her aghast, and say, "Where's Marjorie?" But nobody at the office even mentioned the name. They all knew her by her maiden name, Caroline Gregory. No more Mrs. Lewis. These people, whom she knew she had never met before, talked to her as if she were a daily part of their lives. And everything that was needed for her new life—skill, knowledge, social etiquette—everything that was once Marjorie's—came to her naturally, as if she had been born to it.

It was an odd week. But it was also *exciting*. It was everything Caroline had dreamed of—the fast pace, the interesting people. She even met David Devereaux, and he confirmed their date for Saturday night. God, what more could she ask for?

Ted?

Allison?

At times, she heard the echo of their names in her ear, her own voice calling them. It lessened as the week wore on. But at night, falling off to sleep, she still felt the ghost pressure of someone else in bed beside her.

You just gotta take a step back...

Sometimes her heart squeezed in her chest so tightly, she felt it might burst.

◈

Saturday morning, she drove to Marjorie's house. It felt strange saying that—Marjorie's house. She still remembered—faintly now—she and Ted in the kitchen, signing the mortgage agreement.

But that was another life. She liked this one much better.

When she got there, Ted wasn't home. He was working his usual half-Saturday at the office, tying up loose ends. Marjorie had called in a babysitter to watch Allison while the two of them went out to have their hair appointment. The babysitter let her in.

"Oh, hi, Rachel."

"Hi, Miss Gregory. Mrs. Lewis is still in the shower."

"You can call me Caroline if you want. I don't look that old, do I?"

Rachel smiled shyly. "Okay. *Caroline.*"

Rachel was fourteen years old. She had a refreshing innocence about her that radiated through her pleasant smile and out through the ends of her long, naturally blonde hair.

"Auntie Carol, Auntie Carol..." Allison came running into the kitchen.

"Hi, Peanut." The response came automatically. Allison gave her a big hug.

"Me and Rachel are going to make choca-chip cookies."

"You *are?*" Caroline shared a smile with Rachel.

"Yup!"

Marjorie's voice came from the bathroom. "Carol is that you?"

"It's me."

"I'll be with you in a minute."

"No rush, Marge, we've got plenty of time."

A sudden wave of déjà vu swept over her. But it passed just as quickly.

Seven o'clock brought a knock at Caroline's apartment door. When she opened it, there he was. David Devereaux was soap opera handsome. Well-dressed, dark-haired, neatly groomed; when he smiled he flashed a brilliant set of perfect white teeth. Caroline had been preparing for that smile all evening—new dress, new hair, the entire glamorous package all neatly tied and waiting to be opened.

They drove to an expensive uptown restaurant. Caroline ordered linguini; David, prime rib. The wine was a little too potent for Caroline's taste, but then this was all new to her, in a way. She just let the evening take her. David was a young, up-and-coming lawyer, and had a reputation for being ruthless in the courtroom. Sitting across from him, Caroline could understand how a jury could be persuaded by his disarming nature. His charm was as potent as the wine.

After dinner they drove back to his place. When they entered his apartment, David pinned her against the door with a kiss. His hands traveled up and down the sides of her dress and were probing for more when Caroline broke contact.

"David, I don't think I'm ready for this just yet."

David's eyes suddenly transformed from smoky grey to coal black. "You're kidding, right?"

"No. I think I've had a little too much wine, that's all. I had a nice evening. Maybe some other time, okay?"

David's features softened a bit. "I'll make us some coffee. We'll talk." He went to kiss her again. Caroline accepted it briefly, but turned away.

"No, David, really. I'm not feeling well. Right now, I think it would be best if you just take me home."

He released her then and turned around. He walked two paces, his hand up to his chin. From behind, it looked as if he was contemplating his next line of questioning. When he turned to face her, those dark eyes were back again, accompanied by a strange grin. He was shaking his head.

"Nope, not this time."

He grabbed her by both arms and tried to kiss her again, this time more forcibly. Caroline wrenched herself free and stumbled away

—away from him but also farther into the apartment. Her heart hammered in her chest. What stupid situation did she get herself into now? Her eyes scanned the apartment for something to defend herself with. But her head was spinning—the wine was fermenting inside of her, swirling any possible resolve she had into a helpless kind of panic.

"Caroline, you know I like the challenge." David removed his suit jacket and flung it onto the sofa. He then loosened the knot of his tie.

Caroline backed across the living room, only to realize she was headed toward the bedroom. She quickly circled, but found herself cornered between a bookcase and a large-screen television. That's when she realized she had but one option. She let him come to her.

"I'm sorry, David." She forced her muscles to relax. "I guess I really don't know what I want." She feigned submission, and David's grin widened to a victor's smile. He approached her, gentler this time, and when he attempted to put his arms around her again, Caroline brought her knee up into his groin as hard as she could. The look on David's face was as priceless as his brand-new BMW sport coupe. He crumpled to the floor.

"Sorry, changed my mind again." Caroline quickly stepped past him and out the door.

David's only reply was a restrained "*Bitch!*" before he vomited onto the plush, triple-ply carpet.

Caroline took the elevator down to the street. She walked to a nearby Dunkin' Donuts and called a cab. She kept herself under control the entire way home. Only when she was safely inside her apartment did she let go, burying her face in her pillow. She reached out, her hand searching, but there was nothing there to comfort her but the stale, silent emptiness of her apartment.

The weeks after the incident with David seemed to blend into one long work day. Caroline kept pace with the demands of her job as best she could, but at times she sensed Mr. Thorndike's displeasure; times when, in the midst of performing even the simplest of tasks, such as filing a brief or taking down notes for upcoming appointments, she found herself daydreaming, lost in some inner space filled with unfamiliar thoughts and feelings. It was disorienting when it struck—as if she were in two places at once.

Mostly, she just felt tired. And with tired came lonely. And with lonely came scared—the scared, helpless feeling of growing old and never finding someone to love.

"So, how are you and David doing?" Marjorie asked.

Once again, the three of them were seated at the food court in the Emerald Square Mall. This time it was chef salads for the two of them, Chicken McNuggets for Allison. It was now August. Back-to-school sales, the smell of new clothes, kids everywhere. Grade schoolers with their mothers, teenagers in roving packs, lone college students — all searching the stores for the latest and most hip.

"David?" Caroline thought for a moment, distracted by all the young people walking by. "Oh, David and I are fine," she lied.

"You two aren't getting serious, are you?"

"Oh, no, nothing like that." Caroline hadn't seen David since the "incident." In fact, she hadn't seen anyone since the incident. Dating was getting a bit dangerous nowadays. Who could you trust?

"That's too bad."

Marjorie, if you only knew, Caroline felt like saying. She produced a fake pout for Marjorie's benefit, then smiled. *Oh, well, better luck next time. Maybe next time I'll actually get raped. Maybe next time I'll even get beat up a little. That would be nice. Marjorie, you don't know how lucky you are—to have the security of one man, someone who loves and respects you, someone to come home to and talk to late at night...*

"Hi, Mrs. Lewis. Hi, Caroline. Hey Ally-bear." It was Allison's baby-sitter, Rachel. Rachel stood behind Allison, gathering Allison's hair together behind her neck and then letting it fall. Allison slobbered a honey-coated McNugget into her mouth and smiled at the unexpected attention.

"Hi, Rachel. Getting your school shopping done?" Marjorie asked her.

"Yeah." The young girl rolled her eyes.

"You shopping with your mom?"

"Yeah, she's around here somewhere. I told her I'd meet her in front of Papa Gino's at twelve-thirty, but..." Rachel looked around.

Caroline liked this girl. Rachel reminded her a lot of herself when she was that age—unashamed, innocent, the light of her whole life shining before her. Where did it all go wrong? When she lost her virginity at fifteen? The boy had said he loved her—and she'd believed him! So gullible, so naive. After that there were other guys, repeat performances that left her vengeful. The only way she could get back at them was to become smarter. So, she'd made good grades, graduated with high honors, got accepted into a top college.

Now, here she was, looking at a fourteen-year-old copy of herself and wishing she could somehow turn back the clock and start all over again, never make the mistakes she had made so foolishly.

"There she is." Rachel waved to her mother. "Well, I gotta go. See ya," she told Allison, bopping her on the head. "Bye, Mrs. Lewis. Bye, Caroline."

"Bye, Rachel."

Caroline waved to the girl as she made her way over to join her mother. *On the threshold of life.*

Yes, things would definitely be different.

That night, as Caroline sat in her empty apartment, the loneliness pooled around her. Seeking refuge, she climbed into bed and fell asleep, and into a dream.

Again, the sunny beach, the view from the water—long, smooth waves rolling toward shore, like a carpet of stone. On the beach—a young woman building a sand castle, her concentration single-minded and solitary. Caroline almost hated to disturb her, but the water was pulling at her, a riptide sucking at her feet, and this young woman—this girl—seemed to be the only one who could help her. Caroline waved her arms, called out—the water lapped at the back of her neck. Finally, the girl looked up, and Caroline saw that it was Rachel. She could see Rachel's expression; it was one of surprise, but also joy. She waved excitedly to Caroline and returned to her work. The tide then pulled Caroline's feet out from under her and she drifted away.

Caroline opened her eyes.

It was morning. Sunlight beamed through pastel curtains onto pastel walls. A tall dark dresser, a student desk, a lamp, books, note-books, a pretty pink candy jar holding a fistful of pens and pencils. Posters on the walls—young faces with All American smiles and kiss-able lips. Teen TV idols. Boy bands.

She could hear the sounds of breakfast being cooked in the kitchen. Then footsteps outside the door.

A knock. Caroline's throat caught.

"Caroline, breakfast is ready. C'mon honey, get up and get ready for school."

A mother's voice. Caroline felt a sinking feeling—a sudden *receding*, as in the moments just after waking from a dream—and then relief.

Eagerly, she threw back the covers and climbed out of bed. She knew today would be the start of something very special.

The Blue Delta

by John M. Floyd

I⟨T WAS QUIET⟩ at the edge of the woods.

Leonard Drago crouched in the underbrush and stared out at the flatlands stretching away beyond the last of the forest. He had hoped to cross those treeless fields under the cover of darkness, but the sun was already peeking over another patch of woods to the east. And he couldn't go east. His destination was straight ahead, north past this bone-dry farmland and on into the sad outskirts of his hometown, Bayou LeBlanc, where his dimwitted but loyal third cousin might be convinced to hide him until all this blew over.

Which might take awhile. Leonard Drago wasn't your common criminal, and what they'd be sending after him wasn't your usual pursuit. Drago knew this would be a full-blown, multi-agency manhunt, and for good reason: he had escaped last night from the state prison seven miles from here, murdering a guard in the process and a civilian two hours later. It was this second killing that irked him. He'd

71

encountered a drunk staggering down a gravel road in the middle of the night (how unlucky was *that?*), and in his distinctive orange jumpsuit, Drago had had no choice but to kill him. Even more frustrating was that after strangling the idiot and going through his pockets, Drago had come up with almost nothing useful. No gun, no money, no cellphone. He did discover a fifth of bourbon and a hunting knife, though, both of which might come in handy. He'd also taken the guy's baseball cap and jeans (the shirt was too gaudy and eye-catching). The body Drago had thrown into a ditch beside the road, along with his prison outfit. Orange might be the new black, on TV; in real life, a jailbird jumpsuit was a liability.

He desperately wished that that dirt road had produced a driver instead of a pedestrian. With wheels, there was a chance he could've been out of here, maybe out of the state, before the roadblocks went up—but now here he was, still afoot in an area only a short distance from the town where a bungled bank robbery fifteen years ago had ended a promising career in drug trafficking and petty theft. A young and stoned Drago had happily shot three people in that heist—two bank employees and a policeman. As a result, one of the ladies had died, and he'd later heard the cop had lost an arm. But the really bad thing, at least in Drago's view, was that all those sins lumped together had sent him up the river (literally, since the prison was located on the north bank of the mighty Blue) to serve a life sentence.

Until last night. He was no lifer now. He was free, and he didn't plan to get sent back.

For the tenth time, Albert Leonard "Skinny Lenny" Drago took a swallow of his latest victim's booze and checked his immediate surroundings, looking for snakes. He hated snakes. Satisfied on that score, he capped the bottle, took a deep breath, searched the horizon, and focused on a lone house about a mile away across the fields, the only sign of civilization anywhere in this stretch of the pancake-flat Blue River delta. A small barn and several outbuildings surrounded the house: a struggling farm, probably. But even a struggling farmer might have some cash tucked away, and a gun that Drago could steal.

He left the cover of the trees and headed north.

Jake Greenwood was using strips of cloth to tie his tomato plants to a row of upright poles in the garden that bordered his side yard when he looked behind him and saw the man approaching. A short, pale guy in a white T-shirt and baggy jeans, trudging toward him from the distant woods. On his lowered head was a dark blue baseball cap with something written on the front, still too far away to read.

Jake should probably have been more surprised, to see someone out here alone and on foot—and certainly more suspicious. But right now he was thinking mostly about his dry and droopy garden and the dead battery in his truck, the one that was keeping him from running errands and fetching supplies from town. And about the fact that his best friend, Virgil Woodson, had promised he'd buy a new battery and bring it out this morning. Virgil was supposed to arrive any minute now, and Jake wanted to get these tomato vines squared away first.

He had managed to tie half a dozen more plants to their poles by the time the stranger reached the garden. "Mornin'," a voice said, from behind him. "Sad-looking tomatoes."

"They need rain," Jake replied.

He tucked the remaining ties into his pocket, wiped his hands on his overalls, and turned.

Drago stood there a moment, facing the tall black farmer, thinking hard.

He figured he had two options, one of which was to threaten this guy with his knife, force him into the house, find a gun (in Drago's experience, everybody in the South owned a gun), take him or a member of his family as a hostage, and drive out of here in the car or truck or whatever occupied the little garage he'd seen on the far side of the house. He felt sure there *was* a family. A swing set with a slide stood in the dusty yard, and a girl's bike leaned against a side porch. Drago thought he'd even spotted a small face in one of the back windows, watching him as he crossed the field, but he was so tired he wasn't certain.

The problem was, this fellow didn't look easy to threaten. He was big, and appeared to be strong as an ox. The better option, Drago decided, was to kill him quick—strong wouldn't matter if Drago got in close enough, with the knife. Then he could try to locate a firearm and a vehicle and get going. As for taking a family member along as a hostage, that was probably a bad idea. Leonard Drago's policy was to travel alone and leave no witnesses.

With those things in mind, he relaxed his expression and said, "I need your help."

For a long time, they stood there looking at each other.

Finally the farmer said, "You on the run?"

Drago studied the man's face. There was no friendliness in those eyes, no softening of the solemn features. But something about that face, and that no-nonsense voice, made Drago wonder if the guy might have run afoul of the law too, at some point, and if so, maybe he wasn't a big fan of what he would probably call the po-leece. Maybe the enemy of my enemy is my friend.

Still, it was better to take no chances. As he inched his way closer, Drago slowly reached behind him, lifted the tail of his T-shirt, and gripped the handle of the knife in his belt. "Nothing like that," he said. "I'm just lost. Got separated from my survey team south of here, near Blue River, and when I got through the woods—well, I saw your house, and…" He kept approaching as he talked, and at last he was standing beside the row of tomato poles, right in front of the guy, an arm's length away.

Drago tightened his fingers on the knife, began easing it out—

And heard the distant rumble of a car motor.

Both of them turned to look at the dirt road bordering the property. A mile away, across the flats, a vehicle was headed slowly toward them, pulling a white cloud of dust behind it. Even at that distance Drago could see the rack of lights across the top of the car. A police cruiser.

When he turned again, he found the man staring at him.

"I'll ask you again," the farmer said. "Somebody after you?"

Drago glanced once more at the approaching car, and realized he had to change his plan. He swallowed, let his shoulders sag, lowered the tail of his shirt. "Yeah. The truth is, I been growing some weed, me and my daddy. They arrested him yesterday, but I snuck away. I got relatives in Bayou LeBlanc—if I can get there, I'll be safe." He stepped back behind the corner of the nearest outbuilding. "Help me, mister. Please. At least hide me for a few minutes."

The farmer hesitated a moment more, then nodded toward two slanted wooden doors set into the base of the shed beside them, out of view of the driveway. A storm cellar, Drago figured. In the grass next to the doors lay a pair of gloves and hightopped boots.

"In there," the man said. "It's the one place they won't search."

"Why?"

"Because it's locked. Barred." He pointed to the two-by-four wedged through the two handles of the cellar doors.

"So?"

"So, I'll lock it again after you're inside. You can't very well do it yourself, right?"

"What if they figure out you did it *for* me?"

"Think about it." the farmer said. "Why would I hide a white man?"

That made sense.

Without another word, the farmer walked to the cellar, bent down, slid the board free of the handles, and swung one of the doors open on its hinges. It THUNKed backward against the wooden side of the shed.

Drago followed him, stepping over the boots and gloves. He looked for a long moment at the cellar, at the steps leading down into the darkness under the building. Being locked up—locked up *down there* —gave him goosebumps. But the patrol car was here now; he heard it crunch to a stop at the head of the driveway.

He knew he had no choice.

"Get in," the farmer said.

Minutes later, Leonard Drago stood on tiptoe on the second step inside the cellar, squinting out through the tiny spaces between the slats of one of the closed and barred doors. The cop's car was parked out of sight, and the farmer had strolled out to meet his visitor. A moment later Drago saw them move into view, walking out across the side yard. The cop, a black guy in a uniform and a cowboy hat—was *everybody* black in this state, now?—was holding an unlit cigar in one hand and a notepad in the other. As Drago watched, the cop put the cigar between his teeth, opened the pad, and flipped pages. He seemed to be asking questions, and pointing to the south; the farmer replied with frowns and thoughtful shakes of his head.

Drago felt his heart speeding up. He felt sure the conversation was related to him and his whereabouts. What if the policeman was explaining that the man they were searching for was not a dope grower but was in fact a thief and a murderer and an escaped convict? Drago waited, holding his breath, watching for a raised head and a pointing finger and a drawn gun.

It didn't happen. After a couple more minutes, the cop put his notepad away. He and the farmer wandered back toward the driveway, out of Drago's field of vision, chatting like old friends (so much for the hope that this guy hated cops, Drago thought), and after a moment he heard them pass beside his shed. On the way to the house, presumably.

Time ticked away. At one point Drago again thought he heard footsteps behind his hiding place, going away from the house this time, but he heard no voices.

Then he heard a car cranking, and the crunch of its tires on gravel, and the unmistakable sound of its motor receding in the distance. The cop must have left.

But nothing else happened. Drago waited, sweating, for his unlikely benefactor to return, to open the doors and let him out—after which he planned to repay the farmer by slitting his throat, and anyone else's who happened to be on the premises. But no one showed up.

Five minutes passed. Ten. Drago stepped down and moved to the right, trying to see his surroundings in the almost-darkness, and felt his foot hit something hard. He knelt, probed about, and found a huge rectangular pan containing a couple inches of water. Why was *that* here? No matter—at least he wouldn't die of thirst. As that thought occurred to him, he moved up the steps once more, raised his fists, and pounded on the doors. "Let me out!" he shouted.

Still he saw nothing outside the cellar, and heard nothing. He stepped down again.

And then he did hear something. Something *in*side. A movement, off to his left.

He felt his stomach turn over. *Something was in here with him.*

Drago pulled out his knife, held his breath. Tiny bands of light sliced in through the narrow cracks in the doors, but not enough to allow him to see the rest of the room.

He heard another sound, from the right this time. Quiet, whispery, like something brushing across wood. Then more sounds, behind him.

He felt bile rising in his throat, panic arrowing through him. Leonard Drago had been through hard times and scary situations, but he'd never felt fear like this before. He shouted again, wordless this time, a cry of pure terror.

Now there were more sounds, hissing sounds, sliding sounds, and a dusty, whirring buzz that he couldn't pin down. His knees went weak; he shifted position, and stepped on something thick and soft—he felt it move underneath his foot. Off balance, Drago fell to the floor.

Then everything happened at once. Something heavy and sharp hit him just below his ear, like a club with spikes on it. Something else slammed into his cheek, his forehead, his throat.

By now he knew what was it was.

He started screaming again.

At that moment, eight miles away, Deputy Sheriff Virgil Woodson stood on the front steps of the local library with his friend Jake Greenwood, looking through a window at the meeting room. Inside, Jake's wife Dee and his eleven-year-old daughter Kendra were taking their seats. On a makeshift stage in front of them stood a knight, a lady, and a giant frog.

Watching his family, Jake said, "Thanks for giving us a ride, Virge. And for not asking any questions in front of Dee."

"That's me—protect and serve," the deputy said. He looked around to make sure they were alone. "But I'm asking now. You gonna tell me what's going on?"

"In a minute. I'm just lucky there was a performance here today."

Virgil Woodson looked through the window again at Jake's wife and daughter. "It's the only thing I could think of to get them away from the house. And since I *am* finally asking questions—why did you all of a sudden *need* to get them away from the house?"

Jake gave him a strange look. "Because I didn't want to have to explain the sounds they might hear coming from the storm cellar."

"Say what?"

Jake checked his watch. "But I'm thinking that might be over with, by now. Let's give it a while longer—I'll fill you in on the way back."

"Back where?"

"To my house. I told Dee I'd come back here and pick her and Kendra up later. I need you to help me with something." He looked idly toward Virgil's cruiser, parked at the curb.

"You're taking this 'serve' thing a long way," Virgil said. "You mean you need help with the new battery I brought you for your pick-up? The one you didn't want me to take time to unload when we were *at* your house?"

"Yeah," Jake said. "That, too."

Half an hour later, after the short ride back home and after telling a stunned Virgil about this morning's unexpected visitor, Jake Greenwood dropped a coil of rope onto the ground beside his storm cellar, then knelt and removed the bar from the double doors for the second time that day. He pulled one of the doors open and let it fall against the base of the shed. In the harsh light, he and Virgil saw a body lying on its back, still as a stone, at the bottom of the cellar steps.

Virgil whistled. "You were right. That's him."

"You think I'd have done this if there was any doubt?"

They stayed silent a moment, studying the corpse. That it was a corpse was obvious: the upturned face was swollen and bloody and pale as marble, the eyes open and staring as if wondering who was suddenly letting in all that light. The white T-shirt was speckled with red. Lying on the floorboards beside the body was a hunting knife and an Atlanta Braves ball cap.

"Hard to believe," Virgil said quietly. "What are the odds?"

"What?"

"The odds. That this particular guy, out of all the places he could've gone, would come to this particular farm."

"What are the odds that you'd show up in that patrol car just before he killed me?"

Virgil turned to his friend. "Was it that close?"

"He had his hand behind him, probably on that knife you see there. I'd be dead if you hadn't blundered in to bring me my battery. So would my family." Jake stayed silent a minute, deep in thought. "Divine intervention, maybe."

"Could be," Virgil said. "Funny thing is, I wasn't just coming to help get your car going—in case you don't remember, before you took me inside, I asked you some questions the sheriff told me to ask. Questions you wouldn't answer, about this dude and his escape last night."

"Well, he won't be escaping again. Or killing anybody else."

Virgil wiped a hand over his face and glanced at the road to town. "You sure Dee and Kendra won't leave early, find another way home from the library, and catch us at this?"

"I told you, I'm supposed to pick 'em up. Then I'm taking Dee over to visit her dad."

Virgil was still frowning. "Them LSU folks ain't coming today, are they?"

"Next week," Jake said. "Are you done?"

"Done with what?"

"Are you finished trying to think up reasons we can't do this?"

Virgil blew out a sigh. "I guess."

Jake grabbed the gloves and tall boots sitting beside the cellar doors, pulled them on, threw the coil of rope over his shoulder, and walked straight down the steps. He checked carefully to make sure there was nothing lurking inside the dead man's clothes, then picked him up long enough to work a loop of the rope underneath the body's armpits and lash it tight. Moments later, he and Virgil heaved the limp body out of the cellar and onto the brittle grass outside. Jake wrapped it in a bedsheet and bound it with rope at the neck and knees.

It took five minutes to carry the body the two hundred yards west to an abandoned well. They dumped it, sheet and rope and all, into the well, and tossed the knife and baseball cap in on top. Then they shoveled in several feet of dirt.

Afterward, breathing hard, Virgil said, "Why don't I feel worse about this?"

"Because we were soldiers once," Jake said. "Kill or be killed. This isn't that different."

Virgil thought about that awhile, then nodded sadly. "Yeah, it is. You know it is."

"You saying I shouldn't have done it?"

"No." Virgil picked up his shovel, balanced it on his shoulder like a ditchdigger at quitting time, and stared worriedly up at the sky. "I just wish we'd be given a sign, that's all."

"A what?"

"A sign of some kind. An earthquake, a pillar of pink clouds, a James Earl Jones voice from above." He was still squinting into the clear blue heavens. "Or rain, maybe. That could be our sign, you know? A message, that everything's okay."

"There's no rain in the forecast, Virge. Get hold of yourself."

"All right, all right," he growled, and started toward the house. "Let's go tend to your automotive needs. I'm better at that than this."

"Sounds good to me."

"But I wish we'd get a sign."

At two o'clock that afternoon, yet another patrol car arrived at the Greenwood farm. This one was marked BAYOU LEBLANC PO-LICE DEPARTMENT. Two white men climbed out. Jake, who had been kneeling on the porch beside an upturned rocking chair, rose to his feet, put down his screwdriver, and invited them in. His daughter Kendra was sitting in the kitchen, eating a cookie; her eyes widened when the three men trooped in and joined her at the table.

Police Chief Louis Terrell smiled and said, "Afternoon, young lady." He sat and looked around. "Where's your mother?"

"She stayed in town a while, helping Grandpa," Kendra said.

"Give her my best." Without waiting for a reply, Terrell placed both his hands flat on the tabletop and looked at Jake. "Guess you've heard Lenny Drago escaped last night."

Jake nodded. "One of the sheriff's deputies has already been out here, asking about it."

"They're the parish," Terrell said. "I'm the city."

"Actually, Lou, this *is* the parish."

"Well, I'm just a chauffeur today, so it don't matter anyhow. By the way—Officer Heisley, meet Jacob Greenwood. And this little beauty is Kendra. Y'all, this is Charles Heisley, of the state police."

Jake shook hands, then said, "'Fraid I've already told Deputy Woodson everything I know. Which isn't much."

"Mainly we're just wondering if you might've seen anyone around last night or earlier today," Heisley said. "Especially this guy." He took a photo of Drago from his pocket and showed it to Jake and Kendra. "Thing is, we found a dead body in a ditch this morning near Blue River, about four miles south of here, next to a pile of prison clothes. It occurred to us Mr. Drago might've headed through this area to try to make it to Bayou LeBlanc."

"If you're on the run," Jake said, examining the photo, "why head for a town?"

"It's where he grew up, still has some kinfolks around. You might remember a bank robbery there, years ago. Delta National."

Jake looked sharply at Terrell, but saw nothing in his face. "I've heard about it," Jake said to Heisley.

"Then I take it you haven't seen anyone strange lately?"

"Just my friend—the deputy I mentioned. He likes to mooch a meal now and then."

"Well," Heisley said, tucking the photo back into his pocket, "this visit was more to inform you than to question you." He stood up, prompting everyone except Kendra to stand also. "We'll let you folks get back to whatever you were doing."

"Praying for rain, mostly."

"All farmers do that." He shook hands again with Jake. "But I understand you at least have another source of income."

"The snakes, you mean? It's more of a hobby than a job."

"Jake gets friends and neighbors to bring them to him," Terrell said, "and then zoos and medical centers come get 'em and pay him for 'em."

"Interesting. Where do you keep them?"

"A converted storm cellar," Jake said. "Only in warm weather

—but that's most of the year. Feed 'em mice once a week, plenty of those around."

"What kind of snakes?"

"Cottonmouths, mostly. A few copperheads and rattlers. My biggest customers are medical labs at Tulane and LSU that use them to develop antivenom."

"Interesting," Heisley said again.

As they turned to leave, Chief Terrell lagged behind. "Can I use your facilities, Jake?" he said, pointing to the bathroom down the hall.

Jake nodded. "We'll be outside." He pointed to Kendra to stay put at the table, then followed Heisley through the living room and out the front door.

On the porch, Officer Heisley took a toothpick from a shirt pocket and put it in the corner of his mouth. Wiggling it up and down, he said, "I didn't want to say this in there, in front of your daughter, Mr. Greenwood, but this man Drago—he's a killer. One dead in that bank robbery I mentioned, years ago, and two more in drug deals before that. Not counting a prison guard and the guy we told you they found this morning. He was choked to death."

"I understand," Jake said.

"Make sure you do. Keep doors and windows locked, and be watchful." Heisley paused and seemed to soften a bit. "Terrell says you're a good man. Says he knew your parents."

"Everybody around here knows everybody," Jake said. "Or used to."

"Different world, now," Heisley agreed. He removed the toothpick and flicked it over the porch rail like a cigarette butt. "And that's a shame."

"My friend says we need a sign of some kind."

Heisley turned to look at him. "A sign?"

"You know. A miracle, an act of God. Something to show us we're on the right path."

"Maybe's he's right."

They fell silent. When Chief Terrell came out to join them, the two cops thanked Jake again and stepped down off the porch. Jake watched them walk to their cruiser as Kendra eased out the door and stood beside him. Just before Terrell climbed in behind the wheel, he gave Jake a pleased look, and a solemn little nod. And drove off.

Jake frowned at the dust cloud, thought a moment, and studied his daughter's face. "Did Lou Terrell say anything to you, in there?" Before she could answer, Jake added, "He asked to go to the bathroom. Did he go?"

"No." Kendra suddenly looked older than her years. "Soon as y'all went out onto the porch, he sat back down with me, at the table."

Jake felt a chill go up his spine. "What'd he say to you?"

"He asked me if I'd seen the guy in the picture. Drago."

"What'd you say?"

Kendra shifted from one foot to the other. "I said I did."

"What!?"

"I did, Daddy. I saw him through my window early this morning, coming across the back field from the trees, while you were outside working. He had on a cap and a white T-shirt."

"Why didn't you say something earlier? To me or Virgil?"

"Nobody asked me. I figured it was just somebody out hiking or something, until I saw that picture the Heisley man showed you. And then I was scared to say anything."

"You mention anything about this to your mother this morning?"

"No sir."

"What else did you tell the chief?"

She frowned, remembering. "I said I'd heard somebody talking, outside. Then I'd heard the storm-cellar door slam."

Jake lowered his head, rubbed his eyes with his thumbs. "What did Chief Terrell do?"

"He sort of nodded to himself. Like all of a sudden he understood. Then he patted my head and got up and walked out to where y'all were."

Jake drew a long, shaky breath.

"Did I do something wrong, Daddy?"

"No, honey. I'm just glad it was Lou you told, and not the other guy."

Kendra went quiet. She seemed to think that over. "Can I ask a question?"

"Sure."

"What happened to his hand?"

"What?"

"The chief. His left hand is—well, it's like plastic. What's it called..."

"A prosthetic. You never noticed it before?"

"I never thought to ask before. I know he always wears long sleeves." She paused and said again, "What happened?"

This time it was Jake who hesitated. He stood there leaning against the porch rail, staring out over the delta.

"He got hurt, a long time ago," Jake said. "The day my mother died."

Kendra frowned. "The bank robbery, you mean?"

"Yes. Lou Terrell was there. He was shot." Jake looked his daughter in the eye. "He lost his arm, trying to save your grandma."

Kendra swallowed. He could see her mulling that over.

"But ... Grandma died."

"Yes, she did. I wish you could've known her." He lifted a hand, touched his palm to her cheek. "Take a lesson, honey: Sometimes things don't work out the way they're supposed to."

For several minutes, neither of them spoke. Somewhere in the distance, a train whistle blew. A crow cawed.

At last she said, "The chief—Mr. Terrell. He's a good friend?"

"He's a very good friend."

The silence dragged out. Jake turned to look at her. "What?" he said.

"Well... he's white."

Jake couldn't help smiling. "Friends are friends, Kendra. Another lesson."

He watched her think that over.

"Better get to your chores, kiddo. We need to go pick up your mom soon."

"Okay."

Jake had knelt again beside the broken chair, screwdriver in hand, when he realized his daughter hadn't moved. She was still staring at him, her eyes narrow and focused and—somehow—*knowing*.

"What is it, Kendra?"

"That man. Drago." She paused. "We won't have to worry about him anymore. Will we."

"No."

She walked to the door and stopped, her hand on the knob. After a long wait she said, "Sometimes they do."

He looked at her. "What?"

"Sometimes things *do* work out."

Jake just nodded.

He watched her go inside, then went back to his work. He was tightening the last screw on the mended rocker when he heard something, a soft pattering like the tap of fingertips on a drum. The sound grew, first to a trembling rumble, then to a roar. He turned to look out at the darkening yard, the driveway, the suddenly dripping eaves of the barn roof—and smiled.

It was raining.

Binate

by Gabriella T. Rieger

"Binate (adj., botany): produced or borne in pairs"

It is as if the train will forever sit in Lod
and never move on to Tel Aviv and the great cypress trees of the
        North,
to Caesarea at the edge of the sea,
to the Baha'i Temple and its terraces, an ark to desert flora.

I've been wandering this teeming oasis for awhile now,
watching the bedrock of shifting borders sprouting checkpoints,
grey concrete slabs laid in one by one.
I can see the winnowing away of East Jerusalem from the ramparts,
Ma'arat HaMachpela partitioned and barred in cast iron.

Here in this land where every place has two names
I am one of many
I help the wheel turn, without knowing direction.
On the road to the Dheisha refugee camp, homes of Martyrs once
        stood,
now children gather scrap metal in shopping carts.

I still dream of olive trees, Yousef,
I plant them for you here,
in Palestine.
This is what American Jews do, we plant trees in Eretz Yisrael
and dedicate them to our grandparents.
Our grandparents who survived or did not survive the Holocaust
who sought refuge
who walked the streets with stars sewn to their clothes
who hid, who ran, who crossed the Pyrenees,
who spent three years in a detention camp in Jamaica
who moved boulder by boulder in the Gush irrigating the land

who built universities and hospitals
who thought the Sinai War was the war that would end all wars.
Who closed the streets of Hebron,
the storefronts, for more than 10 years
painted a green line on a cement divider
and directed traffic: Jews to the left, Arabs to the right
HaMachpelah, Al-haram al-ibrahimi, split
the tomb of our ancestors
Jews in one entrance
Arabs another
Al-Khalil, Hebron
Avraham, Ibrahim
the tomb of our forefathers

The Cats of Rome

by Edison Jennings
(for Felicia Mitchell)

George W. Bush / Silvio Berlusconi,
Second Gulf War Summit, Rome, June 4, 2004

The cats of Rome sleep, feed, and breed
among the tumbled travertine, and slip,
tails high, across the flag draped avenues.
Ignoring pomp, alert to circumstance,
they cruise cafes for crumbs or prowl
the Pantheon.
                    Because the ages blaze
and fade, the cats ignore the ranks
of flags and fleets of long black cars.
At the axis of the empire, they curl
round Trajan's column, indifferent
to a fault, at home in a falling world.

Wardrobe Conditional

by Rikki Santer

It would have been smoother
if I hadn't been hijacked by his hat menagerie
crumpled against the circular wall
of a mildewed hat box, faded stripes
in hoarse harmony with themselves, or the
two I had taken from that sack
of discarded neckties left on the freeway's
meridian, three sixes swirled into the flavors
on each of its tongues.

If I could only rewind and unsee
the hawk's crime as it raided the murder
of crows, the limp blackness dragged
across the manicured lawn, the deconstructed
cloak of white down and black feather forsaken
while the helpless opera of grating caws
lingered like ghosts in twilight, or if only
I could reweave the peach and cream
gingham of a ripped party dress and erase
the red palm print stinging a six-year-old's thigh.

Tiger Hill's Thousand-Man Rock:
Two Etymologies
by James Penha

> *It would be a pity if you had been to Suzhou,*
> *but didn't get to visit Tiger Hill.*
> *--Su Shi (Song Dynasty)*

Summer sun incarnadines the Rock in
        Suzhou
as blood evaporates from where it has
        reigned
since King Wu was entombed
with one thousand artisans
who sculpted his mausoleum on Tiger Hill
but might not keep its secrets . . .

or . . .

Sheng Gong, the banished monk
who would not bow to Beijing
found refuge in the rockery
of Tiger Hill.

Suzhou turned away its eyes and ears
from the apostate
so Sheng Gong preached
to Tiger Hill, its stones and trees.
Branches assented noisily;
boulders nodded
and one by one the men
of Suzhou dared
to join a miracle.

They were uplifted
a thousand of them
from the Rock
no one knew
hid the tomb of Wu.
Sheng Gong stood his ground.

Atop Tiger Hill
the brick pagoda
also stands tall . . .
or . . .
leans
depending on one's
perspective

A Knife in the Hand

by Atar J. Hadari

They didn't say it wouldn't be mine.
Looking out the window of the cabin,
looking overboard at that unfolding shore of Arab towers,

I knew whatever I brought with me
when Shmuel whisked me away, and shouted "Marry me"
—whatever I managed to keep in my head of medicine and bandages

was all I was going to get
there was no more of it here to be had,
this was the end of promises.

So we bought bad land. I acknowledge it.
We didn't have money. But we bought.
Whatever these swindlers thought

when we came and bought those shameful acres
that is what we bought.
And then to say—"But it's democracy.

Your husband wants to grow what? He's just crazy!"
If anybody may be foolish
it's me for being here to plant these oranges

rather than in a white coat and stethoscope in Budapest
but let *me* say if my husband is out of it,
I may be mad but he knows about plants.

What is democracy? A bunch of strangers
forcing you to think not what's in your own hand.
I walked the wards, in Budapest, I smelt the vagaries,

laudanum, the gas they burned to boil the instruments,
they just about wore masks when I was trained
—I could have been a surgeon, I, the only girl

to wear a star of David in our whole part of the Pale
with not one Jew but our house in that bit of the Mongol veil—
I was going to treat the lame and sick,

wear an icy gown
walk from bed to bed and nod and frown—
I wanted it so much I still taste sweet

in the back of my throat, sometimes
when I wake up at midnight and the hiss
of laudanum, the fire under instruments boiled red

makes me dig the nails into my palm—
I wanted it so bad I could have bled
from looking at those Jaffa shacks on the shore line

and I did not come here and give all that up
to be told by some socialist whose land
will be given away as a free gift to new inhabitants.

So they had a vote? So what?
So they said the village votes to donate land.
Did *I* say I'd give up some dirt? Did we even raise a hand

when the party owns all the hands that count?
So I went out, at midnight, I admit it,
in my bare feet I ran to the fence post

where the line-man stretched his spool of tin—
and I cut it—I'm not ashamed to recount—
—in two places—wire shone in the moon like a jagged throat

down an old lady's collar bone
where the knife can slip under the wrinkled slit—
I used to be the one holding the knife,

If Shmuel had waited till I wore my graduation gown
to get scared and run out of Poland
I'd have been a qualified surgeon

a potentate
not some thief who has to steal the air to breathe in.
Next day the line-man came and knocked

He says, "Your husband in?"
"Away," I say, "paying the loan
for this land, working other people's farms."

Those bastards wanted to give away our land
away but would not waive one *grush* of loan.
We bought the land all right, just not a say in how things run.

"Funny thing," he says, "I stretched the line
across your land last night. Right through to where you planted ..."
"Rhubarb." "Rhubarb? ... Interesting. In any event,

the wire fell-down, in two places,
Right where it meets the fence in fact.
Exactly as if cut, a perfect slit."

"Do you think it was a good clean cut?" I said.
He looked at me. "Who made that cut can shave me any day."
So we're talking. I tell Him about Shmuel's new ideas in fruit,

The criminal mistakes these fools
running the place took in their heads,
about the leper wards, the syphilis,

The world that's gone and never will repeat
and he says, shyly, "I did come
Back from the old country with a teeny problem."

He was a shtetl boy, turns out,
run off from the yeshiva bench to find
exactly what it is boys usually do find

when they run off with one thing on their mind.
So I told him *peni-ci-llin*.
They were prescribing that when I was first trained, just.

I know a syphilitic can touch a girl again.
He can go back if he wants, to that yeshiva bench.
Not like a woman with a son

Who threw off her white coat and bought the land.
He didn't mention that cut wire again.
We parted like the best of friends.

And while the village had a lot of plots
that much smaller, ours has stayed just the same.
A little bigger now than those Socialist plots with their heroic names.

I treasure it, that time, I got to feel what I could still have been—
getting a patient to open up
takes more than a white gown—

and I walk in the orange buds
and smell the instruments that cut and hear the roar
of all those tiny flaming heads and spread my hands into the clouds

and feel the hot breath of the fruit
and know I will not give an inch of this
before the surgeon comes to take my youth.

Father Pearson's Last Day

by Nick Bouchard

A̲BEL P̲EARSON WOKE from an uncomfortable sleep to sirens scream-ing from the street below. The sound meant there would be work to do. He looked at the one-handed clock on the nightstand—the minute hand had been lost years ago, the hour hand pointed between five and six. The warm glow coming through his curtains told him it was evening.

He got up from his frameless bed and walked to the kitchen, started a pot of coffee, and leaned against the counter. His breathing was heavy and his eyes dry, as though they had run out of tears.

Abel's fingers crackled through the thick stubble on his cheeks. The sound reminded him of work to be done. It was Wednesday. He would have to shave. God was no longer a bearded man smiling down from puffy white clouds. He had become a clean-shaven bureaucrat peering over a clipboard.

Early in his career, Abel tried to maintain a second job, to occupy time. He didn't need money. He had never been comfortable in public. His chosen career did nothing to allay his unease. On his days off he felt suspicious, as though there was a man in a dark suit, lurking in a dark alley with one hand inside his dark jacket. Abel knew he was, in some way, the man in the alley.

Abel's knees ached. He plopped into his kitchen chair—an indestructible relic with a cracked vinyl seat and tubular chrome frame. The sight of the chair brought unbidden memories of Father Tom. It hurt to look at, but he was certain it would hurt more to part with it. Its connection to the hours of conversation and comfortable silence the two of them shared was marrow deep. Tom often chided him for hanging onto such old things. He knew Abel had the means to procure replacements. They all did. Abel, however, derived no joy from the act of buying things. Some indulged more; few indulged less than Abel.

The lone chair in his kitchen creaked as the coffee maker burbled. When it hissed its last drops, he stood and removed the only object within the cabinet above—a large ceramic mug. He once kept two, but Father Tom's mug had been buried with him. Abel smiled sadly at the memory of secreting it into the casket at the sparsely attended funeral.

Even as his shaking left hand placed the mug on the counter, a perfectly steady right hand opened the freezer. It emerged with a half-empty fifth of spiced rum.

He poured two fingers into his mug and filled the rest with coffee. After a couple sips, he tossed the whole mug back.

The first time he tried rum in his coffee was after he said The Prayer with a seven-year-old girl. It was only a splash, and he drank it slowly. Time passed, and he increased the rum and the rate at which he drank it. After the girl, a pint could last him a month. Now a fifth was good for no more than a day.

While he poured his second cup his imagination danced momentarily past a handle of rum nestled into the frost inside his freezer. He imagined it right down to the bright pink price stickers from the package store. A brief smile stretched across his face, thin and pale. He knew he was headed for Section Five. He knew it because he was daydreaming about bigger bottles of liquor. He knew it because his knees refused to hold him up. He knew it because the loss of Father

Tom had left him empty.

Emptiness drove him to the job. Now it would drive him out.

Father Tom went to Section Five in June, just six weeks ago. Father Brian a month earlier. They were both in their thirties, thirty-two and thirty-eight, respectively, and considered old for the job. Abel had outlived most men in their line of work. He thought that at fifty-two he might have reached a milestone of some sort, but not one likely to be celebrated with balloons and cake, nor a brief column with a grainy photo in the local paper.

His third cup emptied both the pot and the bottle. Abel made his way back down the hall to the bathroom. He opened the mirrored medicine cabinet above the sink and removed a can of Barbasol with a steady hand. He turned on the water and, knowing how long it would take to warm up, walked back through the kitchen to the pantry.

Abel's pantry was little more than a closet, well lit, with organized shelves. He pulled the chain and the single, unshaded bulb glared. He squinted as he scanned the shelves. He glanced at the top shelf; certain that it held only condensed soups and canned tuna. The second shelf had more of the same, some instant oatmeal and cold cereal. Abel found what he needed poking out from behind some cans of tomato soup. He grabbed the pack of razors and returned to the bathroom after pulling the light's chain again, plunging the pantry back into darkness.

He opened the package, took out a razor, and placed the other five inside the medicine cabinet. Abel held a hand under the tap. Still cold. He silently cursed the old building.

As much as they annoyed him, Abel was resigned to the building's quirks. The hospital gave a sizeable stipend to priests who lived in Dalton Tower. Not that it mattered much. Abel had no will. All his earthly possessions would revert back to the church when he passed.

Father Tom lived two floors up from him until his recent passing. Tom was the only friend that Abel had made in the nearly thirty years since he started his job at the hospital. Apart from the bland pleasantries of day-to-day life, Tom was the only person Abel had really spoken to during his tenure.

❖

The day he met Tom, Abel took the elevator to the ground floor and stepped into the lobby. The sun slanted in through the glass front and winked off the chrome trim on the wide exit doors as they closed. Abel held his hand up to cut the glare from the polished marble floor. A dark, unsteady silhouette shambled toward him. Abel could smell the man before he could really see him. He smelled like beer.

The drunken shape made its way out of the glare and Abel could see that it was another, younger priest stumbling into Dalton Tower at eight in the morning. Abel was appalled until he saw the hospital ID badge still clipped to the drunk's shirt pocket. He read the name on the badge and tucked it into the pocket.

"Good morning, Father Tom," Abel said.

"Hunh? Who are you?"

"A colleague. Was today your first day?"

"Hunh? Oh, uh, yesh."

"I live in fifty-four-oh-seven. Stop by when you wake up and I'll fix us a pot of coffee."

"Okay." Tom lurched into the elevator.

Thick steam rose from the sink, fogging a wide arc at the bottom of the mirror. Abel fiddled with the taps to balance the temperature.

He cupped his hands under the faucet and splashed water onto his face. The Barbasol puffed up as it squirted into his palm. He worked the thick foam into his beard.

Abel grabbed a towel and turned on the shower, allowing time for the shaving cream to soften his beard, per the can's instructions. He returned to the sink and shaved while he waited for the hot water to make its way to the shower. It seemed that instead of the sink and shower being plumbed off the same line, they were individually supplied from the boilers in the basement.

When Abel finished his shave, he discarded the dulled razor, stepped out of his underthings and over the edge of the claw-foot bathtub. He pulled the curtain shut and rinsed his stinging face.

Abel took a long shower, letting the warm water flow over him. It softened the stiffness of age and heavy drinking. The hiss of the showerhead and the gentle spatter of water on the porcelain drowned out the rest of the world. The noises were the sounds of innocence. Abel had always thought it was a strange association, but if he could still remember the rain thrumming on the vinyl roof of his parents' pop-up camper and the smell of Jiffy-Pop, he wouldn't find it so strange.

Abel's parents loved him. Of that he was certain. Whether he had loved them was unclear. There was the accident when he was ten. Perhaps he loved them but never got the chance to love them enough. The only person he was sure he loved was Father Tom.

It was almost three in the afternoon. Abel sat in his recliner thumbing through *Reader's Digest.* He was reading the *Humor in Uniform* section, which included a particularly funny story about an Army Ranger, an Air-Force private, and a small package of Oreos when an electric buzz filled the apartment.

The strange and insistent clatter reminded him of a wind-up toy from his childhood. A little robot with a ray gun that rolled around in erratic circles.

The buzz stopped. Abel stared, trying to pin down the meaning of this sound. Then it started again, followed by a muffled "Hello?" from the door. Abel did not think his doorbell had ever rung before.

"Hello?" Abel asked the vaguely familiar, tidy young man standing in the doorway.

"Uh, yeah, hi, I'm… well…" The young man's eyes were cast down.

"Father Tom," Abel said when recognition set in. "I thought that you had forgotten my invitation. In fact, I may have forgotten it as well."

"No. I was embarrassed. I almost didn't come at all."

"Better late than never," Abel tried on his smile. It felt false. Father Tom raised an eyebrow as if to ask why they were still in the doorway. Abel invited him in.

Abel led Father Tom to the living room and sat him in the recliner. Father Tom looked around. There were no other chairs. Abel felt a genuine smile cross his face this time.

"Don't worry, I have another chair in the kitchen," Abel said before leaving the room. While Abel busied himself with the coffee filter and the big can of Chock Full O' Nuts, he tried to remember his first day on Five.

He poured water into the coffee maker and set it to brew, all the while realizing that he could not recall his first day. He only remembered that it had been difficult dealing with the reality of his task as an ordained doctor.

"How do you take your coffee?"

"Black."

Abel waited for the coffee to finish, poured two mugs, and brought them out to the living room. He placed them on the TV tray and went back to the kitchen to fetch the only other chair in the apartment. The vinyl had not yet cracked and the chrome was blindingly bright. Abel sat across the tray from Father Tom. Abel brought his mug to his lips and blew lightly. As he watched the steam eddying across the surface of the coffee, he realized something.

"My name is Abel."

"Call me Tom."

"I work the Thursday shift. I'm guessing from when I saw you in the lobby you have the Tuesday shift?"

"Yes," Tom's eyes were fixed, staring at his shoes.

"My first night was rough, too. I don't remember much except that I didn't feel too good when I got home. I was sad."

"But you didn't go get pissdrunk, did you?"

"No. I sat in that chair you're sitting in now for almost two whole days. The training teaches that it will be tough the first few times out, but that it becomes easier with time. I can attest to the truth in that."

"I don't see how it could," Tom said with tears in his eyes. The blue was bright and glassy under his dark black eyebrows. Tom blinked a couple times, and then looked at his coffee. He sipped at it in an effort to avoid eye contact.

"It will get easier, just like everything else."

"I don't know," Tom paused. "After yesterday, I can see why men of our profession have such short lives."

"The Prayer is very stressful. That was a part of the training, too."

"I think there's more to it than that. I think it's bad for our souls. What we are paid to do is a sin. The government, with the full support of the church, *pays* us to commit mortal sins."

"You know that isn't true. We have been exempted. Our place in heaven is reserved. The service we perform is redemption for the sin," he countered.

Abel believed the teachings in those days. But that very night, with the doubts of Father Tom rolling around inside his head like spilled marbles, Abel met a young girl named Brianna Collins, an innocent seven-year-old with luminous, feline green eyes, red hair, and a brain tumor. Abel said The Prayer with her, and then bought a pint of rum on his way home. The next day he visited Father Tom's apartment for more coffee and conversation, a tradition that continued for more than ten years.

A burst of icy water yanked Abel from his memory. He turned the tub handles to their off positions, threw open the curtain, and toweled himself off. Abel took his worn terry-cloth robe off the hook on the back of the door and went into his bedroom.

He grabbed a fresh pair of black socks and clean underthings from his dresser. He put on a pair of black slacks, then took a black dress shirt to the kitchen and hung it over the back of the chair.

Abel went back to the bathroom, splashed aftershave on his face and dusted his underarms with talcum powder. Abel looked in the mirror; his face had aged a decade since yesterday. When he could no longer tolerate his reflection, he returned to his room for an undershirt. He fumbled his belt through the loops on his slacks as he returned to the kitchen.

He made himself a can of tomato soup and took it to the TV tray in front of his recliner. He looked at the tray as he pulled it closer, careful not to spill.

The tray was covered with his brown coffee-stain Venn diagrams and the Olympic rings Tom liked to make.

He constantly missed Tom. Sometimes they sat for hours, and all Tom said was "I don't know," as he stared out the window. He had been much too sensitive for the job. Tom chose the profession out of a sense of duty to help make the world great again. Abel chose it because it held humanity at arm's length.

Abel finished his soup and began to read an old *Reader's Digest* from the magazine rack. He tried to take his mind off Tom, but couldn't, so he dropped the magazine to the floor and put his head back. He closed his eyes. Tom's dark hair and easy smile reminded Abel of his own father. As Abel faded into a dreamless sleep, he thought he smelled popcorn for a moment, and a smile stretched across his pale lips.

Abel awoke feeling weak and shaky. He went straight to the freezer, where he opened a new bottle, pitched the top, and drank directly from it. He drank until the shaking stopped. When the shaking stopped, he drank until the sadness ebbed. He no longer felt weak.

He looked at the clock above the kitchen sink. It read 10:45. He picked up the shirt from the back of his chair, took a deep breath, sighed, and pushed his arms down the sleeves.

Abel's clumsy fingers took minutes to finish buttoning the shirt. He thought another swig of rum would help steady his hands. He tipped the bottle again, emptying the last drops into his mouth with a grimace. Tying his shoes was an ordeal.

By 11:05, Abel was out the door. He walked down the hall and got inside the tarnished brass elevator. The accordion gate rasped shut, and he pushed the L. Abel looked up and watched the arrow move left within its ornate half circle from 5 to 4, 3, 2, and finally to L. Abel opened the gate and made his way across the marble floor.

Outside, he hailed the first cab he saw. He got into the backseat.

"Where to?"

"Northam General, please."

"Righto," the cabbie answered and began to talk to Abel about the ballgame.

Abel's head ached, so he closed his eyes, and lay his head back. He fell asleep for the second time that day. When the cab lurched to a stop in front of Northam General Hospital, Abel woke up. The driver was still yammering about the game. Abel paid the fare and got out, wondering if the driver had been talking for the entire drive.

He reached into his pocket and took out his white collar. He fit it around his neck so that the embroidered emblem was centered below his chin. It was a blue snake wound around a crucifix with its head turned inward, facing Christ. This was the emblem of all priests whose task it was to bring The Prayer to the sick.

Abel looked up at the dimly lit windows of the fifth floor. As with every other visit, he remembered pulling up to this very same door, and one of the redcaps putting a hand on his back to guide him in to see his parents before they prayed.

He entered the HOSPITAL STAFF ONLY door and walked down the hall to the lockers. Turning his key, he removed his ID badge and battered Bible. The book was adorned with an Aesculapian crucifix like the one on his collar—this time of peeling gold leaf. Abel walked back down the hall to the elevator, got inside, and selected number five.

"Would you like me to say The Prayer with you, Mister ah—" Abel glanced at the chart hanging from the bedpost, in search of a name, "Flemming?"

The shriveled man whispered and extended a liver-spotted, arthritic hand toward Abel. Abel opened his Bible to the page marked with a crimson ribbon, even though he knew the verse by heart.

Abel held Mr. Flemming's hand and clicked a syringe into the IV line. He pushed the plunger and they prayed together until Mr. Flemming's breath stopped. Abel prayed until the gentle tapping in Mr. Flemming's wrist stopped. He stood, pressed two fingers into Mr. Flemming's neck, and looked at his watch.

He jotted the time on the line marked Time of Death, checked the box next to Accepted Christ, and collapsed into darkness.

Abel awoke to a gentle hand on his shoulder. Someone was talking to him, but he was unable to understand. He blinked slowly in an attempt to clear his vision. Seconds passed as his eyes cleared enough to discern the outline of a man. A few ticks of the clock, and Abel understood that the man next to him was a young priest. The badge clipped to his pocket read: Father Ryan Cain, MD. Father Ryan looked nervous. It was probably his first day.

"Would you like to say The Prayer with me, Father Pearson?" the young man said to him, as he flicked a syringe with a shaky hand.

Abel laid his head back and closed his eyes.

Drag

by Gina L. Grandi

Try this, he said. Mark your arms with sequins. Use beads instead of blood.

Change your ritual. There's comfort in this kind of ceremony, too. There are tools to be maintained. Strokes to be laid upon the skin. Build, here. Transform.

Get to know these smells. The dusty heat of a blow dryer. The kick of hairspray. The plastic damp of neoprene. These things are not uncommon; you will chance across one or the other in your day to day, and that will bring you comfort. You will find home in pockets of air.

Pull each zipper slowly, the way you'd run your fingers over a scar. Zip and unzip as many times as you'd like—the sound will soothe. It will satisfy.

A fringe will brush your thigh more provocatively than a blade.

A bruise stays silent. A cut keeps secrets. A costume, that screams out loud. Wear your tears on your sleeve. On your hip. In your hair.

Dress up in your pain. Take it for a walk. Let the world marvel.

This mirror, these brushes, this pile of spandex and tulle. This is your armor. These are your weapons. Here is your sanctuary.

This you can take off, he said. This, when you choose, you can leave behind.

Creature of Habit
by Caroline Taylor

She was naked, as usual. Strutting about her tiny apartment without a care as to who might be peeping. I'm no perv. I'm just a human being who happened to live about forty or so feet across an alley in a high-rise on the same floor as the one where she lived.

I'm also a woman with normal hang-ups about modesty. Blinds and drapes covered my windows, but I found myself opening them practically every night to watch the shameless woman. She had a dancer's posture and the long, lithe body that goes with that profession. But I was pretty sure hers had nothing to do with dancing en pointe in a tutu. She had thick, bottle blonde hair and the bust of a stripper and probably earned her money wrapping herself around a pole in a dark, beer-smelling "club" somewhere on the seedy side of town. Or doing lap dances.

Which was none of my business. I plead overexposure to media-induced voyeurism, the kind that has you salivating at the latest celebrity—and, these days, political—antics, watching people fall apart after disasters or scandals or other tragedies, snickering at the rich and famous and their feet of clay. Oh, yeah. I was a media junkie, perhaps even an addict.

I couldn't help making up stories to explain the nightly nudity. She was Swedish (despite the bottle) and preferred going au naturel. She was somehow filming herself for a kinky purpose. She was allergic to cloth of any kind. She only had one set of clothes, and they were either in the washer or dryer. She got off on the idea that lots of peeping toms (tomettes?) like me were enjoying the show. But still...

The night it happened was particularly dark. No moon, lowering clouds. I figured she must have put the thermostat up to 80. Either that or she wasn't human. Then, a man walked into the room. In all the weeks I'd been feeding my inner voyeur, I'd never seen her have any visitors. She didn't look happy to see him. I wouldn't have, either, considering he was dressed head to toe in black, including a black wool cap and gloves. The man took two strides across the room and grabbed her by the throat. She put up a fight, I must admit, dragging him closer and closer to the window. Her back was to me, her hair swinging wildly as she jerked herself from side to side. His grip on her throat tightened as he stared at me. He was strangling the dancer, and there wasn't a damn thing I could do. I pulled my phone out of my pocket and held it up, motioning that I was going to call 9-1-1, which I did, just not hitting "send."

Anyway, it was too late. The woman's body slumped to the floor, and the man gave her a vicious kick. Then he pointed his finger at me like it was a gun and left.

An upright citizen would complete the call. Talk to the cops. Maybe do one of those ID sketches. Although I considered myself to be upright, I was not a citizen. My tourist visa had expired eons ago. Doing my civic duty would get me deported back to Ireland, where the man I'd run away from would find me and—

All the killer had to do was look for a woman living on the 14th floor of the building across the alley. He might already be in the lobby. I grabbed my go kit, left the door unlocked, and fled down the stairs to the garage.

I'd learned some lessons from the thing back home. Always have cash, a weapon, a change of clothes, toiletries, and any useful documents packed up and ready to go. In my case, all I had was a forged Social. It was a good one, and I could use it to find work since my connection to the murder would remain unknown. But the police! I should have shut the damn blinds before running. The cops would notice that, and they would naturally want to ask me if I'd seen anything.

How about plenty. The man was tall, white, and probably young. He moved like an athlete. Oh. And strong. Very strong. The dancer had to be over five and a half feet tall and physically fit, even if not capable of overwhelming a taller, heavier man. Poor thing.

So bye-bye, city of my dreams. Hello, America. I headed west, naturally, thinking I might drive all the way to La La Land where the sunshine and beaches would be a welcome break from polar temps and the boss didn't care what your status was.

When I saw the news from Philly the next morning, I nearly threw up my breakfast. The police were searching for the murderer of an exotic (I was right!) dancer. They also wanted to question a woman who might have witnessed the deed.

Angie, the woman who employed me to clean offices, sent me a text: Where R U?

I didn't answer. Yeah, she owed me some money, but running away means cutting all ties. In fact, I'd probably have to dump the phone at some point. Angie was only one of several people who had my number, and at least three of them knew where I lived. Not that it would—

Oh, shit. I'd told Roberto Capuano about the stripper, hinting I might invite him up for a viewing if he'd like. Roberto and I had enjoyed a couple of wild and crazy bouts between his rumpled sheets until his eye had wandered to a chick three years younger than me with breasts as big as grapefruits and an IQ about the same. I'd dumped Roberto, not very graciously, but the invitation had been extended before the eye had wandered. If the police found anything in my place with his name on it, I was toast.

Why would I have anything with his name on it? That question kept me awake nights as I drove across wild and wonderful West

Virginia and into Ohio. It dogged my wheels as I tried to stay awake while navigating the endless prairies of the hinterland. I worked a couple of weeks at a truck stop outside of Pueblo, Colorado, but had to leave when a zoned-out trucker cornered me in the restroom and I'd had to slice his face open.

I zipped down to New Mexico and landed at a godforsaken town called Los Robles in the middle of the desert, far from anything that could be called a city. Had to stop there because the engine on my shitty Chevy Spark was about to blow, and I couldn't have that happen in the middle of nowhere.

Not that the town was much better. There was a gas station, but the mechanic just shrugged when I asked him if he could fix the car and how much it would cost. There was a diner with a Help Wanted sign in the window. There was a store that sold nearly everything but new Chevy Spark engines. And, of course, a Catholic church, surrounded by a cemetery so bleak the dead must be weeping in their graves.

I was about to cry, when a Greyhound bus pulled up beside the store. The sign at the front of the bus said Los Angeles. I went inside and bought a ticket to Phoenix, which would give me some funds left over to eat. I boarded the bus, thinking maybe I should have tried to negotiate a price for the car—scrap or whatever—but that would have meant spending the night or maybe even longer until the next bus came through.

Well, fuck it.

I was beginning to feel confident I'd cheated death again, until I stupidly decided to check my messages and found one from Roberto Capuano. "Hope your gone, mi inamorata. Cops came by & I told them about the stripper. They said somebody trashed your place. You owe him money?"

I spent the remainder of the journey, telling myself I was still okay. I was more than halfway across the country, after all. They might trace my car to New Mexico, but I could have gone anywhere after that. I was okay. As for the guy trashing my apartment, it had to be the killer. I didn't owe anybody a dime. Yet. At the rate I was going, though, I would be dumpster diving for my next meal.

Time to ditch the phone. I left the bus in Tucson, where I tried to sell it, but got only head shakes. "Old technology, man," said one dude sporting a soul patch and backwards baseball cap that would have been cool ten years ago on the East Coast. So I pitched it.

Luckily, it was easy to find work. I did a stint at McDonald's, where I would use the bathroom to brush my teeth, comb my hair, and once a week, give myself a soap and paper towel "bath." In the evenings, I would hop a bus to the airport and stroll around until the wee hours. There are always people sitting around airports, many of them sleeping while they wait for a delayed flight.

Eventually, I moved on to a Mexican restaurant called Guapos where I earned enough in tips to rent a small furnished efficiency, the veritable lap of luxury after months of being homeless.

The manager at Guapos was a stout, middle-aged woman by the name of Irma, which she pronounced Eerma. She wore her graying hair in a bun at the back of her neck and reeked of cigarette smoke in a place where smoking was banned. "See that fella over there?" she said, my first day on the job. She pointed to a slightly built teenager with a shaved head and glasses who was sitting so stiffly upright, he looked like a crash dummy. On closer inspection, I realized he wasn't a kid. "Always comes in at noon. Not 11:59 or 12:02, but noon. On. The. Dot. Always orders the Combo 3 and coffee," she said. "Always by himself. Always leaves twenty percent. Unless," she squinted at me, "you mess up."

"Like, give him the wrong order?"

"Yeah. Or the coffee's only lukewarm or the enchiladas have been sitting under the heat lamp too long or he has to wait more than ten minutes."

"Sheesh."

"He never makes a fuss, mind you. But he also doesn't leave a dime for a tip if you screw up." She smiled. "Weird, but we take good care of him." Then she narrowed her eyes at me. "You do that, and I won't fire you."

It wasn't hard to do, and the guy did tip generously. But I began to think of him as a robot, he was so eerily punctual and predictable. The lenses of his glasses were so thick, I couldn't see his eyes, not that he ever looked at me. But the daily routine might as well have been programmed into his brain circuits. He would walk in the door at twelve noon. He would sit at the same table, facing away from the front of the restaurant. He would open the menu. He would take a sip of his water before ordering the Combo 3 and coffee. Then he would turn his attention to a paperback book, usually some kind of hard-boiled detective story. He would take about twenty minutes to eat, and then he would leave the money, always cash, without asking for the tab. I wondered if the guy was one of those mildly autistic people, but I didn't dwell on it as I had with the naked dancer. I was too busy making sure Irma didn't decide to fire me. I was also trying to figure out how long I needed to work at Guapos before I could start putting money away for a future that didn't involve going home every night with aching feet and a sore back.

All those thoughts evaporated one morning when I saw somebody tall and athletic going into the McDonald's where I had once worked. The shape of his head set off alarm bells. Or maybe it was the way he moved. There was something eerily familiar about it that did not remind me of Roberto Capuano or any of the other men I'd known Back East. I tried to convince myself it wasn't the killer, but the hairs on the back of my neck wouldn't agree.

And then I realized how stupid I'd been to use the Social to get both jobs. Where the boss at McDonald's had been happy to hand out paychecks every two weeks, Guapos had my address, and that meant not only the killer but the cops would eventually find me. I found myself standing at the window of my efficiency, peering into the darkness, trying to see if anyone was out there watching the building.

In the morning, I hit Mickey Dees for my usual.

"Guy was in here yest'day askin' 'bout you," said Humberto, the morning shift manager, as he handed me my coffee.

"Really." I blew at the coffee, trying to channel Miss Nonchalant.

"Says he got some money for you." Humberto grinned, displaying the wide gap between his teeth. He pulled a scrap of paper out from beneath the cash drawer and handed it to me. "His number. You got a rich uncle died somewhere?"

I forced a laugh. "I wish." Shoving the paper into my jeans pocket,

I sent Humberto an air kiss and left.

At the end of my shift at Guapos, I cornered Irma in the bar. "I have to go Back East," I told her. "Apparently, the police in my home town think I have some useful information in a murder case."

"Do you?" she asked, lighting up a cigarette.

"Probably," I said. "Might you hire me back when I return?"

"Maybe." She took a drag and blew it out through her nostrils. "They going to arrest you?"

"Oh, no. I was just a witness. But I don't want them thinking I ran out on them like some kind of fugitive."

"Are you?"

Shit. Did she know about my immigration status? I shook my head. "Of course, not. This should be settled in a few days."

She walked over to the cash register at the bar and opened the drawer, pulled out a wad of bills, and counted them out. "One seventy-five," she said, handing me the money. "Consider that your last paycheck, minus tomorrow 'cause I won't be able to find somebody that quick to take your shift."

"Thank you," I said, pocketing the money. "I shall hope you're hiring when I come back."

"We'll see," she said. "When you come back."

We both knew that wasn't going to happen. At my efficiency, I left the landlord a similar note, but no money, which would piss him off. Packing my go kit, I left the keys on the kitchen counter and fled.

Again. Only this time I had very little money and no way to get a job since I couldn't use the Social anymore.

The following day, I followed Mr. Robot when he left Guapos. He didn't go back to an office. Instead, he stopped and waited for a bus. I joined him, thinking he might recognize me, but so what? I'd make something up.

When the bus arrived, I walked past him and sat two rows back. The bus was pretty empty, considering it was the middle of the day, but it made every single stop on its route, regardless of whether there was anyone to let off or pick up. We finally reached a neighborhood on the outskirts of the city. These houses were all two-level cinderblock—or maybe adobe?—structures with red tile roofs and desert plants scattered around sandy yards.

When Mr. Robot got off, I made a mental note of the street signs. Then I went on to the next stop and walked back. He'd probably already gone inside his house, but I still had to try. I strolled up the street, trying to imagine where a man like that might live. Three of the houses had tricycles or other children's stuff in their yards. At one house, an elderly man was standing on his porch, smoking. He gave me a tiny wave and then went back inside.

Shit. I turned to go back, and saw Mr. Robot emerge from a neatly kept house at the far end of the street. He climbed onto a dirt bike and pedaled off down a path that seemed to lead straight into the desert.

Once he was out of sight, I retraced my steps and approached his house. White. Like all the others on the street. Red tiled roof. Deep set windows. Cactus-filled front yard. Not very appealing, but aesthetics weren't on my radar at the moment. I made a mental note of the house number and then retraced my steps to the bus stop.

It took several days for me to nail down Mr. Robot's routine. He did seem to have a job, one that had him leaving the house at exactly 7:30 every morning and returning at 1:00 pm for his daily dirt bike trip into the desert. At 2:00 pm, he would return to the house for about thirty minutes, probably to shower and change. Then he would catch the bus downtown and would not return until 7:00 pm. For a few hours, the lights of a TV would flicker sporadically behind the slats of his venetian blinds. At precisely 9:00 pm, the lights would go off. What he did on weekends, I didn't know. But by then my feet were worn to a frazzle, and I was beginning to worry that nosy neighbors would wonder why a strange woman kept wandering through the neighborhood at odd times during the day.

One afternoon at about three o'clock, I used my driver's license to unlock the back door. It led straight into the kitchen, which was so clean I wondered if the guy employed a maid. The living room consisted of a sofa and matching chair of the low-end furniture mart type, a modest sized flat screen TV, a coffee table strewn with biking and outdoor magazines, and a smaller table with a landline telephone that looked like a beige version of my grandmother's sixties-era Princess. I lifted the receiver and got a dial tone.

There were three bedrooms upstairs. One was obviously his. Neat as a pin, with a damp towel flung over the shower curtain rod in the master bathroom. The second was apparently used as a storage room and contained a couple of leather suitcases and several cardboard boxes. No blinds on the window.

The third contained a twin bed and a night table. Not even a rug on the floor. Clearly, he did not entertain even his mother in a room this sparse. I opened the closet to be sure and found only two wire hangers. No dust bunnies on the floor or under the bed. If he had a maid, I was screwed.

There was another bathroom between the storage room and the spare bedroom. It had no shower curtain, and the medicine cabinet looked like it had never been used.

Of course, I had to make modifications. In the guest bedroom closet, I constructed a hidey-hole for my stuff. It was easy enough to do, considering the garage, which held no car, contained every tool a man might need for anything ranging from house repairs to bike repairs to lawn care, to even car repairs. This guy was prepared.

He was also a creature of habit. And that's what made it possible for me to live in his house, use his spare bathroom (not the kitchen), watch his TV, and sleep the night away, secure in the knowledge that Mr. Robot never deviated from his routine.

I made myself scarce on Saturdays, when he cleaned the house and ran errands—to the grocery store, the drugstore, the bike store, the dry cleaners. I stayed away until Monday when I would let myself into the house at around nine in the morning. By then I'd made a duplicate of his key, so I didn't have to jimmy the lock. I'd also noticed that the neighbors on either side did not have a clear line of sight of me approaching the house. One neighbor was an elderly woman who must have been housebound. Meals on Wheels would make regular calls, and a daily caregiver often parked in front. I wasn't sure anyone inhabited the house on the other side. It would have been much safer for me to shelter there, but the place was alarmed.

Then I started counting the days. If the killer hadn't fallen for the false trail I'd laid heading east, then by now all his leads in Tucson should have shriveled up and blown away like tumbleweeds. As for the police, how many resources did they have to hunt down a witness to a murder that had occurred three months ago? But still. I had to be careful. Plus, it was comfortable—more or less—hiding in Mr. Robot's house. The only person who could mess things up was Mr. Robot himself. And he was oblivious. At least that's what I'd been telling myself. It wasn't that he suddenly became less a creature of habit, though. It was simply a trap I'd set for myself.

"What the fuck are you doing in my house?" said the irate man one afternoon when he barged in on Let's Make a Deal. I shrieked, zapping the TV off.

"I'm calling the cops," he said, heading for the Princess phone.

"No! Please. I can explain."

He picked up the receiver and punched in a 9.

"Please," I begged. "They'll send me to jail!"

"As they should." He punched in a 1.

I lunged for the phone, knocking him off balance. He staggered backwards, dropping the receiver. "Don't!" I said, scrabbling for the phone. "I'll explain. I haven't stolen anything. I'm not a burglar or a—"

He was stronger than he looked. He grabbed one wrist and then the other and slammed me into the wall beside the phone. "You have invaded my house. How long have you been using my water and eating my food?"

"I—I haven't eaten any of your food," I said. The eyes behind the thick lenses were a deep blue, like the sky on a June day. He also had incredibly curly lashes and several blackheads decorating his cheeks up near the bottom frames of his glasses. "Water, yes. I couldn't help that. I'll pay you."

"Oh, for fuck's sake," he said. "You'll pay me? For using my house to—to—" he broke off. "To what? Were you casing the joint? There's nothing here to steal!" Then he looked at the TV. "You couldn't carry that," he said. "It's too heavy. Where's your partner in crime?"

"I am not a criminal." Unless he was one of those people who believe undocumented immigrants are breaking the law, although this was Arizona. "I'm sorry," I said. "Really. I meant no harm."

Even behind the glasses I caught the eye roll. With a sigh, he dragged me over to the chair and shoved me down onto a cushion that felt like cement. Then he reached down between the sofa cushions and pulled a gun out, pointing it at me before sitting down. "Talk."

I talked. I told him about the naked dancer and the killer who'd flipped me the finger and trashed my apartment and the friend who'd warned me the cops were after me and my journey across America and having to abandon the Chevy in Los Robles and ditch the phone here.

"You're the waitress from Guapos," he said.

I nodded.

"Sounds like a pulp novel," he said. "And you're full of shit."

I sat there, trying not to fall apart, wondering if I should just throw in the towel, let him call the cops, get arrested and, if not jailed, then certainly deported. "This was my sanctuary," I told him. "You are such a—a creature of habit, it was easy to be here when you weren't."

"All night?"

"Well, you didn't ever check, did you?"

His face flushed. "Why would I? I never for one minute thought— Well, until I saw the water bill. Then I thought it was a leak somewhere. I even called the water company." He looked at his watch. "They're due in about ten minutes."

"Maybe you could cancel?" I offered.

He looked at me like that was the dumbest thing a person could say. "I could—make that should—call the police."

The unspoken *but* hung there in the air between us. I held my breath.

"There's something you're not telling me," he said. "If you turned yourself in, they'd probably interview you on the phone or by Skype. You could describe this so-called killer, maybe even have a local sketch artist do a drawing. What's the big deal?"

"I ran. That automatically makes me into a fugitive, not a witness."

He waved a dismissive hand. "Maybe. But you could still turn yourself in. Take your chances."

"Okay," I said. "You got me."

The look of triumph on his face made my stomach curl. He pointed at the phone. "Go ahead. If you don't call the cops, then I will."

"The killer is here in Tucson," I said. "He somehow traced me through my job. That's why I'm hiding. I figured no way would he think to look here." I waved my arm at the sparsely furnished room.

"Why here?" He fingered the sharp pleat in his khakis.

"Like I said. You have a set routine. You never deviate. I could set my watch by—"

"All right." He waved a dismissive hand. "If what you're saying is true, you still could have run away. Seattle or San Francisco, maybe even Canada."

"I can't get a job," I said. "I don't have any money. Well, I only have about sixty bucks left from Guapos. That wouldn't get me very far."

He rubbed an index finger over his thumb. "Poor little you. And this is somehow my problem?"

I leaned forward. "Please. Just let me go. I'll pay you for the water and anything else you think I owe, like on the electricity." I reached into my jeans and pulled out three twenties. "Here. It's all I have."

"I don't want your fucking money."

I gave him a sorrowful look. "You've heard about sanctuary cities, haven't you?"

He nodded, puzzled.

"I don't know if Tucson is one, but I do know that this house, your house, has been like a haven for me. Here, I've been safe from that killer and safe from the cops, whether or not they are still after me. And," I held up my hand to silence whatever he was about to say, "I am also an illegal. From Ireland. I don't have any papers. If the police find me, they will send me back."

He shook his head. "I suppose you're going to tell me your family kicked you out or maybe your husband beat you."

"I was raped," I said. "By the local priest where I lived. He was going to do it again, simply because nobody would believe me. Just like you don't believe me. And, sure," I held up my hand to stop him, "I don't have to go back to Ballyfermot. But Ireland is totally Catholic,

120

and the priests look after each other. Besides, by now I'm more American than Irish. I'm like those DACA children, born and raised here, who are now looking at deportation to places they've—"

"Oh, cut the crap," he said. "They are breaking the law."

I stared at him, so like a robot in his behavior—and his beliefs. "You're saying the Statue of Liberty's just a lie?" Crossing the room, I punched in 9-1-1 and then pushed the plunger.

"I'd like to turn myself in to the police," I said to the nonexistent dispatcher. "My name is Orla Reilly. No. It's r-e-i-l-l-y. Reilly. I'm wanted by the police in Philadelphia... No. I'm no fugitive. Or at least I don't think I am. More like a witness?"

I watched as Mr. Robot's shoulders relaxed. He leaned forward and picked up the gun, shoving it back between the cushions.

"Yes. It's 94078 Ensenada Terrace."

Mr. Robot nodded, his back turned, as he fumbled for the TV remote. "I'll be here," I said to the dead phone. "Should I pack a bag?" After a couple of seconds, I said, "I'll be ready."

Through the slats of the venetian blinds, I spotted a white van pulling up in front of the house. The water company man had arrived. I ran upstairs and grabbed my go kit. The doorbell rang as I was coming down the stairs.

When I reached the bottom, Mr. Robot looked at me. "I may be a creature of habit," he said. "But I'm not a jerk. Take the bike."

The Afterlife

by Nancy Cook

Fergus Fall News, October, 1907

Man Affected by Recent Murder Becomes Insane.

Albert M, aged 22, the only son of a widowed mother and her sole help has been admitted to the State Hospital. Insanity is due to his physical condition. He is suffering from severe catarrh of the nose and ears, and has suffered from it for years, and this is held partly responsible.

It was actuated by his curiosity about a murder. The man viewed the remains in the morgue. The sight had a strange effect on him and he became possessed with the belief that he was being suspected of being the murderer. During the last six weeks he has had frequent crying spells in which he would weep like a baby.

Neighbors called on him and talked strongly of the hereafter and the future life with the result that Albert also became crazed with religion and wanted to die and go to heaven. He also expressed a desire to go out and save souls.

He probably will recover.

"LET ME HAVE a word with him, Trude," Albert overheard Mrs. Olsen say to his mother.

Albert's mother did not think it such a good idea. It was not the time to be talking about hell, nor heaven either. Pastor Birkeland had already spoken to Albert at some length about God's mercy and so on, and had reminded him of his duty to his mother, also mentioning that his father would be looking down on him from above. Albert's mother explained all this to Mrs. Olsen. Too much gloom in his life already, she said. But she was a persuasive woman, Mrs. Olsen, and strong-willed, as Albert's mother was not. And so, on a Saturday morning, six weeks after a visit to the morgue, Albert found himself seated in the parlor with Mrs. Olsen, as well as with Greta Hanssen, Elmira Scheible, Astrid Hoff, and Karl Peters, all of whom had accompanied the good woman.

"You must not carry on so," Mrs. Olsen said plainly.

"I know," said Albert, "but I can't help thinking about it. About the dead man. How someone killed him, just like that. Took a knife and stabbed him, I suppose. Right in the heart."

"The man is at peace now, Albert. You must believe that," old Mrs. Hoff said.

"Yes," said Miss Greta Hanssen. "A good man, surely he is in heaven."

"It was God's will," said Mrs. Olsen firmly. "God's will, Albert, it's not yours to question."

Albert said nothing. His glance took in six nearly identical brown leather boot tips emerging from under the women's skirts, one pair of narrow, shiny black shoes belonging to Miss Hanssen, and Mr. Peters' pair of toe-capped lace-up boots.

"Is that clear enough?" Mrs. Olsen asked.

"Yes. But—"

"But what?"

"Well, what about the man who killed him?"

"Look up when you speak to me, Albert," said Mrs. Olsen. "What about him?"

Albert raised his eyes, though not his chin. "Is there mercy for him?"

"If God grants it," interjected Mr. Peters. "If he has faith in Jesus."

"But what if he doesn't?" asked Albert. "What if he's not sorry?"

"Then he will burn in hell, as well he should," said Mrs. Olsen.

At this, Albert started to weep uncontrollably, as he had so many times in the past six weeks. He was far too old to cry, a grown man already, and head of the household these four years since his father died. To make matters far worse, Albert had an extreme condition of the nasal passages, catarrh, which caused his nose to expel yellow mucous. Globby tears fell from his eyes, and even his ears dripped. It was a terrible sight.

"Oh, for heaven's sake," said Mrs. Olsen. "That is not your concern, Albert. You've enough to keep your conscience occupied with your own sins, now, haven't you? Think of your own soul! Your mother tells me you've neglected your work on the farm. Will you tempt God's hand by falling prey to the temptation of laziness?"

"Or pride," said Mr. Peters. "Let God deal with the murderer's fate. We are not his judge. Here, take my handkerchief, son."

"God loves us," said Mrs. Scheible, who had not until that moment spoken a word. Albert turned to her soft voice and she caught his eyes with hers. "Remember that, Albert. Remember what waits for you in the hereafter. Bliss. Heavenly bliss. Freedom from all our earthly worries. Eternal peace."

"Elmira, really," said Mrs. Olsen, "what does a boy of twenty-two know about earthly worries? The point is, Albert, you'll not see heaven in your future if you don't straighten up now. God is calling on you to trust in his plan."

"But God will forgive me?"

"Do not doubt it," said old Mrs. Hoff.

"God does not deal in forgiveness," said Mrs. Olsen. "He deals in grace."

"He would extend his grace to a murderer?" asked Albert.

"Even to a murderer, Albert," said Mr. Peters. "Although that has naught to do with you."

"No?"

"Of course not," said Mr. Peters. He turned toward the others. "You know, the authorities are saying the man was an itinerant, a thief. Probably he got off the train from Chicago."

"He's been caught?" Miss Greta Hanssen asked, obviously surprised.

"Well, no. Not as of yet," said Mr. Peters. "But there's speculation."

As that seemed to satisfy Albert, and he remained calm for the next fifteen minutes, the neighbors retired to the kitchen, where Albert's mother had been sitting out the visit, ready with a pot of warm cider and a tray of ginger cookies. The company left her, not long after the cookies were eaten and the cider had turned cold, with the impression that Albert had come to his senses.

It had been almost two months since the murder of a local merchant by an unknown assailant had upset the routine of this western Minnesota farm community. The merchant, Jack Bee to all who regularly did business in town, had been accosted late at night. Two large knife wounds slit his rib cage, and he'd sustained blows to the head as well, which caused bad bruising and swelling, difficult to conceal on the meager resources of the mortuary. With his only relatives requiring three days to travel from Illinois, added to the three days it had taken for the news to reach them in the first place, Jack Bee lay in deathly repose at the morgue almost a week. It was a source of considerable diversion for the town, this cold corpse, something quite remarkable to see, and a refreshing topic of conversation during the first few, otherwise low-entertainment weeks of the harvest season.

Albert was among the first of the viewers. He couldn't say what lured him. It wasn't boredom, like it was for many of his old school pals. With the farm in his hands, he didn't have time to be bored. And it wasn't really curiosity about a mere corpse either, as he'd seen his father in death, and his older brother Kelvin, when he'd been pulled from the lake ten years ago. But Albert had never seen a *murdered* body, and maybe that was the magnet.

Whatever it was, Albert hadn't been prepared for his own reaction. The sight of the remains—they were so ordinary, no more defilement to the man's physique than if Jack Bee had been in a tavern brawl—had a strange effect. Standing by the cadaver, Albert wanted to laugh. But two of the Holmstrom boys, Curtis and Wilbur, had come in, along with their mother, and they appeared as sober as if one of their own corpses were lying in that black box. The Holmstroms always bore a sober countenance, of course, but when Albert started to guffaw, Wilbur shot him an especially disgruntled look. So Albert covered the sound up with a cough and shrugged his shoulders.

Mrs. Holstrom approached him. "Are you well, Albert?"

"Tolerably," he said. He didn't want to stretch the truth too far.

She nodded. "Can't ask the Lord for more. And your mother?"

"She's well." Albert took a step back. Mrs. Holstrom's bonnet was tied at his eye level. All the Holmstroms were tall and sturdy, mother, father, three brothers and four sisters. None of them ever took sick. To Albert it looked easy for them to plow and plant—summer wheat and winter wheat—to raise hogs and cows and even horses, to build a corral and a new stable for the horses.

"Albert?" Mrs. Holmstrom said sharply.

"Ma'am?"

"I said, see that she stays that way, Albert. She depends on you."

"Oh. Yes, I will. Of course."

What Mrs. Holstrom meant was that his mother was weak. Did she know that he was weak, too? Anyone could see that it would take three Alberts to do the work of one Holmstrom brother.

"Well, we've dallied too long," said Mrs. Holmstrom to her sons. "Your sisters will have the evening meal on the table before we reach the farm."

"Yeah," Curtis said. "And Carl will have eaten half of it."

"Ida will've taken more than her share, I'd say," said Wilbur.

Albert found himself wishing the Holstroms would invite him over for supper. It had been a long while since he'd enjoyed the company of so many young people in one place. But no one extended an invitation.

"I should get home, too," Albert said.

His mother had been firmly against it, and they even fought

about it in their own wordless way, but Albert returned to the morgue whenever he could find an excuse to go into town.

"You here again?" Mr. Dunn, the undertaker, had said, the third time Albert asked to see the body. "I'll be charging you a nickel the next time."

"He looks peaceful," Albert said.

"Aye. That's what the embalming will do. He didn't die peacefully, though, that's a fact."

"Why didn't he put up more of a fight? Was he stupid or something?"

"Stupid? No, just unlucky," said Mr. Dunn.

Staring at Jack Bee lying there like a butchered porker, it seemed to Albert there wasn't much difference between unlucky and stupid.

"They haven't found the killer," said Albert.

"It's nothing to sneer at," said the mortician. "It's morbid you are, I'm thinking. What's your interest in this dead man? It's unnatural."

Dunn was looking hard at Albert, trying to see through to something. "And they'll catch the brute that did it," he said.

Albert started to think that maybe Dunn suspected him of being the murderer. Worse, he suspected he might be right, that he *was* the murderer. It wasn't so hard to imagine himself wandering the town at night, mad at the world, coming upon a man even weaker than himself, and letting a butcher knife cry out for all the injustices he'd borne. Albert swiped at the slobber dribbling from his nose and the film coating his eyes.

"Best you go home, son," said the mortician.

That was the last time Albert viewed the body. But even after Jack Bee's family finally came and took the dead man's remains back to Peoria for burying, he continued to fret. For the six weeks since, he'd had these frequent crying spells. It got so he couldn't sleep, couldn't work, could hardly eat. He cried and cried, messing his face with mucous and tears until the skin turned raw. Pressed for explanations, he told his mother it was his conscience at work, that he must leave and go into the world to save lost souls. Or, if he couldn't do that, he just wanted to die and go to heaven.

"What has possessed you, Albert?" his mother asked. "What is this nonsense? You can't possibly think of leaving me."

"I'm guilty, mother! I can feel it. Jack Bee's death is on my conscience. I have to make amends."

"What tommyrot! Who is putting these crazy notions in your head? Your Catholic friends? Is it Lars Loken? Or that Montgomery girl?"

"How could it be? I never see them! Or anyone. I haven't been to a single dance or social since last Christmas."

"You are raising your voice, Albert. Someone must be leading you on, because what you say makes no sense at all."

It was true, what he said made no sense. Because if Albert was guilty of murder, as he himself suspected, evangelizing wasn't the answer. It was his own faith that was deficient. His own soul that needed saving.

His mother sent for the doctor, who declared the severe catarrh to blame, and she called on Pastor Birkeland, who tried to get Albert to seek absolution if there was sinning involved, and encouraging him to have faith in God's mercy, if not the State's. But Albert would not seek absolution, did not know if a pardon was called for, and so Pastor Birkeland told him he must pray, and then quietly told Albert's mother, when he thought Albert could not hear him, that he believed Albert was insane.

It was probably Pastor Birkeland's opinion that convinced Albert's mother to bring him to the asylum—well, and Mrs. Olsen's strong persuasive powers when, after learning that her neighborly advice had not had a salutary impact on Albert, she told practically the entire Lutheran congregation that there was only one thing to be done, "And you know what," she said, gesturing insinuatingly toward the western rise. In any case, the decision was made.

"I told you not to go to that undertaker's," Albert's mother said to him as they were walking up the hill, as if she thought he needed to be persuaded to go to the hospital, as if she thought he'd be angry about *that*. "I said it was disrespectful, didn't I, that there would be consequences, you could never tell, not minding your own business."

"And what will I do now?" she added. "The last of the wheat not in yet, and the earth will need turning before the freeze."

Albert couldn't bear to listen to her. At that moment, in fact, he hated her, he wished she would shut up, he wished she were dead.

At first, when he got settled into the ward, was given a bed, and told he must rest, he was at peace, almost as if he himself had died. As if he'd taken Jack Bee's place. But soon, he could hear the thoughts of others, the nurses and the doctors, and the inmates all around him. Everyone telling him what was wrong with him, what an evil person he was, what he should do now to strengthen his faith. It was all so confusing. Suppose he did the wrong thing? Suppose he'd already done it? Would he burn in hell? And if he was saved, would heaven be like this? Was this heavenly bliss? Heavenly bliss, freedom from all our earthly worries, Mrs. Scheible had said, and in the hospital Albert clung to that. But even in this hospital world it was not all peace. There were the voices, all about. And they sounded like the neighbors, Mrs. Olsen especially.

The troubling thing about the afterlife was that everyone would be there. He wanted to know who he would run into, and under what circumstances. Would he end up being with his father, his brother, and, later, his mother, who would surely be among the saved, and who loved him? That was not Albert's idea of bliss. He hadn't even had a chance to be with a girl yet, to have that kind of love. Would he meet someone special in heaven? Was that how it worked? Maybe there would be barn dances and bandstands, and theaters like they had in Minneapolis and Chicago where you could hold a girl's hand in the dark. Was it sinful to even think about that?

How would it all be managed, time lags, old and new loves, old and new friends, reconciliations with enemies of old? What about meeting up with people who have mistreated you? They could not all be in hell, certainly. Or those you have mistreated, how would those encounters be handled? What about those who simply annoyed you? (He thought of Mrs. Olsen and of his cousin Harold, a pharmacist in Grand Forks who liked practical jokes.) Could you avoid them or would you suddenly love them? And the people who have committed atrocious crimes, yet have been rescued by God, would they be there? Herod and Pontius Pilot? Nero? Jezebel, Judas, Cain, Jacob's brothers, Lizzie Borden? What would anyone say to them? Jack Bee would probably be in heaven, and he would know his killer. That was another thing to think about.

For three days, Albert lay still in his bed at the end of the ward, the last in a line of twenty-two cots jammed together. If he turned his head to the right, he could see outside the window. The yard was yellowing from the center out, a jaundiced color. Maybe a hundred yards across the dying grass, a few storage barns had been erected, and a silo, and out of the withered lawn grew a few spindly trees, inadequate for hanging. That silo though, thought Albert, a man could climb the silo, fall in, dive into oblivion. He started to cry. He could not stay in this place, could not remain by this window with a view toward the hospital's farm buildings, where with an accidental turn of his neck he could see the grandness of the farm, how vast it was, overwhelming in size, but at the same time orderly, efficient, successful.

Like his own family's farm before his father died. Before he was the head of the household, his mother's sole support, before there was no time for dreams or making love or pleasant diversions. Of course he hated her, his mother, of course he longed for death, an afterlife. His, hers. Of course he was compelled to seek absolution. Salvation. Respite.

On the fourth day, his mother was permitted to visit. She brought Mrs. Olsen with her. A doctor stood close by while the women spoke to Albert, asked how he felt, said he looked rather well, inquired after his needs. It was all very civil and a little taxing. After ten minutes or so, the doctor suggested they let Albert rest, and the two visitors moved a short distance from Albert's bed.

His mother would not have had the courage to ask, but Mrs. Olsen did.

"What is your opinion, Doctor? What's wrong with the boy? What can his mother expect?"

The doctor's reply took Albert by the throat, almost cut off his breathing.

"Most likely, he will recover."

Would anyone say such a thing about Jack Bee's murderer? Albert remembered the dead man's corpse. He imagined himself holding a

long, sharp hunting knife, thrusting it into the soft part of the belly—
no, aimed higher, in search of the heart, cracking through the breast-
bone, a gloved hand at the mouth or throat, cutting off cries for mercy.
Stepping back quickly, before the eyes glazed over, just as the first
gurgling sounds of death rose in the victim's throat. In the end death
hadn't appeared so terribly messy. Yet everyone agreed only a depraved
man could have done such an outrage. Such a person certainly would
never be allowed to leave the hospital. Could he, Albert, have done
that? Did he have the strength? The courage?

Albert trembled at the realization of his own inadequacy. He
hadn't the strength to do murder, he knew that now. He hadn't the
courage to admit as much, either. Worst of all, he would never, never
be man enough to go back home, to the big lonely farm and all its
burdens.

"Most likely, he will recover," the doctor had said.

It probably couldn't be helped.

Snot ran from Albert's nose, and a low, continuous moan with it.
He wept.

1956*

by Nancy Scott

Magdolna Ban, oil on canvas, 1988

At first glance you see bands of blue-grey and yellow
dominating the sky, then green hills and a pond replete
with black storks facing the horizon. Tranquil, mystical,
until your eye travels to the barbed wire stretched
to the edges of the painting. And, look, there in the sky,
those are not birds, but rather human bodies, soaring.

That year, like thousands of Hungarians a world away,
the three of us escaped our own barbed wire:
my father ran off with his mistress; I left for college;
my brother for military school. Only my mother
remained to rattle around in a house overflowing
with battle fatigue and sorrow.

At Stanford, I met a student from Budapest
who had been at the barricades. In halting English,
he began to tell me what happened, then stopped
and said, *I am here and want to learn about
your wonderful country.* Only the mustiness
of his frayed jacket betrayed the sacrifice he'd made.

*From October 23 through November 10, over 2500
Hungarians and 700 Soviet troops were killed
in what became known as the Hungarian Revolution,
and 200,000 fled as refugees.

On the Feast of Juan Diego

by Mark Fitzpatrick

So look where I am, Juan Diego / New Haven, a port city, colonial city / in the 60's: Black Panthers, the arrest of Jim Morrison that ended a Doors concert / Yale with its centuries of erudition / explication / re-interpretations /

icy rain pounding down / rain that reflects X-mas lights off the tarmac / wet trees / slick street signs / X-mas colors in each raindrop / X-mas dots on the plexiglass of the F6 bus / slogging its way through New Haven /

out of the tales of my childhood, you arise, Juan Diego / eagle man / mystic / rasta man / hijocito de la Virgen / on the cusp of a New World / arrive out of nowhere / oh lone pilgrim on your way / to the new rite / where the young god dies and rises and becomes bread /

just a man in the morning / hearing music so heavenly / wondering what that light up the hillside is / discovering it to be: / a fourteen year old girl with a map of the universe on her cloak /

that morning / so far away now / the morning of the music and the calling of your name /

I am the same age as you, Juan Diego, when La Morenita stepped out of the sun / like you: / lived in one world all my life / until the storm from another swept it away / everything bathed in blood /

So look where I am, Juan Diego / something inside me is warm / something inside me is lost / something inside me wants to be born /

The same age as you, Juan Diego / riding the F6 bus through this port city I am locked in / the same age as you / I hunger for La Morenita's apparition / the revelation there is some love in the universe / how I would gladly climb any winding Tepeyac I come across / how I would gladly carry a bundle of Castilian roses in my black leather jacket / eagerly knock and knock and knock on the door of prelate and pontificator / yell at them: / the universe is full of flower and song / flower and song /

oh, how desperate we are / to get back there / to see it, hear it, be filled with it / back to the morning of the pregnant girl on the hill / calling my name and yours, Juan Diego.

In Some Future Time

by Jory Mickelson

What if, for us, there is no dark
no cold dripping November spruce, no

headstones, not even
a name, the seasons saying

relent with each drip. What if
vetch and sweet pea tire of their work—

honeysuckle exhausts its bloom? When the last
visitor, a century ago tossed an apple

it grew, but now gives up its twisted limbs, what then,
when one of us is not here to hold

the other crookedly—when even the name of this
small town is smudged, moved

from remember to—I really don't
want this to be melancholy

so the chickadees catch the light at the top
of the alder we know

has to be taken down. Is this departure
or regret—how a constellation

hangs over the house, faithful painting
an entire season, and abruptly

the picture's gone askew? We don't believe:

there is a point beyond what can be
repaired between us,

that there will be a time
without our names.

After Absence
by Lana Bella

Not the moment a quiet sink borne
from the clay bottom creek, nor
the moment a neck-knotting noose
dangled from pillar in the garage,
but rather the yawn of mortar shell
ricocheting between joint and muscle,
snaked through and through even
the battledress can't shield. Inward
we spun on then on, on this roadmap
of pouring into bones, falling, head
over heels for the shadows of old
hills cresting bare spires of the city.
Shouldering our reluctant heads to
chests, we felt an awful thirst for
waking where once was a garden-
bed, blood bleeding in the shrunken
room of all the bodies we have loved
as if there were no winged things
in our ribcages. When the mechanics
of an ending stared over the trench
that divided us, we touched ivory
hands to salt-juked snow, touching
the hesitant art of losing in each
straggler's palm, relaxed into stones.

In Rooms

by Sarah Brown Weitzman

"We have all been in rooms / We cannot die in."
James Dickey

In rooms we must not die in
we defy death for a few hours

though guilt at first makes me worthless
to either of us. Here we are free

to speak of feelings that don't exist
outside such rooms, to make promises

we cannot keep. Here love is multiplied
by mirrors and brought to its knees

on dingy sheets. Here time is only
the hour we cannot stay beyond.

As though love left marks, I shower twice
before I must return to rooms I may,

yes, I may, I may die in.

House for Girls

by Jennifer Stuart

Stretched out on their stomachs, Nina and Monica stare at the same jigsaw puzzle from opposite sides. Both wear yoga pants and baggy T-shirts that arrived in the same donation box addressed to the South Carolina branch of the Mary Magdalene Haven House for Girls. Both wear their thick brown hair in high ponytails away from their amber faces, and both bob their feet around in the air with frenzied teenage energy as they snap puzzle pieces together. Laurel, middle-aged, pasty white, and tired-looking, has just vacuumed around the girls and now walks out of the room with an armful of dirty mugs from the coffee table.

"If that woman ever leaves this room long enough, I'm getting out of here," says Monica.

Nina looks up in surprise. "Where you gonna go?"

Coming back in with a feather duster, Laurel says, "Nina, your court advocate's here. You need to go to talk to her."

"What's a court advocate?" Nina asks, making no effort to get up.

"The lady going to court with you this afternoon."

"What, she gonna guard me or somethin'?"

Laurel sighs and puts her hand on her hip. "Nina, honey, you don't need to be guarded. You ain't the defendant. Just go talk to her please.

"What she want with me?"

"Nina, just go ask her. She don't have all day, and she don't normally even come by this early before court. You're lucky she has time to talk to you now."

Nina takes a long time to pry herself up off the ground and slump down the hallway while Laurel begins dusting.

Straining to reach a cobweb in the corner, Laurel feels Monica's eyes on her back. "How ya sleep last night, hon?" she asks Monica without turning to look at her.

Monica turns her eyes back to the puzzle, tapping the piece in her hand against a completed section.

"You didn't sleep, did ya?" Laurel asks. "You know, you're going to collapse one day if you don't start sleeping."

Monica puts the puzzle piece down and looks at Laurel's back again. "I already told you he's coming for me," she says quietly. "Just a matter of time before he finds me again. I ain't gonna be asleep when he does."

Laurel turns around to look at Monica and sighs. She finds herself sighing a lot since starting this job. "It's been four days since the raid honey, he's probably moved on by now. He probably ain't even in this county no more."

"There ain't no way he don't plan to get me back."

Laurel looks at Monica hard. "You don't *wanna* go back, do ya? I've seen girls wanna go back."

Nina returns, so Monica doesn't answer. Laurel sighs again, grabs a mug she'd missed on the coffee table, and heads into the kitchen. Nina drops to the floor emphatically, crosses her legs, and peers at the puzzle.

"What'd your court lady want?" Monica asks.

"Nothin. She just wanted to introduce herself before we go to court later."

"Why you goin' to court later? I ain't had to go to court."

"You ain't had to go 'cause your daddy still on the loose."

"Where your daddy? In jail?"

"Yeeaah, he in jail, what you think, he gonna show up in court if he ain't in jail?"

"What you gonna say in court?"

"What you care?"

"I don't. I just don't know how you can say nothin' 'gainst him. Prolly he gonna get out soon and whomp your ass if you say shit."

"Bitch, what you know? You don't even know."

Laurel sticks her head back in the room. "Hey, we got rules here. I don't wanna hear that language."

"Why can't we just turn the TV on? Then nobody's gotta hear me at all," Nina fumes.

"Like I said, we got rules. TV for one hour only, after dinner. But then, you already knew that." Laurel retreats with a stern look.

"I hate this place," says Nina.

"I hate it more," says Monica.

Monica's on the floor working on the puzzle again, but Nina now sits motionless on the couch, watching sitcoms, a throw pillow clutched against her belly. Since her return from court, Nina has just stared into her lap with her arms crossed, refusing to speak, so that Laurel has finally turned the TV on, shrugging and rolling her eyes with feigned innocence as she left the room, like she doesn't know what she's just done.

"You really not gonna say nothin all day?" Monica finally asks Nina.

Nina just stares at the TV.

"So was he even there or what?"

Nina just stares.

"What did you say? You had to like swear on the bible and all that shit?"

"Yeah, all that shit," says Nina.

"Is court like it is on TV?"

"Yeah. No. Not really. Shit, you ask more questions than the freakin' judge."

"So what happened, was he taken back to jail?"

"I think so, he like pled guilty or somethin' like that."

"Guilty of what?"

"Human trafficking."

"What the hell is human trafficking?"

"I don't know, what you asking me for? I ain't no judge."

"Well, what did you say when you testified?"

"I didn't say nothing, okay? Nothing at all! They brought him out in chains and he stared at me the whole time while the lawyers and everybody else talked, and I just sat there. Nobody asked me nothing. They just decided there'd be no trial. They decided *everything* after he got to sit there and stare at me. Then they took him away again and nobody told me nothing. I don't even know why I had to go. There, happy?"

Monica rolls her eyes. "Okay, I get it, sounds like it was craydic-ulous, but they're like saying he did human trafficking to *you* right?"

"I don't know, I guess. All I know is that because I'm only fifteen years old, that, like, legally makes him a big sicko pervert. It'll be the same thing for you cause you're sixteen."

With her index finger, Monica picks at the small green dollar sign tattooed above her knee as if she could rub it off. "It ain't the same for me 'cause I won't have to go to court. He'll never get caught."

"Whatever, look, I just want to watch this show now. Leave me the fuck alone."

Laurel sticks her head in the room. "Nina, time for your session."

"Not today, Laurel. Tell her I don't want to today." Nina clutches the pillow harder and sinks lower into the sofa.

Laurel shakes her head. "Not an option, sweetie. Long as you're here you gotta do counseling. We all understand it's been a rough day."

"Yeah, everyone understands, so then why can't everyone just leave me the fuck alone!" Nina bangs her feet down on the coffee table.

"I'll stand here and wait," says Laurel.

Laurel stares at Nina, who stares at the TV, until Nina gets tired of being stared at and finally stomps out of the room with Laurel.

When Laurel comes back five minutes later, Monica is rocking back and forth with her arms wrapped around her bent legs. She looks like she's in a trance.

"Monica, what's happening?" Laurel squats in front of her, but Monica keeps rocking, her eyes looking through Laurel.

"Monica, you know if I go get someone, it's gonna mean everyone will be watching you again 24/7. We just took you off watch. You've been doing so much better."

Monica rocks harder.

"You just need some sleep, baby. You've got to sleep," says Laurel. "He's not gonna find ya here."

"He's gonna find me," Monica blurts, and she stops rocking, the spell broken.

"Look, baby," Laurel sighs, "like we all keep telling you, this place has got great security and they double-check the cameras and the locks every night. I don't see why he'd even try to get in here. Besides, he knows the police are looking for him. And they're going to find him sooner or later."

"He's gonna find me," Monica whispers, running her finger over her dollar tattoo.

Laurel sits back for a moment, watching Monica closely. "You afraid of having to see him in court, like Nina? You afraid of having to testify against him? That it?"

Monica clutches her bent legs more tightly, slowly starts to rock again. "I just want to get it over with," she says.

"Get what over with? Going to court?"

"No. Him finding me again."

Becoming Human

by Gayla Mills

Last Sunday evening I returned to work for a forgotten file. As I slipped through the empty hallway toward my office door, I heard an animal howling from the receiving room nearby.

Receiving, by the way, is where people bring their pets or strays. The animals are sometimes kept there overnight until they're taken back to the kennels to be viewed by the public. People don't like working in receiving, don't like watching the animals stream in. Last Monday fifty-one animals were surrendered. It was a real downer.

The dog's eerie wail was cut short in mid-note as I entered the room. Now her eyes were on me, wondering about me just as I was about her. One of the strange things about working with kenneled animals is the sensation of being watched by multiple eyes each time you enter a new room. So many faces turn toward you, wondering what you'll do next. Sometimes you just look away.

She was a medium-sized blonde, cowering as she pressed against the back of her cage. I walked over and surveyed her space, maybe three feet by four, just enough room to turn around. She had soiled the cage and gotten the runny poop on her coat. Her empty water and food bowls lay in the muck on the right side, with little dry space remaining. No one would be in to clean until the morning.

"Hey, sweetie. How ya doin?"

She thumped her tail a bit and looked up through her eyelashes. I read her card.

"Mandy is an affectionate and friendly one-year-old Lab mix. She loves to play fetch, and gets along well with children. She is housebroken and eats dry food."

I thought of her youth with some family, running around with the kids, sleeping in the house, and dispensing lots of sloppy kisses. Did her family imagine her, caged and soiled, facing weeks of uncertainty with a possible death sentence at the end? Or did they picture her at a spacious farmhouse where she played with other carefree animals and slept by the woodstove in the warm, darkened kitchen?

Animals live in an eternal present—they don't seem to understand that if things are bad now, there is hope for a better future. Like young children, their feelings are intense, immediate, and heartfelt. I couldn't explain to Mandy why she had been surrendered, or how we would try to help, or that she might have a wonderful new family soon. What could I do, now that the real damage had been done?

The first step was to stop being trapped in the moment, moved but unmoving. Speaking gently, I opened her cage and guided her by the collar into a clean one next door. I washed out her bowl and gave her fresh water. Maybe it would make the night easier, hearing a few gentle words and having a clean place to sleep and some water to drink.

Sometimes I get letters from charities that I just can't open. The weight of human and animal suffering can knock you flat. In the face of so much misery, what is a person to do?

What we often do is turn away. We must save ourselves first, and the sadness in the world can be too much to bear. The thought of the suffering wounds us, and so we flee. Yet most of us believe that there's something terribly wrong about not doing anything when what we have is so much. When a child's life in a developing country can be saved with a one-dollar hydration treatment, can we sip our four-dollar cappuccinos each day in good conscience? Yet does it serve any purpose to undermine our own pleasures with guilt or heartache? How can we enjoy our own lives while not dismissing the needs of the many facing genuine misery?

Answering these questions is how I'm learning to become human. I've been working on it for years. Finding a way to help others while preserving myself requires practice and time. It might take my whole lifetime to get it right.

My coworkers and I routinely hear, "I don't know how you work in a shelter. I just couldn't do it." That's because they don't understand how positive the experience can be. Those who work in emotionally challenging places—helping abused children or animals, working with the neglected or elderly, assisting the homeless, teaching the uneducated—do so because they get satisfaction from it. They distinguish the possible from the impossible, and measure success in small steps. They continue because their actions make a bad situation more tolerable.

Those who flee are less fortunate. Visitors to an animal shelter, for example, have few options. They can adopt an animal or two (and probably feel bad about the ones left behind) or they can leave feeling helpless. It is the casual observers' inability to change things that leaves them feeling powerless and despondent.

Those who work or volunteer at these places are not so impotent. There are an infinite variety of things that make me feel good about my day. I can feed biscuits or a leftover sandwich to a few dogs. I can speak kindly to them and make their tails wag. I can bring a scared pet into my office for a day or two to teach her that people can be kind; she'll return to her cage eager to meet the next person, and more likely to be noticed and adopted. I can talk with children when I visit their schools, and listen to their stories, while encouraging them to treat animals with respect and kindness. I can offer a shoulder to someone mourning her ill or deceased pet, and affirm the importance of her loss.

But the greatest feeling of all is when I find a caged animal a good home. One of my favorite adoptions was of a pup named Susie. Hit by a car and suffering from a limp, she was brought in as a ten-week-old stray.

Within a month, she had outgrown her cage in the puppy ward and was moved in with the adults. A gangly shepherd mix, her youthful enthusiasm overwhelmed visitors as she barked excitedly and pawed at them from her upper cage. She would fling water on them, too, and she always looked disheveled. We despaired of anyone favorably noticing her, falling in love with her, rescuing her. As the months passed, it was hard to say what seemed worse—killing her or having her caged during so much of her youth.

One day, a gentleman of about fifty came in. He liked shepherds and he liked SPCA dogs, so I recommended he take a look at Susie. I took her into the petting room and gave them a few minutes to get acquainted. This was the time when she turned people off by jumping and pawing, leaving dirty traces on their clothes. When I returned a few minutes later, though, I was shocked to see her on the floor in a sphinx posture, body erect, gazing calmly up at him. Their eyes were locked, time stopped, as they sat adoring each other. She looked regal rather than manic, lithe rather than gangly. She was beautiful, instantly transformed.

The man's wife appeared, and we spoke of technical matters—Susie's medical condition, their living arrangements, adoption fees. He refused to leave Susie alone for a moment, so his wife completed the paperwork. They called a few weeks later to say that the limp we thought permanent had healed, that the dog we thought irrepressible spent hours lying calmly in his car or at his feet.

There are many dogs I have come to love. I feel privileged to have seen their eyes and touched their fur and seen them begin to love and be loved. Watching them walk out the door lessens the pain of seeing others caged. And when I think of those that don't make it, who die on the table because there aren't enough homes, I have to remember the ones we could help.

The world is filled with stories, and often there are more with sad endings than happy ones. Turning away does little to make us feel better, and nothing to make the world better. But I've discovered that when I do something for others—whether a gesture large or small—it's like stepping through a door into a sun-filled room. Finding these doors and walking through them makes the inevitable sad stories easier to bear. It's what helps us become human.

Down To The River To Pray

by Laurence Jones

IT WAS MOST BEAUTIFUL at dawn on a winter's day when there was no one else to see it. A secluded clearing on the banks of Snake River, hidden deep inside the forests of the Oregon Trail. Marvin Reid remembered clearly the first time his father had taken him there. He was ten years old, a lonely child, lying belly down on the wooden slats of their porch in Oxbow, a pile of crumpled comic books stacked high by his side.

"Marvin," shouted his father. "Come on."

Dewey Reid was an aging man with a penchant for drink. The floorboards groaned beneath his footsteps as he lumbered across them until his mud-stained boots came to a halt inches from Marvin's head. Dewey was often likened to the ashen embers of a bonfire, the flames of which had long since died, but, to Marvin, he was a friend, a father, and a hero. He took the *Detective Comics* from Marvin's hands and tossed it onto their front lawn.

"We're going fishing," he said, his breath ripe with whisky. Marvin had learned long ago not to question his father. He stood up and did exactly what Dewey asked, even though there wasn't a bait box or fishing line in sight.

They walked for an hour through the forest without a single word spoken until at last they reached a wall of thick angry brambles.

"Follow me," said Dewey.

He waded a path straight through the undergrowth, beating back branches and bushes like they were made from cotton wool. Marvin followed close behind, but in truth, he had become afraid. It scared him to think where they were going; how his father had discovered such a place. The path seemed to close up behind them as they walked, and all remnants of daylight were fading bleakly into shadow. He wished they had gone fishing after all.

All that changed as he stepped out into the clearing, his anxiety swept away by the majesty before his eyes. It felt like he had been beamed onto an alien planet or sucked into the pages of a Flash Gordon comic. The earth beneath his feet was scorched, as if some great fire had taken place, and waves of freakish fluorescent bugs took turns divebombing against his bare skin. In front of him, rows of giant pine trees lined the riverbank like citadels, reaching up toward the sun, which fractured through their tops in wide angular shards and partitioned the space in a maze of misty, transparent walls.

It was unlike any place he had ever seen.

It felt magical.

For Marvin, the clearing was a place where the true spirit of nature ruled unencumbered. It was a place he loved more than any other. And, as the years passed, he came to know the trees and rocks as friends, carving his initials into bark and chalking his father's name against smooth gray stone. No matter that Dewey would eventually pass in body. His spirit would always belong to Snake River.

Now, Marvin found himself upon those banks again.

A decade had passed since his last visit, so many years lost in a haze of listless work, blue pills, and alcohol. The sky above him was a sullen gray and an acrid white mist drifted across the surface of the river, rising and falling upon itself like cigarette smoke. Not for the first time, Marvin felt lost. He closed his eyes and sank to the ground. 'God,' he said. 'Help me. Please just help me.' The world felt like it was ending, and all because of her.

Marlene.

He picked up a handful of leaves and dirt, felt them cool and rubbery in his palm, then glanced over at the tightly packed suitcase on the ground beside him. The battered leather tan had darkened in the morning dew, and its contents bulged beneath it, a bloated membrane incubating the toxic remnants of his past. Marvin scratched at the side of his head. The sight of the case troubled him more than he cared to think about. He suddenly felt ill at ease. The last few days had tested him more than ever before, made him question the very fabric of his being. Maybe Marlene was right after all. "You're a boy trying to be a man," she had told him, her teeth stained with cheap red wine. "And we can't be together. Not ever."

Marvin hated her for it. She had caused this mess.

And now the life he had was gone.

The wind picked up suddenly, brought a chill to his bare arms, and the mist on the water shifted in its wake. A voice seemed to murmur beneath the breeze, a seductive call he had heard many times before. He looked down at the river's swirling waters.

Join us, the voice said. *Find salvation in us.*

Marvin couldn't bear it. He touched at the scar across his left wrist, a warning of the siren's song carved into his flesh. A familiar anger overcame him, and he kicked at the suitcase, raging and hating at all the world like a spoiled child.

"God damn you, Marlene," he screamed.

He remembered seeing her for the first time. She had appeared at the call-center like a devil, a twenty-something whirlwind of dark red hair and thick black eyeliner, a perfume of strawberry chewing gum trailing in her wake. Marlene worked on a different bank of desks, but he had watched her from afar, mesmerized, as she spoke to strangers each day like she'd known them her whole life. She was beautiful, confident, and carefree. Marvin was smitten from the start.

And then the recession hit.

The phones stopped ringing and the desks emptied out. Soon,

they were a skeleton crew with no guarantee of a future. They kept Marlene of course. She was too good for morale to let go, but even she was getting nervous. Then one day, she approached his desk for the first time. He could remember it vividly even now. The wiggle in her walk, her bright red lipstick and skinny indigo jeans. He pulled his gut in so tight he could hardly breathe.

"You want to go get a drink," she said. "We got to stick together now."

Marvin's heart soared that day, much as it did each time he came to the clearing, each occasion he heard the river thundering along its banks. It was the thrill of something greater than himself. He had been waiting his whole life to drink with a woman like Marlene. A woman to make his daddy proud. And now he had found her.

She trusted him with her drunken secrets, confided in him about the ones who had gone before, and then, when the time was right, he made his move. Even the thought of it now made his blood pump hard, rushing wild and treacherous as Snake River itself; to experience every part of her, know how it felt to caress her face and kiss her neck, to stare deep into her blue eyes as she trembled beneath him.

But now all that was gone.

He glanced at the suitcase on the sodden earth then looked upward as the day began to break. The sunlight brightened beneath a thick blanket of amorphous clouds and gradually dispersed to reveal a clear blue sky. It reminded him of the first sunrise he ever saw with his father, how a blaze of reds and yellows had spread across the treetops like wildfire. It was perfect. Maybe God was listening after all. Marvin dragged the suitcase to the river's edge, unfastened the straps, and opened it up.

'Morning,' he said, though Marlene could no longer answer back.

Her lifeless body lay contorted inside the case, vacant eyes turned upward and mouth locked open as if trying to release one final scream. Marvin took one look at her and smiled. He tipped the body out of the suitcase like he was emptying a wheel barrow filled with dirt. Another man might have taken a moment to reflect upon the awfulness of what had passed but Marvin found only joy at the sight of Marlene's corpse. He had done his best to clothe her again, to restore some modicum of decency, though her t-shirt was torn and the buttons on her jeans were ripped clean off. Regardless, the fierce anger, so constant inside of him for all those years, seemed to have dissipated with the morning mist. He realized then, in the clearness of day, that what had been was now gone. The last of *them*—Marvin and Marlene—had been snuffed out with the light in her eyes.

It was time to move on.

Marvin scoured the side of the river for loose rocks and stones, then measured their weight in his hands. He stuffed them into Marlene's jeans and the tight fabric of her bra, until he could fit no more inside. He took a moment to admire his handiwork, the strange angles and undulations beneath her clothing, as if her body had been shattered into a thousand tiny pieces. An enormous sense of gratitude swelled within him. The river would make things right again. It always did.

He picked Marlene up over his shoulder and flipped her down the steep incline into the murky water below. Snake River swallowed her up with a single splash, then dragged her quickly against a mass of rocks downstream. There was barely any sight of her, strands of her hair against the rocks perhaps, but Marvin could not be sure. No matter, he thought, he had made his peace. Now, he felt joyous about the journey ahead, so many other women he might meet along the way. And so, he headed back along the Oregon Trail, and left behind his secret clearing, a sacred place beside ancient, violent waters, where the dark denim of a young girl's jeans rose briefly to the water's surface then vanished down below.

What We Leave on the Curb

by Ed McCourt

WHILE MOST OF US have ridden a bicycle, rarely do we consider how such a simple device functions. The entire effect of cruising smoothly, noiseless save the clicking of pawls in the freewheel, is dependent upon ball bearings, a set of twenty or so per wheel, each around 5mm, smaller than a kernel of corn. A wheel affixed directly to an axle would creak along with all the smoothness of a Rubbermaid two-wheeled trash can. Each of the tiny bearings is vital to the functioning of the bike, yet they remain wholly unnoticed, until one fails, or an attempt is made to repair the hub.

I should have been walking the dog by this late in the morning, but instead I was refurbishing the hub of a seven-speed beach cruiser I'd snagged from the curb on trash day. There it sat, with its bell and basket, its rear rack shaped like a surfboard, an insinuative bottle opener affixed to the fender. When I found it, the rear wheel and chain assembly were laying on ground by its side. The owner, it seemed, attempted to replace a tube, and gave up once he realized the cassette and chain would separate and become tangled. Better to place it out with the trash and be done with it. He was not the first, not even in my small neighborhood; I'd found a vintage Trek mountain bike the summer before, a mere block away in a similar wheel-less state of partial decay. Restoring it felt something like a resurrection, and I picked this cruiser up hoping for the same.

❖

The only perpetual fear in my life is that lingering existential dread: the looking into the expanse of space-time and then returning to being itself, through that singular portal (a man staring at his own hand), the perpetuation of self, *Dasein,* and realizing what a blip in the infinite I am, and that in the near future this very being, the only thing I have ever known, which appears to me as if it were here in the beginning and will remain eternally, will end abruptly, time and space carrying on without it.

This fear, I imagine, is exactly how my dog Penny felt about the vacuum.

Annie had put Penny out on the screened porch so that she could vacuum, unaware that I'd yet to walk her. When the whirring of the machine began, the dog, stricken with panic, began urinating all over the braided rug we still had drying on the porch from the last time she had an accident. My hands were full of bicycle parts, so I opened the door gingerly with one leg, and upon doing so, the dog darted between my legs back into the house, toward the very source of her terror. Stuck between me and the churning Charybdis, she defecated all over herself and my legs, spinning in nervous circles and ejecting fecal wads in tangential lines, like spokes from a hub. I shooed her out the door and opened the back screen, but she finished spin-pooping inside before fleeing through the yard and into the road.

She didn't die that day, but the mess was substantial, and having inadvertently stepped into said mess, I had exacerbated it, smearing it liberally around the edge of the living room, the porch, and all the way up the sides of the gray Nike low-tops I usually reserve for the classroom.

I believe that my fear is more real than the dog's. Death is here and is absolute. Is it because the dog does not comprehend the nature of our mortality that she fears the vacuum so much, or are the fears one in the same? Perhaps, to her, that vrooming appliance bespoke the cruelty of nature, but if so, why did she not recognize the same danger in the cars between which she so willingly hurled herself?

At the very least, I feel comfort in knowing that however frightened of the strange tango danced by the certainty of the end and the uncertainty of how and when it will arrive, I have not spun myself in circles propelling shit like a furry cork gun. Not yet, at least.

It wasn't until the next day, bent over a hose in the backyard with a brass-bristled brush and a series of broken toothpicks, wet from the back spray of water (and whatever else) coming from the intricate hieroglyphs of the sneaker's soles that I remembered Mike. I always think to myself how unhealthy it is to have that existential dread rekindled by something as farcical as the dog mess incident, but as is often the case, that scene was not the inception. I had been thinking all week about Mike; he was the co-owner of our local bike shop, and just the summer before, he had helped me to rebuild the crank of the Trek I had saved.

I hadn't been able to budge the lock ring to change out a worn bottom bracket, but he assured me that, with the right wrench and his breaker bar, it wouldn't be a problem. Three days passed, and the ring still did not yield, even after using a dubious trick of his: letting it sit in antifreeze overnight. He let me borrow the wrench, and I went home and took a can of PB blaster and a torch to it, and still it would not budge. When I went back to the shop, Mike was there with his son. He was maybe eleven and diffident in that way eleven year olds are around men.

"No luck."

"Not even with the torch?"

"Nope," I said, and gesturing toward his son, added, "maybe we should bring out the big guns?"

The boy smiled and grabbed the breaker bar to play along. Mike ruffled his son's hair.

"I'll just rebuild what I can without replacing the whole thing," he said. "It will be okay."

And it was: no wobble, no grinding. He charged me next to nothing for it. That is how Mike ran the shop: he invested constant energy into it but seldom asked much in return. When I went back in the spring to pick up some tubes and axle nuts for my new cruiser scavenge, I expected Mike to be there, as always. No sign of him, and when I thought about it, I realized he hadn't answered the phone the last two times I had called.

"Haven't seen Mike in a while..."

"Yeah. Well ... he got ill." The man at the counter was large and distant. He spoke with a lazy, southern drawl. Nothing like Mike.

"How long has he been out?"

"It happened in November."

I prompted him on with my eyes.

"Colon cancer."

"Jesus ... Well what's going on with his treatment?"

"I'm sorry to say it man ... Mike died in November. He was diagnosed in August and it was really advanced and he died just a few months later."

It was July, a month before his diagnosis, that we had worked together. At that moment, my own son was only four months old, so new that even the scent of his scalp was enough to evoke my sentimentality. The demure smile of Mike's son had not left my head since, and it lingered still months later when Penny died unexpectedly of kidney failure. She had liver cancer that had been undiagnosed. She was at the vet for full physicals every year and had been asymptomatic throughout. Her end was quick, but it left me shaken. I try to put it in perspective: today I have my son, and he still has me. What beyond that can one promise?

Riding a freshly rebuilt bike is an improvement over even a brand new one; it is broken-in and seems to know the road better than its rider. I rode out of my neighborhood and up the only hill steep enough for a challenge, so I could enjoy the coast down the other side. I tried not to look at the swing sets in the yards and imagine them decaying in the weather, no longer used by children who had outgrown them, eventually finding their way onto the curb in sawed-off and forgotten segments. Instead, I kept my head up in the sweetness of a breeze that seems only to blow in spring.

Encounter

by Rick Holinger

Barton and I both threw up during the crossing. We weren't ready for the rough waters leaving the Kenai Peninsula and skirting Afognak Island. When the ferry finally pulled into Kodiak Harbor, it must have been nine, ten o'clock at night. We went on deck and surveyed the fields of fishing boats, the shore-lined canneries, and the low-roofed buildings at the foot of a gray-green hill.

I roomed with Barton during our freshman year at Deerfield Academy eight years before. He had called in March to tell me he needed someone to ride shotgun along the unpaved Al-Can Highway to Alaska. He bought a new camera and wanted to work out its kinks, he said. Selling three compositions at his one-man show. Barton thought himself an artist.

I had just graduated from Knox College in Illinois with a teaching degree. A history position at a private school waited for me in St. Louis come Labor Day, but I needed a break from academia. The ponderous

—although rewarding—pace of sixteen years in a schoolroom had made me sick of schedules and bells, as student and student teacher both. They'd taken a toll on my psyche, and after Barton's call, I craved Alaska as much as food and drink.

I guess you could call it dusk when we drove off the ferry, but on Kodiak, when isn't it dusk? Most mid-days pass with a wearying, misting gray, the cloudy half-light ubiquitous as the fish and seaweed odor. Even more dour than the oppressive atmosphere were the Natives, the name we gave to hometown Kodiak men. They stood on the dock and stared at us Rich College Kids (RCKs) walking or driving off the ferry. They wore navy knit caps, olive army jackets or yellow slickers, blue jeans or yellow rubber pants from work, and black pullover boots.

Barton and I checked into a motel that first night. Both hungry after puking our guts out, we found what turned out to be the town's best restaurant, still open. The king crab we ordered might have lived within sight of the large picture window but cost a fortune nonetheless —like everything in Alaska.

Back at the room, Barton exploded, "Jesus, Randolph!"

I was reading *The Arrangement*, a novel by Elia Kazan, in the room's one armchair. "What?"

"Says in this paper a bunch of college kids up here looking for cannery work were living in a World War II Quonset hut where they all got killed." Barton sat on his single bed, three pillows stacked behind his back. "Says they don't have any suspects. The cops don't know who did it. Yeah, right. Says one kid was from Lake Forest College, two from Stanford, one from Wesleyan."

"How?"

"How what?"

"... were they killed?"

"Shot. Says no ballistics report is available."

I closed the novel. "Let's get out of here."

"Jesus, Randolph. We just got here. You gonna let some Kodiak pussies push you around?"

"Maybe."

"This is America, man."

"This is fucked." I opened my book and tried to get back to the story of a husband and father leaving his family. He learns to put himself first rather than continue slogging through his routine life.

"Okay," I said. "But we can't stay in this room many more nights. Too expensive."

Next morning, we splurged on a restaurant breakfast, ordering the usual oatmeal and pancakes, the cheapest, most filling menu items. We sat one table over from a couple dressed more like us than the Natives, so we tried talking to them. James and Ruth were crashing in a church basement where transients could unfold their sleeping bags.

"So tonight, we get religion," Barton said.

"And tomorrow you stand in line for a job you won't get," James said. He told us how each day in the *Kodiak Mirror* he checked to see what canneries, if any, were hiring, thew next day he'd show up for a couple hours before the office door opened. At seven or eight someone opened the door, took a couple people they knew, then shut the door again.

The days unfolded. We got the feel of the place, the pace of life. Each morning we rolled up our sleeping bags and left them and our packs along the fake pine panel walls of the church rec room where we slept and played ping-pong along with twenty other RCKs. If a cannery was hiring, we stood in line, the Natives glaring at us. We tried to look nonchalant, oblivious to their hatred. For the first time in our lives, we were the Other, the Outsider, the Minority. Roaming around town, buying groceries, or sauntering to a pier to fish, we looked over our shoulders for gangs of Natives who, we believed, would kill us and throw our bodies in the harbor. Who would know? Who would care? This was the last frontier.

By then, most of us had beards. They were only a few weeks old, and grown more because it was a hassle to shave. They'd grown driving up here, at nightly campsites and in roadside cafes over burgers and Cokes, facial hair more a mask to disguise an innocence, a puerile nature, a silly hunt for a true adventure in Alaska.

I didn't grow one. I began it, but when I saw a bad Abe Lincoln in my metal camping mirror, off it came, the black hairs dropping into a British Columbia stream where we each caught two Dolly Varden. Once in Kodiak, Barton gave me a lot of bullshit about how I should stop acting like a baby, stop conforming to the Man, the State, the Look. One night after brushing my teeth and shaving, I walked back to the sleeping bags after lights out, where Barton was reading *Sometimes a Great Notion* by flashlight. When I dropped my razor in my shaving kit, his beam of light caught it.

"Throw the goddamned razor away," he whispered.

"Fuck you, Barton."

"Your mother's not here to burn your ass."

"But she knows, man, she knows. Our minds are connected by the rays of the moon. She looks in a mirror and asks who's the fairest of all my sons, and she sees me shaving."

"Keep it up, Randolph. Keep it up."

"Shut the fuck up," someone said. "Lights are out, man."

I crawled inside my bag and pillowed a blue jean shirt. "What can I say? I tried it and it sucked. It grew in splotches."

"Doesn't matter what it looks like." Barton turned off the light. Now only the two red exit signs glowed. "What matters is you have one. What matters is you have balls."

"Yeah, you've got balls, Barton." I gave him the finger in the dark. "You've got balls to do what everyone else is doing. Takes real balls to do that."

"Go to sleep, pussy," he said.

I held up the middle finger of my other hand, too, for emphasis.

Once a week we cleaned up. Public showers cost a dollar, a lot of money back when a gallon of gas in the Lower 48 cost thirty-five cents, and twice that on the Al-Can Highway. I luxuriated in the hot water, washing away the anxiety for the three minutes a buck paid for.

We drove to streams where we caught a few trout and afterwards told ourselves the trip was worth it. We took a gravel road all the way to where it ended in a sign on a metal fence advising "NO TRESPASS-ING" by order of some military department.

One day we drove in the opposite direction and found James and Ruth walking along the one-lane road. They put out their thumbs and we picked them up. They'd walked farther than they thought from the middle school three miles out of town, empty until September, where they had been staying.

"What if we'd been the killers?" Barton joked.

"We'd have fucked you up," James said.

"And I'd have put out for some real men," Ruth said, and we all laughed.

Cliques had formed at the church, they said. They didn't like the social dynamics of the preppies versus the religious versus the hippies. They were right; a few days later, Barton and I decided to join them.

By the time we arrived, James and Ruth had left the island to return to Santa Barbara, but we partied with Josh and Samantha, who'd come with us from the church. We smoked some dope in a geography classroom, its walls papered with maps. The only technology was an opaque projector we plugged in and used to project questionable silhouettes on a cinderblock wall.

"Fuck the military," we yelled. "Fuck Charlie. Fuck the Natives."

That's right. Fuck our own United States' citizens in the same breath as our Vietnamese enemy. Because our own countrymen had become our enemy. Because they had made us their enemy. So fuck them. We hated what we didn't understand. Some radical liberals we were.

It wasn't until after midnight that we went to sleep. Outside, the familiar gray sky filled the large, dirty windows, their sills lined with empty cages we imagined in the fall would hold turtles, rodents, and snakes, anomalies like us this far north.

Next morning, we awoke to a blazing sun and unusual heat.

"Let's go into town for breakfast," I said, tired of Sterno stove oatmeal. "You guys coming?"

Josh and Samantha, sharing a double sleeping bag, shook their heads. "We'll stay," Samantha mumbled.

Barton noticed the tires first. Flat—all four, with identical long, clean cuts. He took photographs, as though someday he would admit them as evidence. We figured the Natives must have waited until we turned out the lights and went to sleep to make sure we didn't catch them at work. That would have been when the clouds were breaking and the sun, for the first time since we landed, began to bleed all over the island.

"What should we do?" I asked.

"Walk," Barton said. "What the fuck else?"

So we did. We wore tennis shoes, figuring a three-mile hike in those better than calf-high boots . However, after the first mile, the rocky gravel felt like spearheads.

"Shit, shit, shit," I said with each step. I tried walking beside the road, but tall, thick growth worked against me.

It was the car's growl that stopped and turned us. From where we'd come, a white cloud billowed above the road. The rumbling grew into thunder, a souped-up engine roaring and wide tires crunching stone. Stepping back into the undergrowth, we watched the dark green hood and silver fender bear down on us, ominous and promising at once. Just before it blew past doing seventy or eighty, we put out our thumbs.

When the taillights glowed red and the car skidded sideways, I knew we were screwed. The locked wheels grasped for traction, and the green body came to rest at a ninety-degree angle, its bumpers above the road's shoulders, the two exhaust pipes belching gray exhaust.

The driver's door opened and a man maybe ten or fifteen years older than us got out. He was tall, thin, bearded, and wore a T-shirt with a faded Old Glory on it. Simultaneously, a face appeared over the roof like a rising moon, chin clean-shaven, head bald. One other person, obscured by the dirty back window, shifted position on the back seat.

"Come on," said the driver. His arm beckoned to us. He sounded excited, like we might make them miss the beginning of a concert. "Hop in, man."

I dug in my front pocket and palmed my Swiss Army knife. I looked at Barton, who seemed calm. "What now?"

"No way," he said so softly I barely heard him.

"Long walk," Baldy called. "We got room. At least for one. The other one can stay till help comes. That's what you need, right? Help?"

"Shit," I said.

"No fucking way I get in that car."

"We're fine," I said. "Thanks."

"Thanks?" Driver said. "For what? We didn't do shit. Just said we'd give you a ride. A ride you asked for. Now you don't want it. Not cool, man. Turn down a ride, someone might think you unfriendly."

"Sorry," Barton said. His voice trembled. "Really sorry."

"Come on!" Baldy pressed. "Take you wherever you want."

There. That's what did it. Not what he said, but the way he said, "Take you wherever you want." Like he wasn't being sarcastic, but saying it like he meant it. All I had to do was go with them, and they'd take me where I wanted to go. Accept their invitation and find out what the world was really like. So I did.

Not that what happened over the next couple of hours hasn't left a scar. It has. I still get nightmares about the encounter, the trauma usually disguised as students I can't control in my Kodiak classroom, no amount of pleading or shouting ever enough to quell the revolution.

I said to Barton, "Let's go."

He swiveled toward me. "What?"

"Let's go," I repeated, this time loud enough for everyone hanging around that boxy Detroit behemoth to hear. "Let's go," I said again.

"You're out of your gourd."

"Hey, you kids want to make out," Baldy called, "or take a ride?"

"We're there," I said. "Stay loose, Barton."

He grabbed my arm. "Where'll we meet?"

"Come with," I said. "That car's Alaska. We drove 3,000 miles to get here. I'm not passing it up."

"You're fucked."

"Hey, shitheads," Driver yelled.

"See ya, Barton."

Who knows what I thought, walking toward that car. Maybe something about the novel I was reading, how I might not get to finish it, how I'd never find out how the husband and father felt after he left his family and job, and if he made a better life than the one he left behind.

Because the car was a two-door, the driver had to pull forward the back of his seat to let me in back, where someone slid over to make room for me. Without turning to see, I pictured Barton standing there trying to look cool, hands on hips, thumbs and forefingers resting on the wide leather belt, one leg straight, the other cocked.

When I was halfway in, the seatback whomped back in place, heaving me sideways, headlong into the belly of the backseat passenger. His elbow caught my chin, and I heard a crack as pain flooded my jaw and bits of tooth splintered. The two doors slammed closed, and the rear wheels spun in reverse, machine-gunning gravel against the metal underbelly. When we jolted to a stop, my head bumped the back window. The car lurched forward and Backseat punched me in the stomach. My lungs deflated. As I bent over, gasping for air, a boot smashed my nose, and the three men laughed.

"How far do we go?" Driver asked.

"Before we kill him?" Backseat asked.

"He wants a cannery job," Baldy said. "I say we give him one."

"Don't bleed on my carpet," Driver said.

"Don't bleed on his carpet," Backseat said, and punched me in the neck. I sagged left, into the window. I felt sick. Baldy punched me in the temple, and my head slammed hard against the glass.

"Tough guy," Driver said. "Going north to Alaska. John Wayne. Too cool to fight in Nam. Too rich for Nam. Too well-connected. Pay off your Congressman? Family friends with your state senator? That how you dodged the draft?" He paused, then said, "Do it, Frank."

Something stung my right forearm, and I screamed like a teenage girl. I tried to cover the pain with my left hand, but Backseat caught my fingers in his fist, pulled my left arm toward him, and put his cigarette out in my palm. I screamed again, but not from pain this time, because the pain that outdid all the burns and punches so far was the pain of not knowing what would come next, the pain I wasn't expecting, the pain I could do nothing to prevent.

That morning, I learned that life was not as Hemingway would have it, lived as though looking in the face of a bull, the alert and vigilant matador sidestepping horns meant to gorge. Old Hem's dictum had it wrong on two counts. First, he spoke in metaphor; my pain was literal. Second, looking at life through a matador's eyes didn't conform to that morning's reality. A quick sidestep fools the bull, after which the cape once again invigorates another charge. Beaten up in that back seat, I had nowhere to step to avoid the horns, and needed no cape to incite another attack.

Was the beating a long overdue rite of passage? Was it therapeutic? Baptismal? Maybe one of those or all of those, at least in part. But I don't think it made me a man or cleansed my sins or offered any epiphany. Afterward, however, I knew I didn't want to live in the middle of the country in an average city, teaching above average kids. Barton's call to accompany him to Alaska had resonated with something inside me that the encounter on that gravel road completed. I had jumped at the chance to leave the Lower 48 because something was pulling me away from ordinariness, away from the academic miasma my life had been. It took getting the shit beaten out of me to realize how close I'd come to embracing mediocrity.

They took me to a deserted coastline of jagged rocks and bristly thistles. An empty, rusting cannery stuck out over the water. They dragged me inside and spent another hour or two with me before driving away. On my knees, I watched through a broken window as their car fishtailed away, gray stones thrown out behind. I stumbled down the rickety steps and across the rocky surface to the dirt road, where eventually a couple of rich fly fishermen picked me up and took me to what Kodiak calls a hospital.

My bruises and burns healed by the end of summer, long after I convinced Barton to leave the island without me. It took a while to persuade him the beating hadn't messed my mind up. I tried to explain it had the opposite effect, and proved it to him by landing a job at the Kodiak middle school. Wasn't hard; not a lot of Lower 48ers applied with a teaching degree from a respectable college in Illinois. The administrators even overlooked my lack of an in-state teaching certificate; I could get one in time.

I rented a room on the second floor of a traditional two-story house owned by a family who had moved there from California twelve years before. The husband owned a gun and tackle shop, and the wife taught third grade; it was she who told me about her family renting out an extra upstairs bedroom. Their two kids went to our school. After Chris and Jeanne got to know me, they suggested for a few dollars extra a week, I could eat my meals with them. They introduced me to their friends, and if I wasn't exactly a Native, by the end of my first year, I had begun to lower my paranoid guard when out fishing or doing errands.

In the fall of my second year, at a parents' conference, in walked a woman wearing a fake leather shirt, ankle-length linen skirt, and sandals. Behind her strode a man I supposed was her husband, instantly recognized as Baldy. They sat down in the student desks facing mine. The man had been looking around the room at the kids' drawings and the 3-D maps, so it wasn't until he turned his head to give me excuses as to why his kid was in so much trouble that he got a good look at me.

"You," he said, and smiled. "Martel, it's the guy I told you about. The guy who took all our shit and then some. You teach here?"

"I'm your son's teacher for geography, English, and social studies."

"You know Mr. Tiskan?" the woman asked.

"This is my old lady, Martel."

"Martel Samuels," she said.

"Let's talk about Axel." I leaned forward. "He's the reason you're here."

"Shoot," Baldy said.

"Your son is at a critical age. He gets it now, or he never gets it."

"Gets what?" Martel asked.

"Compassion. Love. Consideration for others."

"My son's got all those," Martel said.

"No, he doesn't." I listed the bullying incidents, the profanity, the tardiness. "By twelve, kids know right from wrong, but the need for attention and acceptance motivates them to behave, well, badly."

Martel looked at Baldy while responding to me. "He is a handful."

Baldy stood up and walked to the window, the same one where not long ago, if I'd looked out at two or three in the morning, I would have seen him slashing Barton's tires.

"I want my son out of your class," Baldy told his reflection.

"My husband's got a temper," Martel said.

"Sit down," I told the father before, for the second time, saying, "Let's talk about Axel."

Communion on the Road

by Michelle S. Myers

THE STRETCH OF ROAD from Dallas to Houston (antiseptically known as the I-45) is flat and lined in some stretches with eerily dark pine trees. You have to pass the state penitentiary, then you pass the huge statue of Sam Houston, and you feel like you could be any drunken good old boy's easy target practice there on that road.

Once or twice a month, I would make this drive with barely documented Central Americans caravanning behind.

I was the translator for their asylum interview at the Houston Asylum Office. I would be scared and shaky but determined to stand in solidarity with this community of Salvadorans and Guatemalans I had come to love while working as a legal aide at a tiny non-profit in Dallas. Never would the seeker of asylum ride with me, because they were never alone. The entirety of their family—and even some friends —on this, the northern side of the border, would make that perilous drive with them. Imperfect, impatient, messy friends and family, who simply called in sick that day to work and to school, and got in the car, and merged into an authentic arising-from-within accompaniment. Solidarity with their beloved, not borne of one of my freshman philosophy classes taught by some social-justice-minded Jesuit, but put into motion from the kind of love that can only get knitted up from absolute reliance upon each other and God.

Although a cradle Catholic, along with most of the asylum seekers, my gringa-gabacha-white-girl-from-the-burbs will had not yet considered adapting a faith that somehow carries within it a reliance upon that seemingly ungraspable grace and trust. *As if* that kind of faith could ever be "adaptable," or "a consideration." I could not pull that (what I was naming) faith inside myself, but I knew I wanted to stay on that road with the families on this journey. We all wanted the journey to end with the relief and safety of that almighty green card. Survivors of torture exposed once upon a time, exposed again; incredibly, riding down a Texas road, translated paperwork signed, moving toward a nondescript parking lot, and on through doors, and on to a cold line in a big-windowed building, and on, and finally there we were in a smallish, stark room with an officer of asylum.

There, on that road was my car—a miniscule Honda, and then their vehicles—substantial trucks and minivans packed with meaty sandwiches, homemade tortillas, black beans, babies, small children, the Virgin Maria, and soda. At our pitstops on the road, I was religiously offered food, and I devotedly accepted it. There is a way in which I learned, even at 22, that you say 'yes' to food offered to you from people who have known physical hunger and the hunger for their forever-lost homes. We were dependent upon each other's sanctuary and care. They needed the shelter of my white skin and college degree, the safety of my US citizenship, and my language skills. I desperately needed the refuge of their immensely generous and freely offered kindness.

Their asylum testimonies brought wholeness to my assumptions about my country and partial political understandings. I stole a place of refuge in the profundity of their humility and fragility, hoping it would soften the rigidity of my transactional heart, which felt love as tit for tat. As we shared our fears and the deliciousness of their food on the road, these families and I entrusted each other to each other's care. In the communion of caring, it became clear that to walk humbly, with patience, and in a love that came wrapped in merengue music and food, and near to the fissures of traumatic homeland scars, was the only way down that road.

Seeking Asylum

by Lita Kurth

Asylum is a strange word. When I was a child, the only word it ever went with was "insane." An insane asylum was the place people were sent to who were cuckoo, off their rockers, crazy, nuts. We made that circling motion around our ear. It was a place, I gathered, that you went to permanently and against your will.

My *New Century Dictionary* (old century now) defines asylum thus: "an inviolable refuge," but then continues, "a place for criminals and debtors," "any secure retreat," and eventually it gets to, "an institution for the maintenance and care of the blind, the insane, orphans or some other class of unfortunate persons." Suddenly, I flash on a San Jose institution whose name literally was "Home for the Friendless."

Have I ever sought asylum? Yes, many times and not always successfully. Perhaps my greatest asylum was the soft couch and carpeted comfort of my first therapist's office, a cozy room entered by a back door so gossipy neighbors or passersby would not see me admitting to a defect, a "mental illness."

The small lobby offered classical music while I waited for my appointment, not looking at other "patients." The therapy room itself had a bow window, but curtained to, again, protect me from people and their judgments. They could not watch me crying, admitting to weakness, confusion, wrongdoing, and wrong-not-doing.

As virtually all my refuges have, this one had a bookshelf, and my therapist lent me books she thought might give me insight or comfort.

In that room, I could have questions instead of answers. I could be unguarded. I could open doors in my memory that I had feared: cellar doors, attic doors, truck doors. I could ponder dreams and nightmares.

After each session, I left exhausted, yet also unburdened. In the evening dark, I'd walk down the quiet, tree-lined street, emptied out and still. My questions remained, but I no longer felt bleak. For all my life's turmoil and tension, I felt a shaky and tender aliveness. Asylum.

Ward B

by Allen X. Davis

THERE WAS NO warning, said Owen. I had just sold a graphic design app to Adobe for a LOT of money and the next morning I walked out my front door and said, This looks like a good day to die. Two patients behind us were playing ping pong, the *pop* ... *pop* of the ball like a soundtrack to our conversation. Galleries were exhibiting my photos, he said. My design business was growing. Cheryl came over and sat down. She looked like that moody actress in the *Twilight* movies. So I went down to Rhode Island to hook up with this guy one time, she said out of the blue as a small smile formed, and you wouldn't believe what I asked him to do to me. I think Owen and I would like to hear more, I said, but instead she declared, And then Zoloft came along and saved my life. Z, her true lover. I couldn't even do multiplication, she said. I couldn't even do basic activities of daily living. Multiplication is overrated, I offered, trying to help, but quickly realized that my comment might trigger thoughts about multiplication of humans, specifically about the baby she gave up in college and about her mother who had died young before they could make peace. These meds are overrated too, I said. I'll bet ninety-nine percent of the people in here don't even need them. She put her hand on my knee in defiance of the touching taboo and it felt good, like it belonged there. Then why do you take them? If it wasn't for the court order, I replied, I wouldn't be taking anything. Sure, sure, she cooed. She and Owen launched into a discussion about selective serotonin reuptake inhibitors like Zoloft, Prozac, Celexa, tricyclic antidepressants like Trazadone, about bipolar disorder, schizoaffective disorder, depression, anxiety, dual diagnosis, and the underlying cause of it all: a chemical imbalance in the brain. They sounded like scientists. Exactly how do they measure this chemical imbalance? I asked. Cheryl glared at me. They stick a needle into your brain and draw out some of the fluid just like they do with amniotic fluid, silly. Everyone knows that. Her eyes got misty and I knew she was thinking about the baby she gave up and her mother, and I was trying to think of some way to comfort her when the buzzer sounded above the door to our ward. A nurse unlocked it and a beautiful Italian woman with long, lustrous black hair and a black dress walked in, leaning slightly on a black cane. Owen waved to her and told us to come meet his wife. She was mean to him and controlling and I couldn't help but wonder if she just used the cane to get attention. Cheryl and I headed to a yoga group, where we got high on stretching and meditation. I imagined Owen's wife stretching and getting high with us and feeling so unbound that she reared back and flung her cane over the rooftops with a final yell of orgasmic release. On the way back we did a lot of laughing and bumping into each other, but the fun came to a screeching halt when my girlfriend showed up for a surprise visit with lavender-tinted hair and daggers in her eyes. I complimented her on the new hairdo and after a while she cooled off and smiled her beatific smile that made me feel glad to be alive and we snuck into the shared bathroom between my room and the next. Moving quickly so we wouldn't get caught, she clicked the locks on both doors, unbuckled my jeans, and did her best to help me forget about Cheryl. But all I could think of during our desperate race against time, while her purple curls bobbed up and down and I sprinted closer and closer to my own little death, was that captivating woman dressed all in black who had almost destroyed a good man. Oh, the things we could have done together!

El Chucho

by Jim Keller

A sound outside
El Chucho barks
Carlos roused from sleep
opens the door to the ICE men
several and large
El Chucho barks again and growls
But Carlos shakes his finger
and points to his bed
He goes reluctantly
continuing to growl and
stare at the men now in his house
speaking a strange,
harsh tongue
The family all awake
begin gathering their things
into black garbage bags
Maria helping the children

At last a man opens the door
Carlito and Angelina
bawling, hug their Chucho
Outside El Chucho tries to follow
But Carlos says No!
And points to the back yard
El Chucho goes only to the side of the house
and watches his family taken away
in the dark vans

Now El Chucho sleeps under his car
against a wheel that blocks
the wind and the snow
Food left by Carlito and Angelina
is gone
as is the water
He is cold, hungry and very thirsty
El Chucho cries
But no one hears

Ritual

by Bernardine (Dine) Watson

Let's take a walk along the lake
you'd say on summer days
blue eyes longing to look again upon your Harriet
lady of lakes, pride of Minneapolis.
And with these words we would begin again
down the narrow path behind your house
you leading the way because you knew it best.

We'd follow Minnehaha Creek,
named *little river*
by the Dakota people
who were first to watch it flow
into Mother Mississippi
farther north where the waterfall falls.

But we had ritual to keep
and would turn toward Harriet
when her shore was in our view
ambling toward her arm in arm
your arm browning quickly in the summer sun,
till it was almost dark as mine.

At shore we would remove our shoes
to feel the ancient sediment against our toes,
the grey-green shale, the limestone
and the purest ivory quartz,
and pay respect to what and who had come before.

In this place we were connected to everything
the visible, the invisible
the sacred, the profane

the nothingness
as we listened to the Dakota whisper, *wakan*
and stood within the web of all creation.

Here our secrets were as water
flowing gently, sometimes wildly toward the
lake in trails of tears.
Here we prayed as one for absolution
from the burdens of our womaness
your broken body
my battered heart.

Who knew then that fate and time
would ever find us far apart?
And that my broken heart would one day seek its healing
in the places I knew first and best
so distant from your lovely lake?
Or that you would choose to stay the path
beside the little river
that always led you to Lake Harriett
and finally find your solace there?

But it is well, it is well
as it is meant to be.
The Dakota say that everything is one:
love pain loss nothingness.
Everything.
Even us.

Lie If Innocent

by Phillip Bannowsky

¿A quien le importa?:
(Spanish) Who cares?
Alhamdulillah:
(Arabic) Thanks be to God. Interjected by Muslims whenever
some blessing is remembered.
"Insha'Allah:
(Arabic) God willing"

I lied, and for a treat, I was unstrung
and seated in a splintered chair.
More lies got me an indoor cell
(for non-compliant brothers), with blanket, soap,
and, under my mattress, a stenciled arrow: Mecca.
Pues, it's somewhere.

Billy, my interrogator, now sees me daily,
sometimes twice, in luxury:
metal chair, Formica table, VCR and TV
(12-inch, always off).
Once I concede I'm born in Lebanon, who cares
if my Arabic is scant, French scanter? *¿A quien le importa?*
I insist the hash was only for the money,
I don't smoke it, don't care for politics, and
I'm Maronite (almost), not Muslim.
I did not care if Beheshti was Hezbollah. *Everyone* was.
That got them so pissed, yelling at me about martyred Marines,
I had to think up five more lies to get them off my case.
Alhamdulillah, they had Hamoudi's name wrong;
it's short for Ahmed, not Muhammad, who's
in trouble if *he* ever gets to Norway,
not Hamoudi; may there he find
himself a wife, *insha'Allah.*

Great news: I will be tried, and Billy shows me *Black Hawk Down*,
so I'll accept my punishment when they find me guilty.
I used to love movies like this,
but nineteen US martyrs looked like Gitmo guards;
the thousand dead Somali looked like us.

After My Mother Has Been Attacked and I Have Been Ordered to Leave

by Alice Morris

I have torn myself out of many bitter places. —James Wright

I am nine years old, running down Second Avenue
toward the Black Dog Power Plant set on a bluff
across the Minnesota River. I flee for the woods, eyes fixed
on coal-burning stacks. I remember how the plant was named for
     Chief Black Dog.
Although my heart is stinging as though filled with angry bees, I
imagine the Sioux
dancing on the bluff above the river.
It is their horses that graze these lands.
I imagine scouts pointing to a lone figure running, their drums
     beating
to the sound of my feet against pavement.
I think what I am seeing are real spirits returned to an ancestral camp.
Off the asphalt, I am breaking through brambles onto softened
     ground, deer trail lit in
sunlight, smells of leaves decaying. Birds rustle in a thicket.
I do not wish to disturb the sparrows
flitting from trees to underbrush,
gathering red berries,
wings so gentle on the air I can scarcely hear them,
I close my eyes, tilt my head and listen.

The old crickets are resting,
they jump slowly now, their backs are burdened,
I wish to hear them,
they have wisdom to impart.
Then kindly, nearby, one begins to sing
in the cattails.
I realize,
perhaps soon, I will have the strength
to return home.

I Live Inside an Accordion

by Pamela Ahlen

I live inside an accordion,
and every day I need his attention—
push/pull   push and pull
one canoodle at a time
until notes become phrases
phrases become songs
songs become two-part inventions
and we hold a lover's conversation
among the rosy tulips of the music room—
me and my main squeeze
my personal protection sounding device.
I hoist him front and center
all susurration and inspiration
my breasts entirely his—
for better/for worse
my body shielded in his.

In the Whispering Breezes

by Joyce Kryszak

"God's voice was not in the earthquake, not in the fire, nor the storm, but in the whispering breezes." —Henry Wadsworth Longfellow

IF YOU LIVE at the epicenter of an earthquake, it's hard to imagine whispering breezes. It's hard to imagine them putting out the fire or giving shelter from the storm. Yet behind the doors of family violence shelters, women and children come to know the meaning of whispering breezes. Resting in the whispers at one of them, I found sanctuary —and hope.

Splintered families like mine find refuge here, breathing for the first time, unstifled by fear and guilt, anger and sadness. These are the first moments of peace and safety, allowing quiet time to think, without fighting fires and storms of abuse. A calm, at first confusing, greeted me at the shelter door and wrapped its arms around me as I walked through it. I had never known the order, respect and tranquility that filled the rooms, that provided structure and ensured my safety. Like anything foreign, it was instantly feared—though eventually it was trusted. I saw another shaken woman enter in, arms burdened with babies and paper bags overflowing with teddy bears and clothes. She looked up with unearned shame and hard-earned sadness, and meeting my eyes, realized that we shared the same burdens.

There are too many of us.

Double-door security, entry buzzers, cameras, motion detectors, and the shelter staff double checking IDs to make sure no one gets in who shouldn't. I learned, as would the new woman, that these security features were tangible proof of how dangerous the person is from whom I fled. The one I shared a home with, a bed with, children with —and a life never truly lived. Anywhere else, he could get to me, his undying "love" and rage, relentless. How did I let it get this bad? How did I fail so completely at the one thing in life that I willed to work? Could anyone ever forgive me? My children? They never forgave me for staying, and learned from me that leaving was wrong. Our families? They never knew. I never let them. My God? My church? They told me to stay, or I thought they did. One thing is certain. The one I ran from, my husband, my batterer, will not forgive. Once these doors are locked behind me, The Secret is out. That is never forgiven.

Also gone beyond these doors is the illusion that I am, or ever was, in control of his behavior. The hardest lesson learned here is that nothing I did for him or with him would ever change him. Our advocate, our friend, leads the new woman slowly through unfamiliar rooms and unfamiliar faces. The advocate takes the woman's trembling hand, holds it gently, and will throughout her long journey from fear to understanding. One day the woman will find answers, with help from advocates, counselors, and other survivors, those whose names she'll forget but not the friendship they gave. One day she'll let go of the undeserved guilt and shame. We are the ones who must forgive ourselves.

Messages of support, empathy, inspiration, and empowerment cover the tables and line the walls. Books and posters, woman after crying woman saying, "You are not alone." A knowledge that doesn't make the pain go away but blankets it in comfort. The healing process begins.

Tending to the order, supplying the routine, is the duty of the veterans. We cook the meals, wash the dishes, sweep the floors, and watch the children. All by schedule, all by turn, all without yelling, all without ridicule. Tending to daily tasks, we stay busy while sorting through plans and preparations for the future. It is the job of the new women, the new survivors, to cry. Deep, sobbing, desperate cries, filled with longing for sleep without terror, time without decisions. The sobbing ceases, finally, with an aching hunger to learn how to live without violence.

One by one, the ranks of those who function grow from those who once only cried, begged pitifully, hoped foolishly, and cried still more. They, too, begin to share their stories and their pain, share in the responsibility of their healing. The counselors never let on how many times they've heard the same tragic story, told with different names. Their patience is unfailing, their tears of empathy real. Most are past victims of abuse themselves, recognizing, too well, the bruised bodies and battered souls bent before them. Shattered women, racked with grief and indecision, flinching at the ring of the phone, the close of a door, and the memories of what is on the other side. The threat of violence, though locked out, is still a powerful weapon. The promise of peace and safety is still not trusted.

Those who leave the shelter pass those entering, swapping places in the worlds of shelter and possibility. Some of us who leave take tools with us—self-worth, self-control, self-confidence—tools that make building a new life a little easier. Some take only the strength gathered here, returning to houses built on terror, ridicule, and intimidation. Lives built on fault lines in raging fires and storms. When the empty promises of change and the strength drain away, they return again to the shelter's bolted doors and the peace. They come back to rest in the whispering breezes. Ever welcoming, the shelter stands, arms open, like a loving grandmother—unjudging, uncritical, undemanding—assuring those who leave: "Call if you need anything. I'll always be here for you. I'll always protect you."

The Other Side

by Jennifer Stuart

Never before in her twenty-two years has Florencia stood completely naked, outside in daylight, with strangers. Yet, here she stands now, naked and right out in the open, tightly clutching two plastic garbage bags filled with her only remaining possessions. She has already tried pleading for some other way, any other way. But it's for your own good, they told her. And you'll regret it later if you get your clothes wet, they repeated. So here she stands. Still, her feet will not move.

The descending sun spreads a preposterously gentle luminosity across the barren, brown landscape around her, as if across a place of beauty. The shifting golden light obscures the empty bottles and food wrappers nestled against branches poking out of the river. An occasional breeze cools Florencia's sweaty skin, lulling her physically into a trancelike sense of calmness.

She cannot make herself move. She stares at the milky brown water and trembles with fear of what might be below the surface. She tries to think of anything at all except snakes. What comes to mind are the gunshots she heard hours earlier in Ciudad Juarez, when she almost died from being in the wrong place at the wrong time. That incident threatens to take over her mind again like a song that won't stop re-playing even though it's driving her crazy.

So, in her mind's eye, to calm herself, she conjures up the home she left behind two days ago. She imagines walking back through her *mamá's* arched kitchen doorway and smelling the rich undertone of chocolate in a pot of mole simmering on the stove.

"What are you waiting for, you idiot?" Carlos now yells from the opposite river bank. He holds Florencia's naked three-year-old daughter in his hands, dangling her out in front of him at arm's length. The child still drips rivulets of water and her mouth gapes in disbelief at her situation. Even from across the river, the girl's plump, round face contrasts comically with her straight stick limbs. Florencia's heart surges.

"You want little Rosa? You better come get her." For his exclamation point, Carlos opens his hands with a flourish so that Rosa plops down into the thick, soft mud. The little girl whimpers and stares at Florencia across the river. Florencia clutches the two plastic bags more tightly, her heart pounding in her ears.

"C'mon, little chicken," Carlos taunts. If you don't get in the water, we're leaving without you, and I'll take the girl with me."

The other naked women crouch awkwardly on the bank around Carlos, trying futilely to brush sticky dirt off their legs before pulling their dry clothes out of plastic bags. They look across the river with alarm at Florencia, their faces pleading with her to get in the water.

For the first time, but not the last, Florencia wonders if Rosa might be better off as an orphan on the other side.

Carlos makes a braying noise across the river. "Hey Donkey, we're about to leave without you now. But don't worry, I'll take good care of your little girl."

Florencia's feet still feel more permanently affixed than the dirt underneath them. She looks again at the brown water and tries unsuccessfully, again, not to think about snakes. Without moving her feet, she twists in desperation to look behind her at the many dim lights covering the slopes of the city. The air keeps cooling as the sun lowers, reminding her more and more of her small, hilly home-town. She pictures her mamá' sitting hunched over her sewing right now, hundreds of miles behind the city lights of Ciudad Juarez, surrounded by the life Florencia had always known before this.

A mosquito dives at Florencia's neck and she flinches, shrugs it away, but still her feet do not move. She remembers the day she left home, longing to live it over again so she can change her mind and stay. At this moment, Florencia's memories of her mamá' have not yet begun to fade, though they soon will, so for now she can see every wrinkle and curve of her mamá's face next to the white lace curtain of the front window. Florencia can still feel the warmth of her mamá's calloused hands clutching her face, can still see her mamá staring back at her hungrily, trying to memorize her, before pressing the largest wad of cash either of them has ever seen into Florencia's hands. Everything her mamá' has ever saved as well as plenty she's borrowed. Then the sound of hens squawking in the yard and commotion from the dirt road outside and her mamá' moving to the window and pulling back the curtain to shake her head with disdain. A group of machismo-filled boys in the road jeering at a girl and picking fights with each other just to show off, jabbing each other in the chest with their scrawny arms. Mamá musing under her breath, "Those boys over-compensate for how scared they are. You know, they say true bravery is not about being fearless. If you have no fear, then nothing is ever difficult. True bravery is doing what must be done, even when you're terrified."

"That's enough, you idiot!" Carlos now bellows across the river. "You're not worth waiting for." He scoops up the astonished child, holding her around her torso with one muscular arm, her skinny arms and legs dangling around him so that in the tricky light of the deepening dusk he seems to be holding a small octopus. The sun's nearly down now and Carlos's smooth, shaved head seems to melt into the darkness as he walks away from the river. Still adjusting their now re-donned clothing, the other women glance toward Florencia remorsefully, but they waste no time turning away from the river and following

Carlos through shadows toward the last gold flecks of light. They seem to be chasing the vanishing sun. The girl's moon face still strains back toward Florencia as Carlos walks into the tall brush with his human cargo tucked under his arm.

Florencia feels the shock of cold water before she realizes her feet are moving.

With Every Thought

by Jesse Falzoi

IT WAS MY DAUGHTER who arranged it. She promised that it would only be temporary. They have a little baby, she said and, Please Mom, just a couple of weeks, until they found a new place for them.

"They" meant my daughter's new friends. She'd taken some kind of political elective and through that got involved with a group of volunteers who helped the "Newcomers"—that's how they called them —in all imaginable ways, i.e. housing them with family members. You'd be paid, she added, and when she said how much, my heart skipped a beat. If I wanted to stay in the apartment in which we'd lived for more than two decades, where I'd given birth to three children, breastfed them, brought them through sickness, puberty, and *Abitur*, I would have to take boarders some time soon anyway. To share my place for one month with these refugees could postpone that for at least another year.

They were from Syria. A young couple and their newborn baby, and the grandfather. They would be happy with the living room, my daughter said.

"It's the biggest room!"

"Exactly. And you never use it."

When the kids were still living with me, we often sat there, playing board games, bending our heads over jigsaw puzzles, celebrating birthdays, Christmases, and graduations. But they hardly showed up together anymore and never long enough to play games. I couldn't remember when I last sat on one of the sofas, and sometimes I even forgot to water the flowers, but to see someone else inhabit it brought tears to my eyes. My daughter took me into her arms. "The baby's so cute, Mom. You always wanted to have grandchildren."

The family was supposed to arrive by the end of the week. I removed personal stuff from the living room, emptied dressers and shelves, exchanged one of the sofas with my queen-size bed. I got the crib out of the cellar, the one bought for my first child and kept for the other two though none of them ever slept in it. Even when they were older and the crib had been replaced by a child's bed, it had taken a long time to get them out of mine.

The next day I had a last glance at the room that held so many memories of my family. It looked like a hotel room now. Except for the pictures on the wall. There was an oversized photograph of my still small children; a friend of mine, now a famous photographer, had taken it while I was offering her shelter after she'd left her then boyfriend. There was a reproduction of a Hopper painting; the woman wasn't nude but the legs and knees were well visible, and with a little bit of imagination, one could take the black shadow for her crotch, so I took it off and my children as well. They were neatly dressed and looked innocent enough but I didn't remember when girls started to wear hijabs in Syria. It also would remind them that it wasn't their home, and at least in their room, I wanted them to feel welcome.

When we traveled I often rented our place to tourists. It was the only way we could afford flights and hostels. There was a group of students from France, handsome young men sitting bare-chested on the balcony until the wee hours, smoking, laughing, drinking caipirinha, as a neighbor reported later, a linguistics professor from Italy, families from Spain and the Netherlands, and three Swedish students who looked like actresses from Bergman movies.

My friends always asked me whether I wasn't worried, and I laughed it off, saying that we owned nothing valuable. Our TV or stereo or laptops were old, our furniture, even though antique, run-down. Renters would probably have newer, pricier things. "But what about your personal stuff? Photographs, letters ..." Here they usually stopped, and I often wondered what they expected to find in my drawers. I answered that nowadays people expose more on Facebook. Their presence was not real without me being there. Their ghosts didn't linger. So why was I afraid of taking in this Syrian family in need of a home? My daughter was right. I couldn't say no.

Even though I already missed my bed. But I didn't really need a bed for two, did I?

Then they arrived, the couple with a baby car seat, behind them a man around my age. I smiled and said, *"Salam alaikum."*

"Guten tag," they said.

I offered my hand, then remembered that some Muslim men didn't shake hands with women, and put an extra effort into my smile while pulling my hand back, but the father had already reached for it and so stumbled forward. Fortunately he wasn't holding the baby but a huge Tupperware bowl that fell on the floor instead. Rice salad spread all over us. "I'm so sorry," I said, bending down to save at least some of it, and he said, "It's my fault, please let me do it."

The mother started to laugh, which woke up the baby, and the grandfather said in accent-free German, "Just remember, once you're over the hill you begin to pick up speed."

I looked up in astonishment.

"Schopenhauer." He smiled. "Didn't mean it that literally, I suppose."

"You speak German?"

"I should. I've been teaching it long enough."

"Hold on." I ran inside and to the kitchen, grabbed some kitchen wipes, and returned. They were taken out of my hands, and the son continued to clean the stairs while his wife said, "I'm Sara. Thank you so much. Hopefully we won't need it for long." Her English was better than mine.

I cleared my throat and said, "Come in, please. I am very happy to help."

◆

My father emigrated from Italy during the Sixties. He was one of the millions of migrant workers hired during the *Wirtschaftswunder*. He met my mother and married her, but since she spoke Italian fluently, he never bothered to take German lessons. Fifty years later, he still made so many mistakes that it was difficult to have a conversation with him, one of the reasons that he didn't have any real friends. "I'll show you around," I said in German but very slowly, very clearly.

"Speak normal, please," the grandfather said. "They have to get used to it."

His son raised his eyebrows. "Daddy, can you shut the fuck up, just for once?"

"No, speak English," his father said with a big smile.

I showed them their rooms, the kitchen and the bathroom, my study, and after some hesitation, my bedroom. "If one of you ever needs a moment of peace and I'm not here, please feel free to use it. I know how it is." I smiled at the baby. "At that age you'd give anything to sleep for a couple of hours."

"How many children do you have?" Sara asked.

I nodded toward one of the few remaining photographs. "Three. All grown up now."

"They're beautiful. Must have been sweet as babies."

I took some linen from the dresser and said to the grandfather, "You can have my son's room. Let me just make your bed."

"Call me Khaled." He gently but firmly took the bed linen out of my hands and accompanied me. A lot of my son's stuff was still there, I'd left his laundry on the unmade bed, and his desk was covered with exercise books and pencils, all of which he'd been planning to take to his new place months ago.

"I'm sorry. It's a mess, I know. Why don't you have a seat in the kitchen?" I said.

Khaled smiled. "Sure."

I returned with all the Ikea bags I could find and when they were full, I carried them to the hall. Another five minutes later, I had removed dust and trash. When the girls were gone, it didn't take me long to give their rooms new meanings, but with my son's room, I had postponed any action time and again.

As I joined my new cohabitants in the kitchen, they'd already prepared coffee, "It's all a bit chaotic here, sorry." My kids had been responsible for the household. Every pocket money raise meant a new chore, and since parties and clothes were expensive, I didn't have to do anything in the end. But they always neglected one tiny thing—dirt in the sink or an undusted shelf or an overflowing trash bin, their small revolutionary act of which I couldn't complain since the rest of the apartment was in perfect shape. After they'd all moved out I tried to demonstrate that I was capable of taking care of it myself, but after a few weeks, I lost interest.

I opened the cabinet. "You already found cups and plates. Glasses." I opened the hanging locker. "Pots and pans." The drawer. "Knives, forks, and spoons." And another drawer. "Other useful items." I turned around and opened the fridge, which was nearly empty. "Feel free to use any space. I mostly eat out that's why…" I looked up. Their close attention made me nervous. I shifted my gaze and said, "Dishwasher. Tabs are here. Do you know how …? Of course you do." I bent forward to open the sink cabinet. "There's all kinds of cleaning stuff. It's a mess, I know." I noticed the dirt on the floor, straightened myself, and said, "I am going to the library. You can take a shower, a bath, anything. Make yourselves at home!"

Khaled laughed. "Sit down. Have a scone. Make yourself at home."

I looked at him, frowning.

"Monty Python? Life of Brian?"

He reached for my mug and held it up to me. "Sit down for a minute. Tell us about yourself. Tell us what you like and what you hate. The latter is even more important since we took over your sanctuary."

I looked at Sara and her husband who were smiling politely, the way you smile when you only understand half of the conversation.

"Shouldn't we switch to English for a while? You must all be tired."

"They do understand. They are only sulking."

"We wanted to go to the States in the first place," Sara said. "It would have been much easier."

"Not for me," Khaled said.

"Yale wanted you."

"Johann, let's not discuss this in front of our host!"

At my puzzled look the son started to laugh. "First it was Goethe, then Celan. I would have preferred Paul though." He got up and kissed the baby on the forehead. "Let me put her to bed. We'll talk later."

We had another round of coffee while Sara told me that she and her husband were medics and fell in love at work, while operating on a five-year-old girl. He proposed to her during another operation, and they were again looking like vampires having a feast. Even as a married couple, they continued saving lives at the last practicing hospital in Aleppo but when Sara became pregnant, they decided to leave.

"How long have you been here?" I asked.

"Six months," Khaled said.

"Was it difficult?" I cleared my throat and said, "Did you have a long journey?" I felt heat rising up my neck, how stupid of me, as if I'd inquired about a holiday trip. And wasn't "journey" the most inadequate word I could choose? "It must be hard to leave everything behind," I added.

"I was an exchange student in Tübingen," Khaled said. "I always wanted to return."

When Sara went to the bathroom, he told me that he'd written a book on Paul Celan. I was sick while we discussed him at school and later never got interested enough to even google his poems. I looked at the clock and quickly stood up. "The library's closing soon. Do you need something? A book? CDs? They have tons of audio books. Maybe you want to come next time? It's not far."

"Thank you," Khaled said. "We have our Kindle. We learned to travel light."

"Right," I said.

"But maybe I could have a look at your books? If you don't mind?"

"Take anything you want. Most of it is English though."

"Why?"

"I have the classics, of course." I felt the heat rising up my neck and turned away as if checking the clock again. "Well, have a look. There are also books in my study." I went to the hall to put on my shoes and then I called out, "See you later!"

I didn't go to the library. I wanted to give them some time for themselves and went to my daughter's place. "How did it go?" she asked.

"Fine."

"I told you." She looked at her smart phone. "I have to run. There's tea in the kitchen. Are you hungry?"

"No." I kissed her on the cheek and said, "I'll just lie down on your bed and read a bit."

She hugged me. "Thank you, Mom."

I took one of her books but didn't get past the first page. It was the first time I was alone in her room and I felt strange and uncomfortable. I didn't dare to go to the kitchen either, out of fear that I might run into one of her flat-mates, most of whom I hadn't even met.

When I came home at half past ten, the apartment was quiet. I sat in my study for some time to read my e-mail and browse over several news sites, then I went to the bathroom and locked myself in. While I was storing personal items away, I realized that I'd forgotten to give them towels, put a pile onto the kitchen table, with a note, saying that there were more in the dresser. Before going to bed I browsed over the bookshelves. My English version of Kafka's short stories looked as if it had been taken out, but then I remembered that I'd removed it myself a couple of days before in order to reread *A Dream*. I took it to my room and hid it under the bed. He wasn't even German, I told myself. "But it was his native language!" I imagined Khaled saying, with that disconcerted look in his eyes.

The next morning they were having breakfast when I woke up. I could hear their quiet chatter in the kitchen. I stayed in bed, hoping that they would leave soon since it was already half past nine, but then

I remembered that it was Sunday. Even if they went to German classes or other activities during the week, today nothing would be on their program. Unfortunately it was raining heavily, so even a stroll outside was out of the question, especially with such a small baby. I put my new nightgown over my pajamas and carefully opened the door. As I walked along the closed kitchen door, I could hear them speaking in German.

Showered and dressed, a welcoming smile on my face, I came out of the bathroom. My guests stood at the front door, Khaled and Sara dressed in raincoats, Johann equipped with an umbrella and the baby in a front carrier.

"Good morning," Sara said. "There's breakfast for you in the kitchen."

"We're going to the library," Khaled said.

"But it's not open on Sundays."

Sara buttoned up her coat. "The one at Humboldt Universität is. We'll be home around six. Do you want me to cook dinner?"

"That would be nice." I held the door open and looked after them, then I called, "Looking forward to it!"

They must have gone to the bakery, there was a croissant and rolls and coffee and a glass of freshly pressed orange juice. The kitchen looked cleaner than ever before. After pouring some milk into my coffee I went to put the carton back into the fridge and found it filled. When I opened the sink cabinet to get a bag, I noticed that here too they had cleaned up and put everything in order.

I had breakfast in bed and read until afternoon, then I got up and sat at the desk to prepare my lessons. I wanted to read a story with my class. I'd given it much thought and in the end went for the German translation of *The Lottery*.

I was in the middle of preparing a questionnaire when the Syrian family returned. They rang the bell even though they could have let themselves in, and I opened and waited for them at the door. When Johann freed the baby from its carrier, I stretched out my arms. "Give her to me."

I carried the little girl around the rooms, telling her about the child that once slept and did homework in it, showing her the remaining photographs. Then Johann came and took her to the bathroom. Khaled asked me what I had been doing, and I told him.

He took a tattered Reclam out of the inner pocket of his jacket. "Why don't you read them a German story?"

It was Kleist's *Marquise of O*. Didn't he say that he only had his Kindle? "Too complicated," I said.

"The words?"

"Everything." I smiled. "Do you guys like Italian food?"

He laughed. "We like everything."

Once he'd gone into his room I checked the shelf where I stored my *Reclams*. My copy was still there.

Dinner reminded me of my classes, when the task was to play a scene at a restaurant. Only Khaled seemed confident and relaxed. He asked me harmless questions about my past and my family, which I took great pains to answer in a simple and clear language and pronunciation, so that the others could understand. But with me they were shy to speak German and only made short, risk-free remarks, and there were a lot of uncomfortable pauses. After less than half an hour, I pretended to have a headache and retired to my bedroom.

The next day I read *The Marquise*. I read it a second time after collecting smart phones. Then I told my pupils about my new guests. "They know a lot about German literature," I said to my Syrian students. "But I don't know anything about yours."

"Adonis," Sami said.

Hala raised her hand. "Maryana Marrash."

I wrote the names down and when school was over went to the library where I found a book by Adonis. I copied *Desert* and *The Beginning of Speech*. When I asked for Syrian novels, the librarian recommended Fawwaz Haddad's *God's Soldiers*, which I read there, and finished shortly before closing time.

On my way home I realized how hungry I was. I hadn't eaten anything since breakfast. Passing the falafel vendor at Rosenthaler Platz I was pulled in by the smell like a magnet and I ordered grilled haloumi, which I ate staring at a large photograph of two men riding camels in a desert. When I paid I asked where it had been taken, but the vendor said that he had no idea. All these places looked alike to him, he'd never even wanted to go. "I was born in Wuppertal. I never really learned Arabic. Had to take lessons for this job." He looked at the photograph, then back at me. "I'd put up something else, but the boss says that it's good for business."

When I came home all was quiet again. They had left dinner for me on the kitchen table. It looked delicious but I was so stuffed that I couldn't bring myself to take at least a spoonful. I took the plate to the bathroom and poured it into the toilet, cleaning thoroughly afterward. Here too everything had been put in order. Here too one of them—or all?—had dusted and swept and wiped. They'd even done the laundry.

I tiptoed to my study and browsed over a few Facebook posts. A friend of mine, who moved from Kreuzberg to a Bavarian village when she got pregnant, had shared an article about a gang rape of a 15-year-old girl. Only one of them was third generation Turkish, the rest a hundred percent German, yet she'd commented: *German girls aren't safe anymore. Wake up, Merkel!*

It was hardly nine when I went to bed. I tried to read but couldn't concentrate, knowing that Khaled and I were only separated by a wall. I couldn't fall asleep for a long time but must have eventually since I was woken by the crying of the baby. Soon I heard someone hurrying along the hallway, then steps again, slow and soft this time. I stood up and held my ear to the door. Khaled was singing Schubert's *Schlummerlied*:

> Ins frische Gras legt er sich hin,
> Lässt über sich die Wolken ziehn,
> An seine Mutter angeschmiegt,
> Hat ihn der Traumgott eingewiegt.

I waited, hoping that the baby would start crying again so that I could offer my help, take over from him, but after he'd sung all three verses a second time I heard him bringing the baby back to her parents

The next day a boy from Afghanistan was missing. During the

final lesson Hala shouted out, "They arrested Amir." She held up her smart phone and now there was no stopping the others from getting theirs out of the bags again. I leaned back and looked at the clock. There were only ten minutes left anyway. When the school bell rang, all uncertainties were cleared: He would be taken back to Kabul.

Before they all left the classroom I took Sami aside. "This cannot happen to people from your country, can it? You're allowed to stay permanently, right?"

"I don't care. As soon I turn eighteen I'm going home." He turned his gaze to the window, behind which the trees were all green now. "I rather die there than stay a day longer here."

"But why?"

He shrugged. It was clear that he didn't want to confide in me. Maybe he just had a bad day, I told myself, but a soft voice inside of me began to whisper, ISIS.

As I came up the stairs, I could hear Bach's *Chaconne* at top volume, coming from my apartment. They must have found my Hilary Hahn CD, I thought, smiling. Then I remembered that I'd last been listening to it in my bedroom. Maybe one of them was lying on my bed now, enjoying the peace, while everybody else was out.

I unlocked the door slowly and noisily. "Anybody home?" I shouted.

The music stopped. A second later Khaled appeared, a violin in his left hand, a bow in the other. "I hope you don't mind. Or your neighbors."

"Not at all!" I smiled. "How have you all been? We hardly see each other."

"Fine," he said.

I realized that he wasn't finished playing but didn't dare to go on. "I have a lot of baby clothes." I said, "They are totally cute, but we have been asked to clear our cellars. They want to do some paintwork."

"You just came home, please sit down. I'll make coffee for you."

"I just had coffee." I left my coat on and said, "Really, I wanted to check things out down there anyway." As soon as I closed the door behind me I heard the first notes of Beethoven's violin concerto. A little later I opened the big suitcase in which I'd stored our baby clothes. I held the tiny rompers and socks and dresses in my hands, and long lost memories flashed through my head, and I started to cry and couldn't stop. In the end I closed the suitcase again, shoved it back into a safe corner, and took the subway to the next H&M that had a children's section. I came back home with two big shopping bags. The complete family was waiting for me at the dinner table.

"There must have been a pipe break," I said. "Everything was wet and moldy. Had to throw it all away. But these are cute too, aren't they?" I took out piece after piece and hung it over the chair. "Please, don't say no. It really made me happy to choose them. It can take ages until my kids show up with a baby."

Sara smiled. "Do you eat meat?"

I looked at the table. "It's bœuf bourguignon, isn't it? I love it."

Later, when father and son went for a walk with the baby and we cleaned the kitchen together, Sara switched to English and told me that they'd applied for jobs in NYC. They could live with friends in the beginning. Khaled didn't know.

"But why? Aren't you much safer here? With things going on over there right now? What if they send you back at the airport?" I remembered the horror stories I'd read about and the photographs of small kids in handcuffs. "They might even take away your baby."

"Here we lost our ability to dream. Maybe we're safe. But life's worthless without dreaming."

I cleared my throat. "What about Khaled?"

"We've been studying, we've been working. Here, we can get cleaning jobs, if we're lucky." When the men returned, she whispered, "Don't tell him."

Khaled had a cup of tea with me in the kitchen after the little family had retreated to my living room. We talked about teaching. We raved and complained about the same things. We were both tired of it and couldn't imagine a life without it at the same time.

"What happened to your wife?" I asked as I put our cups into the dishwasher.

"She died of cancer a year ago."

"I'm sorry." I closed the dishwasher and filled a glass with water, which I would put on my nightstand. Then I emptied it again and left it in the sink, remembering that I'd stopped that habit in order not to have to go to the toilet at night. I turned around and said, "She would have been happy to become a grandmother I guess."

"We lost touch. She was living in Egypt." He looked around the kitchen, as if wanting to make sure that they removed every sign of their presence. "We've been divorced for years."

"Really?"

He smiled. "Our countries have much more in common than you think."

The next morning I was working late. I could hear them moving in the hallway for a while, then I fell asleep again, and when I woke up they were gone. At school, as I was clearing my pigeonhole, the head had just said goodbye to a woman wearing a hijab. "She claimed to be a French teacher, but my long forgotten school French was better than hers," my boss said when the woman had closed the door behind her. "I don't want to be mean but with all the papers lost they can claim to be anything, can't they?"

"I wouldn't want to clean toilets if I'd been a university professor before," I said.

"A lot of people from the GDR had to do it," she said.

I glanced at the book where the secretary wrote down the names of the students excused that day. "Aren't we doing something about Amir?"

My boss looked at me, frowning.

"The kid from Afghanistan?"

"Well, that's sad." She shrugged, then she smiled and said, "Let's concentrate on the ones who are staying."

Today I'd brought Kafka's *Homecoming*. I had to borrow the German edition from our school library. At the end of the lesson I gave Hala and Sami a *Reclam*. "Always carry it with you," I said. "People will show more respect. And it'll make it harder for them to throw you out."

On the week-end I visited a friend in Hamburg I hadn't seen in

211

years, wanting my new cohabitants to have some time for themselves, and when I returned, it was only my daughter waiting for me. "I told you that it wouldn't be for long. We helped with their application and everything, but none of us thought that it would work out that quickly, with things going on over there right now." She smiled and said, "I tried to call you. They wanted to say goodbye."

"I forgot the charger."

She had already put on new sheets. Theirs were spinning around in the washing machine, together with the towels. On the kitchen table I found a thank-you note written by Sara and signed by Johann as well. Next to it two books: Kafka's complete work in German with a note inside by Khaled. He wasn't happy, he explained, but wanted to see his granddaughter growing up. The second book was in Arabic. I opened it where he'd left the book ribbon. Next to a poem he'd written

> With every Thought I went
> out of the World: there you were,
> you my Gentle One, you my Open One, and—
> you received us.

By the end of the month a large sum was transferred to my account. "Aren't you happy now?" my daughter asked.

Piano
by Laura Foley

A late spring afternoon, the river
just beginning to thaw, ice about to give way.
I look out at the large grey puddles of rain
and want it all to remain just like this:
softening hills of snow, Billy's music
spilling over me.

Keeping the Quiet

by Rick Kempa

The other creatures give no sign,
except the bat's thin screech, torn air,
a drift of skunk. We two kneel
before the fire, tending it.

Your face toward me a bed for shifting coals,
a blanket moon. Off to one side
you have made a pile of wood
too beautiful to burn.

A curl of wind. The oak lets go
a spray of last year's leaves. The new growth
has more room to breathe.

Water runs its fingers over
every boulder in the creek. Each one
sounds a separate note.

Somewhere high up in the cliffs,
a great-horned owl's cry
reverberates.

I hold the cup—
this is what makes us human—
you pour the tea.

Yukon Artists' Co-op

by Kersten Christianson

I blame you, of course,
for opening the doors

your arms outstretched
like raven's wings

your trickster smile,
the understanding

of no cost too high
within this nest

of bright art: waning
yellow moon, shapeshifters,

strokes of beryl & ochre,
handmade journals, felted

hats, your dream of the north,
wrapped in handmade paper.

Sanctuary with Internment Camp and Shrinking Glacier
by Jory Mickelson

1.

Lorna kept a single, orphaned fawn
it was fragile; she was not. Slash

logging stripped the mountain, left her
broke. Though she afforded patience enough to tame

& raise the fawn indoors, teaching it to piss
in the wading pool she kept in her bedroom

Mother and child neither city or wild
has room for, so they occupy

the border places. If I scrubbed
this into something cleaner

polished the woman and her fawn
from the ramshackle trailer—

But I won't.

They cling more tightly than lichen
to the crumbling granite.

There is something fragile in her, the bending of its head
two crushed water bottles left along the gravel road.

2.

The crumbled asphalt streets of Butte are fading in the sun

their names a power to smoke (again and again) the mystery
of substance: Galena & Porphyry

Gagnon curling into itself just off Main
Platinum, Mercury, Dakota, The Knobby Hill at Walkerville.

My grandfather coming home each night from below the earth
riding the shaking elevator up the Orphan Girl's throat

a homecoming song, the only thing not caked in soot

his shiny eyes, my grandfather, stumbling down the hall
and through the bathroom door

with the pistol in his hand—

sits down on the toilet, looking at the whiteness of the tub
stops when he realizes he will regret this, decides he won't.

3.

At Spanaway all the fencing's been taken
down the razor wire rusted in some dump five decades

now. As the barren field is silent & longtime residents too
as a bottle after it's broken quiets. As the breaking demonstrates.

Forty miles from where my grandmother was born—internment
camp
housing dozens of Italian families.

In wind scrubbed barracks with row after row of misshaped
beds, cracks in the walls let

damp crawl in & sink and spill
another blanket over the bed

making it hard to ever

warm. Hands and feet balled into siblings' bodies
whole families, bunched cold clouds.

What do you remember, I asked her once
at her home overlooking the Sound, holy cards

stuck in the mirror's corner & Frank Sinatra soothing
behind us, what can you tell me about the war? *I don't know*

what you're talking about then
They finally gave my camera back.

4.

When I catch sight of them

two young does, one watches
while the other bends to graze.

One watches the busy road leading to the dormant
volcano buried in wind, until they can chance to

cross. The shrinking glaciers & basalt giving way
to evergreens and on clear days a dazzled view

for everyone else, the mountain unable to catch
itself—& the thrown sky blue about

its head & wind &
clouds coming down to cover everything, grey endlessly

in the green dripping valleys & the wide mouthed bay
& under the earth.

I called those the yearlings, what else, mistake & remedy
Every time their tails flag white at the approach of the neighbor's

dog & vanish without looking back finally as the lab crosses
the field with the sound of pursuit still caught in its throat.

Claim Sanctuary

by Charlotte Platt

PUSHING AGAINST the door, Marc forced his frozen hands to work at the handle. Hearing the unmistakable snap of the lock breaking, he smirked to himself. He was good at this. The gale pulled at his coat, almost tugging it from his body and whipping his tangle of hair about his face, but he managed to fall unceremoniously into the St. Magnus Cathedral.

He hated these islands.

Pulling himself up, he took in the silent building. He grabbed a chair and jammed the door shut, sealing himself in for the night. The few lights on left an eerie shadow clinging to the chasm of the rising roof. So, this was a church at night, he pondered, his eyes wandering over every inch they could find.

The stones were amazing, sandstone of contrasting colours that stood against the gloom. A dull red, the colour of dead blood to Marc's eyes, mixed with bone white to form the body of the leviathan church.

Woven wooden chairs sat like soldiers on uniform parade, with a tile spine running the length of the main wing. Rib-like pillars supported the roof, and an alter sat proud at the heart of the cathedral.

He let out low whistle, walking between the columns and the walls, along a wide corridor that seemed to span the whole cathedral. In the mid-winter darkness, the stained-glass windows weren't at their best, but the images were still enchanting, even to a little heathen like Marc. Magnificent shades depicted valiant knights, tragic saints, and intricately detailed biblical scenes. He recognised a few, long ago memories of Sunday school meetings he'd almost slept through stabbing at his mind. He didn't care for the headstones upon the walls—the dead held no interest for him—but he knew it would be a safe enough place to sleep for two or three hours. They'd open the doors at around seven; he would have to leave at around six, so it would be two hours. Better than nothing, he supposed.

He was right at the back of the cathedral now, looking up at an immense, flower-like main window. The glass branched off into thin slices of colour and shape from a sphere in the centre, some pattern he couldn't identify snaking through them.

"It's beautiful, isn't it?" A voice rang through the darkness. Marc spun around, fists up: living rough had taught him to keep his guard up. He saw someone approaching, and mentally cursed: he should have checked if anyone else was sleeping here. Or waiting.

"What, can't you speak?" she asked, and now he could tell it was a woman. She entered the sparse light and he saw she was only a touch older than him, twenty-two to his twenty, he supposed. She wore a short denim skirt and black halter-neck top, with knee length boots that held a wicked heel. Her hair was in a messy bun with a few soft curls falling about her face. He thought she looked amazing. She looked him up and down slowly, her emerald eyes, rimmed with dark eyelashes, he noted, meeting his thunder-grey ones briefly.

"Is there something wrong with your voice?" she pushed, smiling. Her glossed lips shone a pale blue, an odd choice, to his mind, but it complimented the outfit.

"No, my voice his fine," he replied, frowning at her.

"You're not from Orkney, are you?" she asked, the smile broadening. "I'm not taking the Mick, it's your accent. It's different."

"It will be. I'm from Southport."

"Never heard of it." She laughed.

"I'd never heard of this place until last week."

"So how come you're up here?" she asked, leaning against one of the pillars.

"Why do you care?" he asked, unused to anyone asking. You didn't, living rough. No one cared. His family hadn't, that was why he'd been living on the streets for the past four years.

"I'm being polite. And I'm interested. That so rare?" she asked, bristling just a touch at his tone.

"Yeah," he bit back. Deafening chimes rang through the air, making him flinch. Quarter past four then.

"Oh well. So, how come you're up here?" she pushed, not letting the question drop.

"Why are you here?" he questioned back, assuming she wouldn't want to tell him.

"I had an argument with my colleagues on a staff night out. We split up, I couldn't get home because I live in the middle of nowhere —also known as South Ronaldsay—and there are no busses this late, so I went to the graveyard. It's the most sheltered spot on the main street. You?"

He sighed, knowing she wouldn't let it drop.

"I'm hiding from someone. Okay?"

"I'd ask who, but I doubt you'd tell me. I'm Elsbeth, by the way."

"From someone I was supposed to meet up here," he said, crouching with his back against the rough stone. He could easily outrun her if he had to, so he saw no harm in it.

"Where's Southport?" she asked, changing track.

"It's in England, South Lancashire. Near Liverpool."

"Now there I've heard of. Must have been a hard job if you needed to come this far north. And if you have to claim sanctuary," she said, a hint of knowledge in her voice.

He looked at her with a raised eyebrow. "Claim sanctuary?"

223

"In the old days, when someone was on the run, from the law or anyone else, they could enter a church and stay there. No one could take them out of the church, and they could live there as long as they needed to. You're sleeping here, right?" she asked with a sad smile.

"Look, why are you asking this?" He was too tired to be bothered with this, or manners, or retelling his life story.

"You look like you could use a chat. And a good meal," she added, nodding to his loose clothes.

"Well I don't. Why don't you just run off and find your friends?"

"Because it's four AM and they'll all have crashed out somewhere. I won't be able to find them. And because I would like to keep talking to you, if you don't mind."

He stared at her, willing her to be a symptom of sleep deprivation. She took his silence to mean he didn't, so began to quiz him once more.

"So, why do you need to hide: running from the law? Dodging some big villain? Were you delivering drugs or something?" she laughed. He stayed silent, avoiding her gaze. "You were, weren't you? Are you Marc?"

"How do you know my name?" he growled, jumping up.

"Good old Radio Orkney. Your name and appearance were broadcast today as a missing person. But you're deliberately missing, aren't you?"

"And? What does it matter to you?" he snarled, ready to walk away. He did not need this right now, he only had to last till tomorrow and make it onto the boat, he didn't want the police involved.

"I'm interested. I'd like to help you, if I can," she shrugged.

"Why?" He paused, curiosity niggling at his mind. Help never came for free.

"Tell me about yourself and I'll tell you why," she offered, her head tilting to one side.

He briefly described his past four years, and why he'd left home. He explained his dad's drinking problem, the frequent beatings, the fights, Mum dying. He was never going to meet Elsbeth again, it didn't matter what she knew. He could have made it all up for all she knew.

"So why the drugs?" she asked after he'd stopped.

"I was sleeping rough in Aberdeen, and someone approached me. Offered four hundred pounds if I'd take a rucksack on the next ferry up here, then give it to someone on this side. Gave me an address and a ticket, just asked my name for the booking. I accepted."

"Where was the problem? Sounds like good money."

"I got curious. I opened the bag, found drugs. There were clothes on the top, you know, the main compartment, but in the bottom, there were bags of stuff. White powder, some tablets, resin too, pretty sure I saw some scragg in there, you name it. Easily a few thousand quid, probably more," he sighed, rubbing the back of his neck.

"And?" she ventured. "You said you didn't do the deal."

"And I got scared! I don't get involved in drugs; the odd joint now and again, sure I'll turn a blind eye, but that was way too much. Too deep. I've seen people OD on that kind of thing, not always accidentally. As soon as I got to dry land I dumped the bag over the harbor and bolted. I've been sleeping here and there for two days, but the wind's as cold as hell. I'd freeze outside tonight."

"Aye, you would," she nodded with a thin smile. "So, what are you going to do?"

"I've got a ticket. I'm gone tomorrow. Keep my hood up, don't talk much, and stay in the corners of the boat where I won't be found."

"How'd you get a ticket?"

"First rule my mum taught me; keep enough cash on you to get out of a bad situation. You learn that quickly. What did they say?" he asked, wondering if he'd be able to get out of these islands.

"Who?" she yelled over the clanging of the bells once more. Half past four now.

"On the radio," he explained, rolling his eyes.

"Just that you were missing, that your family was worried for you, and that if you were seen it should be reported. You'll need to be careful."

Danny cursed as he neared the hulking stone cathedral. It was too early in the morning for this shit, it was cold as an icebox, and he should have either been in bed or partying: he didn't mind which.

Thousands of pounds worth of drugs that boy was supposed to

carry, that was his selling supply for the next three months, riding out the January blues through to when the kids were on holiday. He'd got the call from Aberdeen, been given a name and a meeting place. The only problem? The boy hadn't turned up.

He'd been looking for the brat for the last two days, then had finally got his details on the radio to try and drum up interest. No one on the scene had seen him, so he must have been lying low. Danny needed to find the idiot, Marc his name was. Marc had seen the main supplier, he knew who the stuff came from. Marc had to be dealt with.

An overdose somewhere quiet, maybe a doorway. He'd just be another junkie on too much of a high, with a cold, lonely body found the next morning. Rare in Orkney but not unheard of; all it needed was a bit of some powder and a bubble in the syringe. Easy way to get rid of a problem.

He knew, in this weather, there were only two places a street sleeper would go, either the graveyard or the cathedral. They'd never upgraded the back doors to that place; anyone with half a brain could get in there. He pulled himself up to peek through one of the warped glass windows and saw a chair pushed up against it. Yeah, Marc was in there.

They heard the slamming against the door at the same time, Marc was back on his feet immediately.

"Oh shit, that'll be him!" he cussed, his eyes frantically searching for the other exits. He reminded Elsbeth of a fox hearing the dogs.

"How do you know it's him?" Elsbeth asked, watching the alcove of the door. The chair was beginning to give way, another few minutes and whoever was at it would be inside.

"Oh, who else is it going to be?" He rounded on her, glaring. "Shit! How do I get out of here?" He was scared out of his wits. He'd thrown too much over that harbour wall—if he was found, he wouldn't survive the night. He looked hopelessly at Elsbeth.

"I know somewhere you can hide. I know my way around this place better than you, I can lead him out of here and be safe enough," she smiled, flashing surprisingly white teeth. He frowned, chewing his lower lip. Guilt nagged in his gut. This was his mess; he should deal with it

"Are you sure?" he asked after another round of hammering against what was apparently his only exit.

"What's he going to do, kill me?" she asked with a laugh. "Even if he gets hold of me, I'll just say I was staying here because I got separated from my friends. Now come on," she assured, grabbing his painfully thin wrist by the coat sleeve and pulling him down a set of dark stone steps. She shoved him into a small, cramped toilet.

"Are you really sure about this, Elsbeth?" he asked once more. "He'll hurt you if he finds you."

"*If* being the important word there. Now shut up and stay here until half past six; they'll be opening up just after then, so it'll be safe for you to leave. Good luck." She smiled, pecking a kiss to his head and running back up the steps. He heard the heavy door shut and was left in the brooding darkness.

Marc didn't know how long he sat there for before the quarter-to-five chimes. He could hear the sounds of someone walking around the cathedral in heavy boots, then someone with heels running across the floor. She must have been slamming her feet; he'd not heard her make that noise with him. The boots gave chase, a door slammed shut, the wind howled just once, and then he could only hear his own shallow breathing.

He carefully made his way up the steps, tugging the door open a sliver. There was no one else in the echoing space, the door he had used was closed, and the chair discarded beside it. He was safe for now, but he decided not to sleep. He didn't bother to put the chair back either.

The bells rang for their final time in Marc's ears; it was half past six and time for him to get the hell out of there. He'd spent all night pacing underneath the largest stained-glass window, worrying over Elsbeth. That was rare for him, really, the only person he usually cared for was himself. He hoped she got away. The guy hadn't come back, so he'd presumed she had managed to at least lead him away.

Marc rubbed his hands over his face as if to wash away his

fatigue, then went back towards the door he'd first broken through. As he emerged from his hiding place he saw the unmistakable blue flashes of an emergency vehicle at the wall of the graveyard.

She turned him in: the thought stabbed through his mind quicker than any needle. Panic jolted through him and he felt his heart jump but saw now it was an ambulance, not a police van. Panic filled his heart, and he ran deeper into the graveyard. The guy must have caught her, there must have been an accident around the stones.

He saw the crowd of spectators gathered about one of the taller monuments, milling around a cordon line. There was a stretcher, blanketed and full, it's burden hidden from the curious bodies dotted about.

Marc approached a small older woman with hair the colour of frost.

"What's happened?" he asked, knowing she wouldn't recognise him. She didn't have any glasses.

"It's tragic, some poor young lass has frozen to death last night! Name of Elsbeth Tait, the policeman said, she's been there all night, died of exposure. They said she's frozen stiff, probably slipped away with that wind around midnight. He's over by the ambulance; he'll be able to tell you some more. Oh, it is tragic," she sighed.

Marc stepped back, looking over at the trolley once more. The height was about the same, but that could be coincidence. One of the paramedics came over to him, putting a hand to his shoulder.

"Are you all right son? You look ill." He was a tall man, older, with grey encroaching on his dark blond hair.

"The girl, what was her name?" he asked, praying the old woman was just a gossip, she'd gotten the names confused.

"Elsbeth Tait. It was in her purse."

"Could I see her?" Marc asked uneasily, the panic in his system spiking. He couldn't tear his eyes away from the trolley now.

"You family?" the paramedic asked.

"No. I was out with a girl called Elsbeth last night, she got separated from the group and she's not answering her phone. Please, just to put my mind at rest," he implored. Sighing, the paramedic nodded.

"I shouldn't really be doing this," he muttered. "But just so you know it's not your friend. It looks like she froze last night. We have to do an examination of course, but we think she'd be dead by around one o'clock" he explained as they walked.

He led Marc to the stretcher and pulled the blanket away. Marc's eyes widened; tears springing up at the sight. Pale skin with blue lips, soft brown hair, and such dark lashes, laid upon the carrying board, a small smile still playing on her mouth.

"Is that her?" the paramedic prompted.

"No," Marc lied, "Thank goodness, it's not. My Elsbeth is probably on someone's sofa. Sorry to have bothered you mate: I was just worried when I heard the name."

He nodded to the paramedic and left, dodging the policemen at the gate. He stuffed his hands into his pockets and made for the library, another sanctuary, until his boat. He just had to last till the ferry. He could hold it together till then. If she could haunt a damned cathedral till morning, he could last until lunchtime.

The First Lo'ihian

by Sage Kalmus

Aᴌᴏʜᴀ, ᴍʏ ɴᴀᴍᴇ is Kale (that's KA-le) Kahananui, and if you're reading this, then I'm already food for the *i'a* (that's the fishes, in case you haven't kept the old language). I was born on the Big Island of Hawai'i as one century was coming to a close and the next was gearing up for its big cue. I don't know when it is for you now, but I have to believe it's better than this.

You're probably wondering what's with this bundle—that is if any of it's even still intact when you find it, which is why I'm adding this message. I'm racing sunup to write this in the gear hut where I work on Punalu'u beach, before all the people start showing up. This is where you'd normally find me every weekday before and after school, and all day most weekends, in this thatch hut on this black sand beach on the island's southeast shore, renting snorkel and scuba gear to tourists (though mostly all they end up seeing down here are sea turtles).

231

Locals come here mostly to spearfish. My brothers and his brahs surf. I just like to swim.

I love the feeling of weightlessness in the water, and freedom of motion in every direction. I like to get deep under the surface and spin like a porpoise, lose all sense of up and down. I never go out too far. It's easy to get disoriented and find yourself too far out to return. I'm a strong swimmer, but I know better than to get too cocky with the *kai*. I swim out just far enough to turn back and gaze at the shore. I watch the lava trickling down Kilauea, like the Goddess Pele's veins spilling red liquid fire into the *kai* in a geyser of steam. When it hardens, it'll turn into more *aina*: a reminder that the island is always expanding, always growing—one molten trickle at a time. After that, I always return to the shore feeling cleansed.

In the gear hut I spend all my time in between customers staring back out at the water: at a particular spot twenty miles offshore where, 10,000 feet below the surface, scientists in the early 1970s discovered an underwater volcano they named the Lo'ihi seamount. They said in 50,000 years, this seamount will break through the surface to join its sisters as the newest island in the Hawaiian chain. Every day, I watch that spot as the minutes tick by, imagining what the island Lo'ihi will become after it breaks through the surface. I imagine its landscape: tree-lined plains sweeping up into a majestic peak, and its coastline, weaving in and out of lagoons. And I imagine its people: simple, uncorrupted, genuine, kind. Even in this moonless black, I know right where it will be. I don't need my eyes to see it.

Looking out there now, I imagine you, kneeling at this strange, decaying bundle stuck in the reeds, this note in your hands. And I imagine you pausing as you read to gaze back across the water at that ocean wall of a land mass blocking out your view from north to west, imagining me 50,000 years in your past, trying to figure out the best place to start this story.

Did it start last night, when I found this offering washed up on the beach? Or did it start seventeen years before, with my untimely birth? The answer I came to, right or wrong, is it would probably be simplest to start yesterday morning, a Saturday, when me and Lina were in my bedroom clipping orchid buds for hula.

"What about dese?" Lina said, holding up a hanging chocolate orchid by the stem, like a chick by its neck. She's what we call around here a real *tita!* True Polynesian, not like those skinny bitches they slap a grass skirt on and make into bobble-heads for *haoles'* dashboards (*haoles*—pronounced *HOW-lees*—are whites, and it's not a compliment.) When you look at statues of Pele, you don't see narrow waists and perky tits. You see sagging mounds of boobs and butt: a volcanic mountain in female flesh. You see Lina.

I'm somewhere between the two: an elephant seal to Lina's walrus, which for a *kanaka maoli* is on the paler side of the scale. But when most people look at me they don't see my size. They see the tri-color neon hair, tattoos down my neck, silver dollar holes in my ears. And they squint behind their sunglasses to figure out if I'm a boy or a girl. Needless to say, they don't make a bobble-head or deity statue the likes of me.

I live in my own room, the size of a walk-in closet, crammed into a leaky, corrugated shack of mostly hallway, with both my parents, my two sisters, and two of my brothers (the two remaining, who, like me, have yet to fly this rusty coop—and at the rate they're going, probably never will). Everyone else shares their room with someone, but since no one wants to share space with me, the arrangement suits us all just fine.

"Easy with that, yeah?" I said as I plucked a ripe dendrobium clean.

Lina snuffled at me. "I not gonna break it. Jesus! Like you no got plenty more." She made a big sweeping gesture to the jungle of orchids overrunning my room. Purple dendrobium, looking like a thick-lipped choir. Lavender vanda, like swans stretching out their golden necks. *Ohai ali'i* like bright orange ruffled bowties. Mauna Loa beallara, like pink and white speckled starfish. I grew them all. Even some that weren't orchids, like the leafy maile I used to make the Lei of Royalty, mostly for Torao.

Oh Torao.

It's amazing what I hear people pay for orchids on the mainland; out here they grow like weeds.

"People want to smell flowery smells at hula," I explained, waving my hands through the air. "Sweet and perfumy, yeah?" Most orchids don't have a smell, but I only grow the ones that do, because that's how the crowds prefer it. It's too bad. Some of the prettiest flowers don't have scents.

Lina wrinkled her radish nose at me. "People *lolo.*"

"You don't need to tell me that," I said, as she buried that radish into one of those tiger-spotted buds and drew in deep, letting it out in a sensual, "Mmmm."

"Okay, enough!" I shot my hand up between us to block out the image. "You win. Just put that face away. Go... box them up."

With a smug grin I've grown to hate but that I was suddenly overwhelmed with how much I was going to miss, she snatched up one of the last empty plastic boxes on my bed, the rest were filled with bunches of buds, one type in each. Arrayed on my bed that way, it looked like a patchwork quilt of a fabulous garden with each patch its own bright swath of color. Watching her for a second busying about, unaware of being watched, I wanted to hold her there in time, like you do when you see a perfect lei. But you know those aren't made to last. This is the best you get of them, before they wither and fade.

I heard Lina's voice in the background: "All dese orchid you grow for dem—" and I wondered if she'd just started up or had I missed something, off in what she calls: La-La Land. "You show up and you string for dem for free for every week."

"So? It's how I do my part."

"And what dey do for you?"

"What are they supposed to do for me?"

"Let you dance wit dem. Howzat?"

I let out a short laugh with a "Yeah!" that sounded like a deep, open puka in the ground, venting steam.

"See?" she said. "You bad as dey."

"I just get where they're coming from is all," I said.

I'm an excellent dancer, actually, and I know it—just not at the part they make me dance at every tryout. The *kane* part should be powerful and strong. But no matter how sharp I shoot my arms around my head like arrows or stomp the ground like a boar, I still always look like I'm swatting and squashing bugs. And no one wants a *moke* like me swishing my hips and shaking my man-boobs with the *wahine*. And Lina knows it.

I turned my head so she couldn't see me blush. With this Polynesian skin tone, it always looks like a rash (you may have noticed this too.) "I don't like it," I went on, "but I understand."

My first name, Kale, means manly, and my last name, Kahananui, means the hard work. So you could say my full name translates to the hard work of being manly. Tell me about it. I was the sixth boy of six *keiki*. We have two younger sisters now, but right before them was me. In *kanaka maoli* tradition if the first five *keiki* are boys then the sixth, whatever its gender, is raised to help the mother with the household chores: *wahine* work. Oftentimes, if this was a boy, he grew up to become *mahu*. Personally, I think that's all coincidence. My parents didn't even follow that tradition. But still there's not a Polynesian from here to Hilo who doesn't believe that when I popped out with an *ule* instead of a *kohe*, my parents were performing some sort of preemptive *huna* mysticism in naming me.

"Well, you ditch this joint for New York wit me, you won't have to deal wit dat bullshit anymore."

Now it was my turn to snuffle. "Right, 'cause the mainland's so much less judgmental." Just the thought of a thousand times more people looking down their noses at me, and more in every direction for miles and miles, made my stomach squirm.

"No, dumbshit. Cause anyone bother you, I kick em in de *ala alas!* Dat's why." She pumped out her torso and face at me like a puffer fish and stayed that way till I couldn't help but crack a smile.

"Please, sistah," I said. "As soon as your feet hit the mainland you'll turn haole like the rest of them." Then steeled myself for her retaliation. She wants to know why I won't go with her? She doesn't realize, it has nothing to do with New York or the mainland. I won't go anywhere to live that's not here: not with her, not with anyone. I'm Hawaiian and Hawai'i is my home, even if I don't always feel so welcome or at home here. That's not Hawai'i's fault, it's not the *aina's* fault, or the Goddess Pele's. It's not even the people's fault (though boy, can it feel like it most times). It's the timing. It's because the Hawaiian island where I belong, where I was meant to be born, won't break sea level for another 50,000 years.

As I expected, Lina charged me, lunging across the four-foot gap between us, shoving me backward toward the bed. I yelped and threw myself to the side, doing a sort of twisting scuttle to avoid crashing down and crushing all our hard work. As I regained my balance I heard applause behind me, but not from Lina. It was coming from across the room, at my doorway, where my two brothers, Ken and Luke, stood clapping with wide, fake grins. I call them Cheech and Chong, for what should be obvious reasons to anyone who gets downwind of them. Though sometimes I think they like the names too much.

"You go an try out for hula wit dat tonight, sistah-boy?" said Cheech, aka Ken.

"You make it for *shoah*," said Chong, aka Luke. "But where dey go and find grass skirt and coconut bra dat fit you?"

"Why don't you two go back to your room and smoke some more *pakalolo?*" I said. "You're still conscious."

"Conscious," Cheech repeated all mock impressed. "Would ya listen to him, with such fancy word?" He turned to Chong. "You see how much better than we he is?"

"Yeah," Chong joined in, "it like he come out a book instead of he own *kine.*"

"Not our *kine,*" Cheech mock protested. "Him don't got a *kine.*"

"Hey wahine," Chong directed at me. "Why you not move to *haole*-land with your boyfriend over dere?" He flashed a sideways smirk at Lina, who gave him stink-eye as he kept on at me, "You belong over dere a whole lot better den dis moke here do."

"This *moke* here make poi out of you," Lina said, lunging at them and halting a foot from their faces, and several inches lower. They only burst out snickering, of course, but also turned from the room as they did so, and tripped off down the hall, snorting and clapping each other's backs. I wondered if they'd be so easy to get rid of when Lina was on the other side of an ocean and not just a room. She turned back into the room and scanned my face like a nurse performing triage.

But she wouldn't get to play bodyguard or therapist to me anymore. From here on, my problems were my own. "I need to get ready," I said, turning to my wardrobe rack and pulling down an outfit. "Bring those to the car," I added, nodding behind me at the plastic boxes of flowers as I headed from the room. "I'll be ready by the time you're done."

"Oh Kale, you lie," Lina shot at my back.

In the bathroom, I found my littlest sister smearing on makeup like it was warrior face paint. "Mom know you doing that?" I asked.

"You shut up," she said, and before I could kick her in the fanny she stomped past me out the door. But once turning the corner she called out behind her with false bravery, "Mahu!" before tittering and skittering away. I don't even know if she understands what that word means yet. No one does, really, 'cause there's too many meanings for it; it means something different to every person. To some people mahu is just gay. Or homosexual (which is gay without the lifestyle.) To other people it's a full-on crossdressing wannabe wahine. That's why I don't like the word. Not because people say it to be mean. I can take mean.

I peered into the hallway, making ugly-face, and snarled, "You call me that again, I'll sneak into your room while you're sleeping and smother you with your mermaid doll," bursting out a cartoon villain laugh as she ran off screeching, "Mommy!"

I don't think of myself as wahine trapped in *kane* skin. I like being a boy. I look this way because I like it. Not because it makes me feel wahine. So, am I mahu, or am I not mahu?

Knock-knock.

Who dere?

Mima.

Mima who?

Ha-ha. You mahu!

You wouldn't want to let my father hear you tell that joke, though. He doesn't think it's very funny.

"Would you come on!" Lina hollered from the lanai. "We go and make late."

"Hold your horses!" I hollered back.

"Why you get so worked up making pretty for that boy? He kine no even know you alive."

"I don't do it for Torao," I said, stepping out in a subdued bamboo aloha shirt—vertical stripes—and matching shorts, reaching

behind my neck to clasp shut a cowry shell necklace. "I do it for me."
Bamboo and cowry shells are symbols of good luck.

We took off in Lina's little canary yellow Jeep that she was having
shipped on Monday to Oakland, California, for more than the heap
was worth, tearing out of Na'alehu, my hometown, like we were never
coming back, which at least for one of us was still like always. Na'alehu
looks like a Dutch farm village from a fairy tale that got locked in a
drawer and never again taken out and read. The name means literally
volcanic ash, since that's what this was before man came and brought
all the green. It's better than where Lina's from, at least, on the other
side of South Point in HOVE: Hawaiian Ocean View Estates, which
is just a fancy name for Big Neighborhood On Steep Slope. It's a tract
neighborhood slapped onto a wasteland, so it's not like I don't understand her urge to escape. Everything you see on that mountainside that
isn't solid rock was shipped in from the mainland and placed there by
someone, the yards looking all like hedged-in patches of the moon.
But that's how all the towns on this island started out: on all the islands.
As gray, lifeless moonscapes formed by cooling lava. A civilization taking up on a chain of active volcanos. All that's needed to make it able
to support life, shipped in.

Leaving Na'alehu we passed through the last bit of farmland and
crossed into more moonscape, only the real deal this time: barren and
void, like before man landed. Even the road we were riding on didn't
used to be there. We were driving straight over the side of Mauna Loa,
an active volcano, probably still. About twenty years before Lina and
me were born, she erupted and covered the beautiful tropical landscape and million dollar houses and the former road connecting the
two sides of the island by the south in an even coating of *a'a*: molten
red at first; hard, grey, and shockingly sharp like broken glass after.
This, class, is how continents are born. Nothing grows on it naturally.
Nothing survives to penetrate through it, as if it could.

We cruised through like the place would suck us down into it,
like a *puka* would open up in one of these craters and swallow us right
in—though I don't think this was ever in Lina's conscious awareness.
Then again, it could explain New York.

In any case, we pinned it at a steady ninety, as always, the whole time Lina yammering on about Times Square and Central Park and subways while I lapsed into my usual daydreams about Torao. About what I'd say to him if we ran into each other at practice, which never happened. But that never stopped the daydreams from coming. Only this time, every time I tried to conjure his image, all I could see in my mind's eye was my nine-year-old sister calling me "Mahu!" and tittering away.

"Now entering Puna!" Lina bellowed beside me like an Aloha Air attendant, secretly satisfied for having just scared your ass awake. "All arrivals from La-La Land will now come in for landing. Snap back, zombie. Dere yo boy."

I jolted alert and saw we'd arrived at the Puna community center, where hula rehearsals were held ever since enough members threatened to drop out because they didn't want to make the drive to Hilo —even though the facilities there were better. And like Lina said, there was Torao, walking up the steps into the lanai where all the dancers and musicians hung out before practice got started. Torao's impossible to miss around here. His Japanese half gives him a lighter skin tone, for one. Plus, he's all arms and legs. We have a saying: there are no skinny Hawaiians. If you're skinny, then you must have Japanese blood mixed in you somewhere. But skinny wasn't the right word for Torao, because he surfed. So, his legs were stacked like those balancing rock sculptures people build on the beach, and his stomach was like a boogie board I craved to ride.

"Quit looking at his ass!" Lina railed, much louder than necessary, as we pulled into a free spot alongside the other cars.

I rolled up the window, turning away before I could see if Torao had heard her, glancing up instead to the lanai, where I knew everyone would be ignoring us for sure. "I'm not looking at his *okole*," I rasped. Although now that she'd planted the seed, I had a hard time not looking at it. It was such a nice *okole*. The seat of his surfer shorts hugging his thighs as he climbed those stairs.

Half-Japanese guys have the smallest, tightest *okoles*. Like two fresh Hawaiian sweet rolls that haven't yet been separated.

Lina harrumphed at me as she got out and started loading up

with boxes. But I waited until Torao turned into the practice room before getting out to help her.

❖

Lina and I sat in the back of the room, like always. For two hours twice a week and four hours on Saturdays, you would find us back there stringing pink, gold, and fiery red orchid buds to the rhythms of the *ipu* drums and *pu'ili* shakers.

The way we'd get into it back there you'd think the dancers would be swimming in leis. You'd expect waves of flowers to be spilling over the seats and into the aisles. But hula's not like stepping off the plane in an Aloha Air ad: a sorry, dinky excuse for a lei draped over your head by a smiling native girl. In hula there's more than necks to lei: there's ankles and wrists, and one that goes around the top of the head like a crown or a halo (on Torao it looks like both). It's true you don't need leis for practice, just for performance. But we thought it made practice better. And while none of the dancers or musicians ever said as much themselves, no one was kicking us out of there either.

So, we stayed invisible and did our thing while the dancers executed their routines one by one. They had a lot of routines too, like a dozen at any point, and they spent like ten, fifteen, twenty minutes working on each. Always, they split it up evenly, between all-wahine, all-kane, and mixed. I liked the all-wahine and all-kane best; I had trouble watching the mixed.

When the kane danced their dances, the wahine all sat in the front rows tittering like my little sister. When it was the wahine's turn, the men went out for a smoke or piss or to use the vending machine. Most times Cheech and Chong waited out in the parking lot in their over-pimped Chevy with the rest of the brahs waiting for Torao to come out for a hit off the pipe.

I resented my brothers more at these times than most, because these were the only times when I could catch a glimpse of the real Torao beneath all the show. I knew he had a softer side, when he wasn't playing gangsta with his brahs or up there playing young King Kamehameha. He couldn't dance like that if he didn't. You could see it especially in the mixed numbers, which are usually traditional courtship rituals. But he'd never show that for real, not offstage. Never in front of the brahs.

The *kane* dances are usually war dances—a lot of thrusting out of chests at imagined enemies—and prayers to the Gods for a successful hunt. Most times they all dance the same moves in unison, except when they're telling a story. And because Torao was the only one up there who wasn't a big *moke,* it was almost always him up front taking those solos. For the most part, none of the other *mokes* complained because they all knew the crowds and judges wanted to eat him up. So, they were always making him the Prince, the Hero, the Lover, the Returned Soldier. Only when they needed a real *moke* did they go for one of the others.

After hula ended, Lina and I took our time packing up, like always. Usually at that point, once everyone had cleared out, I would slip into one of those grass skirts, sneak out onstage, and start dancing the wahine part without anyone but Lina knowing. She always liked to whistle and cat-call from the back. "Woo-hoo! Shake it, bruddah! You go!" All good things. It made me dance better.

So that night—last night—I was doing my thing as she started lugging boxes out to the Jeep. I started humming a little hula tune to move to and picked up a pair of *uli'uli* to shake to the rhythm. I got so into it, I didn't even hear the side door open. All I heard was, "So dat *was* chocolate I smell," and not in Lina's voice, of course, or any wahine's. This was all kane. It was Torao.

In the back of the room. Nose buried in a box with a few stray brown and white petals held in his pale, lithe fingers, facing the stage.

Immediately that Polynesian rash started creeping over my skin, and I slipped off the skirt. Let it drop with a swish to the wood-panel floor. "No, don't stop," he practically cried out, looking straight at me now. Half-Japanese guys have these eyes: not almonds or teardrops; more like sunflower seeds. And his hair was a thin dusting of fine black; I imagined it felt like fleece. "You make good dance for dat part." Then he started walking toward me, down the aisle between the rows of chairs. "Why you not try out for dis?"

I didn't answer, just kept my head down and snaked along the side of the room to go finish packing up. That's when Lina blew through the door and, taking notice of what was going on (or what she thought was) slipped back out with a sly grin, waving the *shaka* sign at me: middle and ring fingers down.

"What? You no talk?" Torao said, as though offended, standing even now with the front row. "I know." He nodded. "You no like me."

"No!" I blurted out. Then, shyly: "No. I just… know you're messing with me. That's all."

"You don't know nothing," he said. "Now *hana hou.*" It means: Do it again.

I shook my head a little too rapid, and feeling dizzy, giggled out another: "No."

"Yeah, brah," he said, waving me over. "C'mon." He called me brah. "For me."

I shuffled my feet a minute and then gave in: stepping back to the stage area and starting up again, swinging my hips and rocking my arms, though understandably with less exuberance than when I thought I was alone.

"No, do it for real. Like befoah."

I sighed and rolled my eyes and then did as he told, getting more into it.

"Yeah, like dat!" He started clapping, not to my rhythm but like applause.

"Now put dis back on." With his foot he scooted the grass skirt back across the floor at me.

"Nice slippahs," I said, trying to keep my gaze from moving up to the narrow ankles above them.

"Put it on." He looked at me and pointed to the skirt.

I knew there was a chance I was being toyed with—a good chance —but I also knew that for the first time, Torao was paying attention to me, and in that moment it was enough. Whatever his reason, all I wanted was to keep it going and never let it stop. So, I stepped into the skirt, slid it up to my waist, and danced some more. He pulled back those tight, almost pencilled-on lips, baring those bleach-white teeth. His sunflower seed eyes pointed straight at me. All making me shimmy, sashay, and grind like none of those wimpy wahine would ever dare.

"Yeah, now dis too," he said, tossing a coconut shell bra at me. It hit me in the stomach and I cringed as it clattered to the floor. He laughed. "It no gonna bite you, brah." There was that word again: brah. A term of endearment. Of familiarity, friendship. Intimacy even.

I picked up by its strings, a piece made for a body half my size, and wrapped it around my chest as best as I could, pulling the strings taut in front, pinching a groove in my skin as I tied them in a knot. Then rotating the piece around, I put the shells in their proper positions. Gave a nervous chuckle, and went back to it: hips swinging, arms swaying.

And to my shock, his hips started swinging too, and his shoulders started bouncing, a little more hip-hop than hula, and still down in the audience, but just the same, it was like we were dancing a duet.

Until out of nowhere he says to me, "Now, c'mere." And I stopped dancing, his stare paralyzing me.

"Why?" I asked, my insides churning, and I wondered if he could hear it.

"What you scared of?" he asked. "Don't you trust me?"

I waddled over, feeling like a little *keiki*. And when I got up to him, like a foot away, he held my gaze and I held his. He lowered his hands and I felt sure he was about to touch me. To grab a handful of caramel flesh on each side of my waist and pull me in until our lips collided and our tongues locked. Instead he laid his hands on his own hips, yanked his shorts down to those narrow ankles, and said, "Go on. Touch it." Adding, when he saw my stupid-face, "It no gonna bite eitha, brah."

There was that word again. Only it didn't feel so special now, his thing sticking halfway out at me, like punctuation. The hooded tip bent down, like it was taking a bow. "You like it, don't you?" he said in a tone I could only call coy.

I'd never seen one so long before. It wasn't as thick as mine or any of my brothers', but it looked like it could reach right over and yank me in if it wanted to.

"C'mon," he said. "I know you wanna."

"It's not that..." I started. This was all wrong. This was not how this was supposed to go at all.

243

"What's a matter? You mahu, isn't you?"

And for the first time of all the times anyone has asked me that, I nodded. Slow and small.

"Then what you waitin' foah? I ain't got all night." He wagged his thing at me like a dead *'opelu*. "Now get down here and get to work."

And with that I scampered to the door.

Lina and I drove around for a while afterward like we always do, neither of us ever ready to go home yet, let alone after this. I still hadn't told her what happened, and didn't plan to. She had her guesses, a few of them close, but I didn't confirm or deny anything. I didn't utter a word the whole ride; I couldn't help it. At that moment, I blamed her for everything. I blamed her for encouraging me in a hopeless crush. (Did she know Torao liked chocolate?) I blamed her for leaving me alone with him, and for probably keeping everyone else out, like I was sure she would have. And I blamed her for leaving the island the day after next. For throwing my whole world into upheaval and making me a coqui frog peep away from a total meltdown. For making me so blind and weak I couldn't even see what I was letting happen. Helping to happen. I wasn't myself anymore and I blamed her for it.

When she finally dropped me off after midnight and drove off fuming about how I was choosing to leave things, I sulked to my room, only to stumble into the aftermath of an orchid massacre.

Pots were all toppled and smashed, baskets all torn from their hooks. And the flowers: they smothered the floor, the shelves, my bedspread, like a swamp, all their colors all bled out. And not caring who saw me, I collapsed into the swamp and bawled and bawled as my thumbs sought out individual petals to stroke. When finally words could form, all I could say was, "For what? For what!"

"You know for what!" I heard Cheech's voice say behind me. And I turned to see his head sticking through the doorway.

"You did this?" I said, unable to hold back my trembling.

"Naw, brah," he said, stepping in.

"You did," Chong finished, stepping in after him.

"What did I do?" I asked, clenching every muscle to stop from crying in front of these two.

"What you do, you fucking mahu?" Cheech railed in genuine disbelief.

"You want make walk and talk like wahine that fine." The pair
stormed up to me and towered over me, and he went on, "But you
make move on our brah, you cross a line."

"Make a move?" I said. "On who?"

"You know who," said Chong.

"You mean Torao?"

"See? You know."

"He came on to me!"

Cheech hoisted his fist as if to strike me, and even though I knew
it was only a fakeout, still I flinched. "Don't you lie to me."

"I'm not!" I said, and tried to get out what really happened, but
they didn't want to hear it. "You stay away from our friends," Cheech
cut me off, his ash-stained finger popping out from his fist and pointing at me. "Or next time it won't be your flowers."

I swiped his finger out of my face and turned to look anywhere
but at my twin tormentors. Which meant taking in again the slaughter-
house the unholy duo had made of my nursery. (And where was the
rest of my family when this happened?) My brothers stared a few extra
moments, reading my face to be sure we were clear, then, satisfied,
marched out, making sure their four heels pounded down extra hard
on the orchid corpses in their path.

I stood there for a while, trying to muster the strength to start
the hard work—the *kahananui*—of cleaning up, but I couldn't bring
myself to do it. The room didn't feel mine anymore. It was just a room.
Like HOVE before the people came. All the life razed out of it.

I strolled past the gear hut onto the black sands of Punalu'u
Beach. Black for the *a'a* it used to be before the pressures of time
crushed it into this. I stepped out over those volcanic smithereens,
gazing out at Lo'ihi like I always had, thinking about starting again.
Not sure if I'd go back to growing orchids or making leis or watching
hula. Forget about dancing it. But still sure I wasn't about to jet off to
the mainland either.

Maybe a different island, I thought. Everyone says all the mahu move to Molokai and love it. Except I don't get along with other mahu either. I'm not cute enough or slutty enough. And with them, if you're not one you'd better darn well be the other.

I decided to take a swim. But as I started to peel my shirt over my head, I caught a glimpse of something up the beach, glowing blue in the moonlight.

Straightening my shirt again, I stepped toward it, still unsure what I was looking at. At first, I thought it was seaweed, and then just a stingray, both which I normally ignore, but I'd never seen seaweed or a stingray that color before. I stepped toward it slowly, until I was sure it wasn't moving. And when I got up close enough, I saw that it wasn't seaweed or a stingray, but an octopus. An inky blue octopus, with see-through skin, blue as the *kai,* looking like it washed up from some little keiki's dream. All its innards on display to the world. Just like I felt, all my deepest parts exposed.

It still gave off such an iridescent glow, I had a hard time believing it was dead. And then I realized, I'd seen a picture of a glowing blue octopus just like this once before.

In a newspaper. The story was about one of the first creatures discovered off the Lo'ihi seamount. A blue octopus. About three feet long, with spikes instead of suckers. A blue Lo'ihi octopus. Possibly the first Lo'ihian. I looked around to see if there was anyone I could call over to show this. Share in the wonder. Someone who could help me figure out what to do about it.

I thought about calling Lina down, but what for? I could already hear the conversation in my head:

"Blech! That what you bring me here for?"

"But it's Lo'ihian!"

"Oh, of course, it's Lo'ihian. I should have guessed."

"It is!"

"And so? Why you want me for? Call the cops. Call the scientists. I don't know."

"Don't you think I already thought of that? The cops wouldn't care. And scientists will just dissect it under a microscope."

"So, call the TV. The newspaper. Maybe they put in a museum instead. Make you hero."

"I don't want that. And sticking him in a glass box to be gawked at as a freak of nature for eternity is no better than being studied by science."

"Well, what you want me to say? You going *lolo* on me, Kale? Right before I take off? Real aloha, brah."

"Forget it."

There's no one I could bring here who wouldn't defile him. Which would defile you, and I couldn't let that happen. But I couldn't just leave him out here for the gulls either. I knew that's how Mama's cycle goes, but this was different.

He was sacred: a link to our future, and your past. A link between you and us. For that alone, he deserved better than any fate this shore might have for him. I had no choice, I realized. I had to take him home.

With this newfound clarity, I turned from the *kai* and headed into the brush to scavenge whatever flowers I could: morning glory, hibiscus, pansy, yellow ilima—no orchids, unfortunately, but these would have to do. Loaded up, I returned to the gear hut and started plucking the buds from their stems and stringing them on a fishing line as I scanned the *kai's* surface to seek out the spot where your home and this offering's proper burial ground lay in the blackness.

Holding the finished lei up for inspection, I had to admit, it wasn't bad for not bearing a single orchid. And come to think of it, I realized, maybe it's perfect this way. Orchids are what everyone thinks of when they think of leis, but there's always other flowers in there too. Ones they probably don't even notice, let alone know the names of. Like when people think about people, they don't think about folks like me. They think about Torao or my kid sister. (And why wouldn't they?)

And when people think about Hawai'i, they don't think about the Big Island that actually bears its name. They think about Oahu, two islands over, and even then, most don't know its name; they only know Honolulu. No one thinks about you. No one but me, that is. So, under the circumstances, I believe an orchid-less lei is about as fitting as they come.

I retrieved my shirt from the sand, wrapped up the corpse, and secured it with the lei. Then I tromped upshore and rummaged through the scrub until I found a bottle with the top still on. I brought the bottle into the hut to find a full tank and wetsuit. Then I sat down to write this message.

I don't have to make it the whole twenty miles, I realized: just far enough to be out from the pull of the undertow. Then, of course, there's getting back. But don't worry about me. Like I said before, I'm a strong swimmer, and if you're reading this, then I'm already food for the *i'a* either way, or the worms or gulls; we all end up there eventually. What's important now is that what's yours has been returned to you. The world I live in is no place for it. But for you this place is already dead and gone. For you the world is new again.

About This Book

The typeface in this book is 11 point Garamond with Gill Sans headings. The title on the cover is set in Aniron. Funky typesetting reflects the requests of the authors.

Thank you to Peter Bradbury for finding our cover photo.

About Darkhouse Books

Darkhouse Books is a publisher of mystery and science fiction, as well as literary prose and poetry. We are located in Niles, California, an inadvertently preserved, 120-year-old one-sided railtown, forty miles from San Francisco.

Please visit us at **www.darkhousebooks.com** and **www.facebook.com/darkhousebooks/** for more information.

Authors' Notes

Pamela Ahlen / *I Live Inside an Accordion*

"My father loved the bully pulpit, my mother was a worrier. What better place for an only child to retreat than behind the immensity of an instrument that could make fierce and sweet music."

Pamela Ahlen is program coordinator for Bookstock Literary Festival, in Woodstock, Vermont. She organizes literary events for Osher, and recently compiled the *Anthology of Poets and Writers: Celebrating Twenty-Five Years at Dartmouth*. She is the author of the chapbook *Gather Every Little Thing* (Finishing Line Press).

Phillip Bannowsky *Lie if Innocent*

"*Lie if Innocent* comes near the end of my novel in verse *Jacobo the Turko*, which concerns a man from Ecuador of indigenous and Lebanese parentage who seeks the American dream, working a summer job on the beaches of Delaware, only to be deported to Lebanon (where he has never been before), abducted to Bagram, and ultimately confined at Guantanamo Prison. Jacobo's interrogation is partly based on an incident recounted in *Guantánamo Diary*, written in 2005 by prisoner Mohamedou Ould Slahi, who had been detained in Cuba since 2002."

Phillip Bannowsky is a retired auto-worker, human rights activist, and teacher of the Poetry of Empowerment at the University of Delaware. Published works include *The Milk of Human Kindness* (poetry), *Autoplant: A Poetic Monologue*, and *The Mother Earth Inn* (novel). In 2017 he was awarded a Delaware Division of the Arts Established Artist Fellowship for Literature: Poetry. Recently, his poems have appeared in *Dreamstreets*, *Broadkill Review*, the anthology *Bad Hombres and Nasty Women*, *Armarolla*, and *Meat for Tea: The Valley Review*.

Aileen Bassis *Drawing Home*

"I was thinking about refugees and migrants, moved by the many news stories about desperate people drowning in the Mediterranean, longing for a better life and yet longing for home."

Aileen Bassis is a visual artist in Jersey City working in book arts, printmaking, photography and installation. Her use of text in art led her to explore another creative life as a poet. She was awarded an artist residency in poetry to the Atlantic Center for the Arts. Her poems have appeared in *B o d y Literature*, *Spillway*, *Grey Sparrow Journal*, *Canary*, *Amoskeag*, *Stone Canoe*, *The Pinch Journal*, and *Pittsburgh Poetry Review*.

Lana Bella *After Absence*

A four-time Pushcart Prize nominee, five-time Best of the Net, and Bettering American Poetry nominee, Lana Bella is an author of three chapbooks, *Under My Dark* (Crisis Chronicles Press, 2016), *Adagio* (Finishing Line Press, 2016), and *Dear Suki: Letters* (Platypus 2412 Mini Chapbook Series, 2016). Her work has featured in over 500 journals, *Barzakh*, *EVENT*, *The Fortnightly Review*, *Ilanot Review*, *Midwest Quarterly*, *New Reader*, *Notre Dame Review*, *Sundress Publications*, and *Whiskey Island*, among others, and *Aeolian Harp Anthology* Volume 3. She lives in the US and the coastal town of Nha Trang, Vietnam, where she is mom to two far-too-clever-frolicsome imps.

Lana has chosen to let her poem speak for itself.

Peter Bradbury *Poetry Editor*

Peter Bradbury's first sanctuary was the kitchen in his childhood home in Hong Kong, ruled over by Ah Weh and Ah Hung, the language a creole of Mandarin and Cantonese. As a teenager, he discovered the haven of poetry in Keats and Plath. Since then he's written about and taught poetry, and his poems and stories have been published in *Sewanee Review, New Poetry, Malahat Review, Poetry Australia, Seam, Stand, Staple,* and *Big Flame.* He has taught writing at the City Lit in London and the Universities of London and Oxford. He lives in San Francisco where he writes, teaches, and edits other people's work.

Nick Bouchard *Father Pearson's Last Day*

"*Father Pearson's Last Day* was inspired twenty years ago by a classroom debate about the rights and fate of Terry Schiavo. I like to think he has matured since the original, hastily scribbled first draft, in which Father Pearson carried a silenced pistol and wore a plastic apron."

Nick is a father, husband, and writer living in Vermont. He likes baseball, old cars, and typewriters. He works in a print shop to be close to the magic. He can be found online @ nicktionary19.

Susannah Carlson *Prose and General Editor*

"The idea for this anthology was born out of current events, which have only gotten worse in the months between the book's conception and its production. I am utterly appalled at the catastrophic rise of heartlessness and hatred in this world, and I hope this book will help in some small way to nudge things back toward decency."

Susannah's poetry, essays, and short stories have appeared in numerous literary journals over three decades, including *Sequoia, The SFSU Review, Narrative, Reed Magazine,* and *Sixfold.* She has won numerous awards for her work, including a national essay contest (The Fund for Animals National Vanishing Species Essay Contest) when she was twelve, which resulted in a three-day "safari" in Los Angeles with Cleveland Amory, and lunch poolside at Joan Rivers' house. This is the second anthology she has edited for Darkhouse Books, the previous being *Descansos: Words from the Wayside.* She lives in the San Francisco Bay Area with her boyfriend, her grad-student son, Lily the elderly craigslist mutt, and Kyle the one-eyed chiweenie.

Kersten Christianson *Yukon Artists Co-op*

"I'm fascinated by all things north, including this art gallery in the heart of Whitehorse. From this lovely space, I've hauled home many a raven in various forms: acrylic, paint, print, sculpture. It's my homage."

Kersten Christianson is a raven-watching, moon-gazing Alaskan. When not exploring the summer lands and dark winter of the Yukon, she lives in Sitka, Alaska. She holds an MFA in Creative Writing (University of Alaska Anchorage) and recently published her first collection of poetry *Something Yet to Be Named* (Aldrich Press, 2017). Kersten is the poetry editor of the quarterly journal, *Alaska Women Speak.* www.kerstenchristianson.com.

Nancy Cook *Illuminations and Illusions; The Afterlife*

"The stories come out of a recent residency on the grounds of the former Fergus Fall State Hospital, built in 1896. During my residency, I spent many hours at the local historical society, combing through news items about the hospital and its residents from the late nineteenth and early twentieth century. Excerpts from those news items are the epigraphs to these stories."

Nancy Cook is a writer whose wanderlust has taken her from the shores of Lake Erie to New England, New Mexico, New York's Finger Lakes, Maryland's Eastern Shore, and, most recently, to the frozen lakes of Minnesota. She is a 2017 recipient of a National Parks Arts Foundation residency at Gettysburg. Nancy also runs a "Witness Project," a series of free community writing workshops in Minneapolis designed to enable creative work by underrepresented voices. Her newest work can be found in *Stoneboat, The Ocotillo Review*, and *The Centrifugal Eye*.

Allen X. Davis *Ward B*

"I met a man like Owen in a place like Ward B. He was a smart, kind, creative man who was told that the underlying problem was not anything he did, or anything in his life, but something he had no control over: a chemical imbalance in his brain. In real life, his wife was an angel, but I reversed that for the purposes of the story. I am appalled by lazy psychiatrists and psychologists who send patients to the 'sanctuary' of medication and hospitalization at resorts paid for by insurance companies instead of identifying and treating the true underlying issues. Everyone's a victim. Everyone needs medication. And Big Pharma profits from it all."

Allen X. Davis' recent stories appear in *Ragazine, Tinge Magazine, Gravel*, and *Literally Stories*. One of his stories was recently nominated for the Pushcart Prize.

Mark Fitzpatrick *On the Feast of Juan Diego*

"I wrote *On the Feast of Juan Diego* because I felt trapped in my life, a bit depressed, and yet I had a feeling of hope because it was Christmas. I wrote it on the F6 bus heading home through New Haven."

Mark Fitzpatrick is an ESL teacher who has lived and worked in Brazil, Somaliland, Haiti, Honduras, and New Haven, CT. He tutored a child in the early Project Sanctuary days, for a church. That child is now a grown woman who lives in Canada and still keeps in touch with him.

John M. Floyd *The Blue Delta*

"Three things, I think, inspired me to write *The Blue Delta*: (1) I spent a lot of childhood vacations visiting relatives in the Mississippi Delta, not too far from where this story is set; (2) I liked the idea of a regular working-man—a family man—being thrust into a life-or-death situation that required fast and smart decisions; and (3) I hate snakes. I can't say much more without giving away plot secrets, but I also discovered (after I started the writing and editing) that I wanted to include a few backstory surprises and a few 'lessons' for those readers who might not have grown up in this corner of the US. Why try to do that? Well, in some ways, the Deep South—and its people—are just like everywhere and everyone else. In other ways, there's no other place like it on Earth. I hope I've done it justice."

John M. Floyd's work has appeared in more than 250 different publications, including *Ellery Queen's Mystery Magazine, Alfred Hitchcock's Mystery Magazine, The Strand Magazine, The Saturday Evening Post*, and *The Best American Mystery Stories*. A former Air Force captain and IBM systems engineer, John is also an Edgar Award nominee, a three-time Derringer Award winner, and a three-time Pushcart Prize nominee. His seventh book, *The Barrens*, is scheduled for release in fall 2018.

Laura Foley *Piano*

"I wrote *Piano* at the time my grown musician-son and I shared living quarters. My husband, his father, had died, and my other children were away in school or college. It was a tender, creative time, in our house on the river. Billy was working on a haunting piece of music, his own composition."

Laura Foley is the author of six poetry collections, including, most recently, *WTF* and *Night Ringing*. Her poem *Gratitude List* won the Common Good Books poetry contest and was read by Garrison Keillor on The Writer's Almanac. Her poem *Nine Ways of Looking at Light* won the Joe Gouveia Outermost Poetry Contest, judged by Marge Piercy. Her book,

The Glass Tree, won a *Foreword Review* Prize for Poetry. Her poems have appeared widely in journals and magazines. A palliative care volunteer in hospitals, with an M. Phil. in English Literature from Columbia University, she lives with her wife and their two dogs among the hills of Vermont.

Gina L. Grandi *Drag*

"*Drag* began as a one-hour writing exercise; the challenge was to draw inspiration from a *Humans of New York* photo. The figure in the photo I chose was dressed in an elaborate costume, and the description included the words, *I used to self-harm*. It reminded me of my friend Eddie's beautiful drama therapy thesis presentation on drag as therapy."

Gina taught public school in San Francisco for 13 years before moving to New York to toil valiantly and temporarily in the non-profit, arts education world. She recently completed her doctorate at NYU, where she teaches theatre and theatre education. She is also the founder and artistic director of The Bechdel Group, a theatre company that works to challenge the role of women on stage. Her fiction has appeared in *Cicada, Apex Magazine, 100wordstory*, and *Gold Fever Press*. She can be found on twitter at @yonderpaw.

Atar J. Hadari *A Knife in the Hand*

"A story about Ariel Sharon's mother seemed to me to sum up a lot about her and her relationship to the country she wound up in, and the relationship of both herself and her son to Israeli society."

Atar Hadari's *Songs from Bialik: Selected Poems of H. N. Bialik* (Syracuse University Press) was a finalist for the American Literary Translators' Association Award and his debut collection, *Rembrandt's Bible*, was published by Indigo Dreams in 2013. *Lives of the Dead: Collected Poems of Hanoch Levin* won a PEN Translates award and is out now from Arc Publications. He contributes a monthly verse Bible translation column to *MOSAIC* magazine.

Richard Holinger *Encounter*

"In the summer of 1970, between my junior and senior year of college, my roommate from boarding school asked if I wanted to drive to Alaska, camping and fishing on the way, to look for jobs. Reaching the border, we heard there were cannery jobs on Kodiak Island, so we ferried over, only to find hostile Alaskans had killed some college students from the "Lower 48" who'd come there, as we had, to have an adventure and land a job. According to the *Kodiak Mirror*, as well as anecdotal evidence, they were murdered because they were taking jobs that Kodiak natives wanted for themselves. *Encounter* follows a relatively auto-biographical plot path up to the scene in which the car skids to a stop on the gravel road. After the driver hops out and offers a 'ride,' my friend and I, in the real world, turned down the invitation; for dramatic effect, the story invents a crueler and more violent scenario, one that will lead to the protagonist's epiphany and subsequent decision to stay on Kodiak and teach. It is, above all, a story above all that exposes a young man to hostility and bigotry never before encountered, that throws him into the position of a hated and scapegoated minority; finding himself defined for the first time as an outsider, he learns the outsider's pain and must decide what will heal it."

Richard Holinger's poetry, fiction, and nonfiction have appeared in *The Southern Review, The Iowa Review, Boulevard, Witness*, and elsewhere. His short story collection, *Not Everybody's Nice*, won the 2012 Split Oak Press Flash Prose Chapbook Contest, and Kattywampus Press published his innovative fiction chapbook, *Hybrid Seeds: Little Fictions*. He writes a column for the *Kane County Chronicle*, teaches in a parochial high school, facilitates a writing workshop, and lives with his wife, dog, and, occasionally, his two twenty-something children in the Fox Valley, an hour west of Chicago.

Edison Jennings *Cats of Rome*

"I wrote *Cats of Rome* when I and my friend, Dr. Felicia Mitchell, were sightseeing on the Via dei Fori Imperiali near the Coliseum the day President George W. Bush was due to arrive in Rome to consult with Prime Minister Silvio Berlusconi regarding the Second Gulf War. The boulevards were lined with bleachers and draped with flags. Carabinieri armed with machine pistols were on every corner. Felicia was very concerned about the welfare of the famous Roman cats that prowl the Coliseum. I wrote this poem with her in mind."

Edison Jennings lives in the western Appalachian region of Virginia. His poetry has appeared in a variety of journals and anthologies. His chapbook, *Reckoning*, is available at Jacar Press (http://www.jacarpress.com/reckoning).

Laurence Jones *Down to the River to Pray*

"*Down to the River to Pray* is about getting back to basics. I grew up with shows like *The Twilight Zone* and *Tales of the Unexpected* and always loved the format, particularly the sucker-punch twist in the tale. For me, such stories are an exercise in sleight of hand: is it possible to lead a reader in one direction, avoid their guesswork, and still deliver a satisfactory revelation? One which, on re-reading, somehow seems inevitable? Hard to plan, harder to achieve but sometimes, just sometimes, it works."

Laurence Jones was born and raised in London. His short stories have been published in literary journals including *Storgy, New Zenith Magazine* and *Collages,* as well as the forthcoming *Seven Hills Review* and *Impermanent Facts* anthologies. He won the Conville & Walsh Discovery Day in 2013 and has been shortlisted/longlisted for multiple literary prizes including the Commonwealth Short Story Prize and TLC's Pen Factor.

Scott Archer Jones *Contentment*

"I belonged to a health facility in Taos where the clientele ranged all the way from bruisers (female and male) drenched in tattoos through to extreme and aging narcissists fighting their chin sag and wrinkled triceps. I've slow-cooked in the hot tub described in the story's beginning. Youth attracted me for one story, and mortality for another."

Scotts Archer Jones is currently living and working on his fifth novel and second novella in northern New Mexico, after stints in the Netherlands, Scotland, and Norway, plus less exotic locations. He's worked for a power company, a grocer, a lumberyard, an energy company (for a very long time), and a winery. His first novel was published by Southern Yellow Pine, *Jupiter and Gilgamesh, a Novel of Sumeria and Texas. Jupiter* was a finalist in four categories of the 2014 New Mexico-Arizona Book Awards. The next book *The Big Wheel*, arrived in 2015. *A rising tide of people swept away* was released by Fomite Press in 2016. All have won FAPA awards, and *Jupiter* took an IPPY Bronze and was a finalist in two Eric Hoffer Award categories. Scott cuts all his own firewood, lives a mile from his nearest neighbor, and writes grant applications for the community. He is the Treasurer of Shuter Library of Angel Fire, a private 501.C3, and desperately needs your money to keep the doors open.

Sage Kalmus *The First Lo'ihian*

"My husband and I lived on the Big Island of Hawaii for five years, and spent a great deal of time in the areas described in this story. While there, we experienced the profound spirituality of the culture and witnessed firsthand how different people experienced and interpreted it differently. Kale is an expression of that ever-present pull between self-actualization and belonging. *The First Lo'ihian* was to be the first of a series of short stories set in the Puna district of Hawaii with a follow-up TV pilot, only, given the 'big one' volcanic eruption taking place there at the very moment of this note's writing, those projects may be on hold for a while. As Kale would say, 'That's Pele for you.'"

Sage Kalmus is co-founder, co-CEO, and senior editor of Qommunicate Media, publisher of *Hashtag Queer: LGBTQ+ Creative Anthology, Volumes 1 & 2; Queer Families: LGBTQ+ True Stories Anthology*, and the upcoming anthologies *Queer Around the World* and *Geek Out!*. His writing has appeared in *The Writer, Whisperings Magazine, Carnival Online Literary Journal, Rose Red Review, The Hampshire Gazette*, and *Livestrong.com*. He has taught writing in Lesley University's MFA creative writing program, been an editorial intern at Dzanc Books, was a three-time contest reader for *Salamander Magazine*, and wrote and directed three plays in San Francisco. Since 2004, Sage has worked as a freelance writer, editor, and ghostwriter. He holds an MFA in creative writing from Lesley University and a BS in Film and Broadcasting from Boston University. He currently lives in the lush and lovely Berkshires of western Massachusetts with his adored and adoring husband and their four-legged family.

Jim Keller *El Chucho*

"Dual empathies, for poor and abused immigrants and for discarded dogs."

Jim Keller is a recently retired chemical engineer. Some of his poems were published some years ago in the excellent little magazine *Mad Blood*. More recently, several of his poems have been published online in *Verse-virtual, The Shrike* is featured in the online and print journal *Poetry City, USA. Till Death Do Us Part I, II* was in last year's *Porter Gulch Review* of Cabrillo College.

Rick Kempa *Keeping the Quiet*

"*Keeping the Quiet* arises from a place of utter peace shared with a loved one—the only other human in that wilderness world."

Rick Kempa lives in Rock Springs, Wyoming, where he is finishing his thirtieth and final year as a teacher of writing and philosophy at Western Wyoming College. *Ten Thousand Voices*, his most recent book of poems, was published in 2014 by Littoral Press. Rickkempa.com.

Joyce Kryszak *In the Whispering Breezes*

"*In the Whispering Breezes* was born of my personal experience as a survivor of domestic violence. For obvious reasons, shelters for domestic violence victims are hidden from public view. This piece was my way of helping people better understand the fear, the loss, and the trauma of being uprooted from your life. It was also my way of saying thank you to the shelter that saved my sanity and my life."

Joyce Kryszak is an award-winning former journalist who reported for NPR, the BBC, Voice of America, and others. During Joyce's twenty-plus years as a reporter, she won more than three dozen Associated Press Awards, and a prestigious Edward R. Murrow Award. Joyce's in-depth work regularly examined poverty, racial disparities, politics, and culture. As an interviewer, Joyce has spoken with hundreds of remarkable people, among them; Bob Woodward, Salmon Rushdie, and mime artist, Marcel Marceau (yes, he spoke.) Joyce has reported from as far away as Singapore, and has performed as a singer off Broadway with the legendary Mabou Mines. She continues her writing passion now as a freelance writer telling stories that are true, and stories wanting to be true. Joyce is currently writing a novel of historical fiction about an unconventional woman growing up in and with the 20th century. Joyce is a Buffalo Gal transplanted in Maine where she lives with her composer husband, Alan, and their neurotic Great Pyrenees, Kashmir. When she isn't writing, or finagling visits from their children, Joyce likes to kayak, hike, garden, cook, and read four books at the same time.

Lita Kurth *Seeking Asylum*

"Where did *Seeking Asylum* come from? At first, I thought I should choose a more outward, activist, and overtly political treatment of the word, because God knows we have a need for asylum in so many areas, but when I thought back to my first encounter with the word, it was the negative "insane asylum," so I continued in that vein, and it occurs to me now that therapy does have a relationship with activism, if it makes us more capable of working with others in the long and difficult struggle to promote fairness and reduce avoidable calamities."

Lita Kurth holds an MFA from Pacific Lutheran University and has published poetry, creative nonfiction, and various sizes of fiction. Several of her works have been nominated for Pushcart Prizes and one for Best of the Net. In 2013, she co-founded the Flash Fiction Forum, a reading series in San Jose, CA. She teaches publicly at De Anza College and privately at CreatorSchoolCA, The ArsenalSJ, online, and in her home.

Ellaraine Lockie *White Noise and Other Muses*

"I wrote *White Noise and Other Muses* because I write at a coffee shop every morning no matter where I am. I never intend to write *about* the coffee shops, however enough of what goes on around me there sinks in to the extent that I have a chapbook, *Coffee House Confessions*, which is a collection of poems inspired by and about coffee shops."

Ellaraine Lockie is widely published and awarded as a poet, nonfiction book author, and essayist. *Tripping with the Top Down* is her thirteenth chapbook. Earlier collections have won Poetry Forum's Chapbook Contest Prize, San Gabriel Valley Poetry Festival Chapbook Competition, Encircle Publications Chapbook Contest, Best Individual Poetry Collection Award from Purple Patch magazine in England, and the Aurorean's Chapbook Choice Award. Ellaraine has received multiple nominations for the Pushcart Prize, teaches writing workshops, and serves as poetry editor for the lifestyles magazine, *Lilipoh*.

Kathleen McClung *Perfect Game*

"I saw a child throwing orange peels at birds. Because dumps fascinate me, I used one as the setting for a tiny narrative about a kid using imagination as a form of strength and solace. At first, this kid was a boy, but I had an aha, changed the gender to a girl, and the poem felt finished."

Kathleen McClung is the author of two poetry collections, *The Typists Play Monopoly* (2018) and *Almost the Rowboat* (2013.) Her work appears widely in journals and anthologies and has received the Rita Dove, Shirley McClure, and Maria W. Faust poetry prizes. She teaches at Skyline College and The Writing Salon, and is associate director of the Soul-Making Keats literary competition. She lives in San Francisco. www.kathleenmcclung.com.

Ed McCourt *What We Leave on the Curb*

"I've often found myself rescuing and refurbishing broken things: vintage hifi equipment and electronics, various furniture, and, of course, bikes. Our dining room set, foyer table, and nicest bookshelf were all saved from the curbside. I wrote *What We Leave on the Curb* with the concurrent realization that this hobby is about more than thrift; it is about the benevolence of second chances. If true for these objects, maybe there is hope for us, too."

Ed McCourt is an Associate Professor of English at Jacksonville University. His prose and verse has appeared in the *Little Patuxent Review*, the *Citron Review*, the *Portland Review*, and many others. While he enjoys the outdoors, flea markets, sports, and numerous other hobbies, he now spends his time convincing a one-year-old boy not to stick his tongue into an electrical socket.

Jory Mickelson *In Some Future Time; Sanctuary with Internment Camp and Shrinking Glacier*

"*In Some Future Time* came about when I read in a book that the real history of the town isn't in the town, but in the cemetery, and it got me thinking about the small rural towns in America and all of the small, forgotten cemeteries on the outskirts. The title comes from a fragment of Sappho's poetry: *someone in / some future time / will think of us.* The genesis of *Sanctuary with Internment Camp and Shrinking Glacier* came from reading an article about a woman in British Columbia who had tamed a fawn after its mother died, innocuous enough, but the story wouldn't leave me alone. The other sections are built upon snippets of stories I have heard as well."

Jory Mickelson is a writer whose work has appeared or is forthcoming in *The Rumpus, Ninth Letter, Vinyl Poetry, The Florida Review, Superstition Review, The Collagist, The Los Angeles Review,* and other journals. She is the recipient of an Academy of American Poets Prize and a Lambda Literary Fellowship in Poetry. Her most recent chapbook *Slow Depth* was published by Argus House Press.

Gayla Mills *Becoming Human*

"I wrote *Becoming Human* when I worked as the director of education at the SPCA. My coworkers and I struggled to help as many as we could while knowing many more would be lost. Daily, the eyes of these sentient creatures challenged me to do what I could without losing myself to the tragedies in the world."

Formerly a writing professor, Gayla Mills has published in *Little Patuxent Review, Spry, Prairie Wolf Press, Skirt!,* and more. Her essay collection *Finite* won the RED OCHRE LiT Chapbook contest. Also a musician, she is currently writing a how-to book, *Making Music After 40.* www.gaylamills.com.

Alice Morris *After My Mother Has Been Attacked and I Have Been Asked to Leave*

"For over five decades, I found that the events of *After My Mother Has Been Attacked* often returned to me, which led me to believe I needed to explore this experience through poetry. When the poem was completed, I was hesitant to send it out until I noticed the word *sanctuary* in a submission call. Immediately, as though a spark had jumped off the page, I knew this poem needed to be placed within the context of sanctuary, only in this environment could my poem rest easy."

Alice Morris comes to writing with a background in art—published in *The New York Art Review,* and a West Virginia textbook. Her poetry appears in *The Broadkill Review, Delaware Beach Life, The White Space,* in numerous anthologies and collections, and in several online publications. She is a member of Coastal Writers and the Rehoboth Beach Writer's Guild.

Leslie Muzingo *Heroes on the Ceiling*

"While *Heroes on the Ceiling* is not based on true events, the spirit of the story is based on my experiences while working at a domestic violence shelter. I was a shelter-aide from 1986–1987. One thing I did was to try to connect with the children, especially the older, withdrawn ones. This was a confusing time for all family members living there, but I think it hit the children aged eight and above the hardest. These children were old enough to feel the stigma of living in a shelter, and they were more likely to be upset about having to change schools. Their resentment toward their mother often ran deep. Many expressed feelings that the main character in the story, Clancy, kept to himself. These children often worried about their father being alone and wanted to go home to care for him. Many became reclusive and depressed or seemed to live in another world. I wrote this story because, yes, we want to help these women get away from their abusive partners, but let's not forget how the children are affected. The mothers need help in building a new life, but many times the children need help in keeping a piece of the old one. Validating their feelings is a step in the right direction."

Leslie Muzingo grew up in Iowa but relocated to the Deep South some years ago. She has recently begun spending her summers on Prince Edward Island, and finds great similarities between PEI and the rural Iowa of her youth. Her recent publications include a fairy tale in *The Forgotten and the Fantastical, IV*, and three stories in the *Two Sisters Writing Anthology of Fresh Writers*. Her stories are also found in last year's Canadian anthology, *Two Eyes Open, The World Retold*, (2016); *Literary Mama*, (2015); and *Puff Puff Prose Poetry and a Play* (2015). She considers herself an emerging writer. Her emergence is a slow one, as she has so many things she likes to do, and there are only so many hours in a day.

Michelle S. Myers *Communion on the Road*

"In writing *Communion on the Road*, I wanted to honor the children, women, and men from El Salvador, Guatemala, and Honduras whom I encountered in my service work in Dallas, Texas, during the late 1990's. Writing anything about 'them,' I am very conscious that I get to be an 'I,' and have the power to be an 'I'—publicly using my first and last name. I can be out in the world, speed in my car, pay my taxes late(ish!), protest in the street, and never be afraid that I will be incarcerated or deported. This piece is told from the limited and partial stance of power, safety, and privilege as a middle-class, white, US citizen. My hope is that, somehow, through these words, a greater awareness is created of how precarious, exhausting, and dangerous it can feel—then and now—to be a person who is an immigrant or an asylum seeker in this country. More importantly however, I want to stress the essence of goodness inherent in each person, the want to connect, and the need to give and to receive from each other the sacred gifts of belonging and gentleness."

Born in San Jose, CA, while it was still the Valley of the Heart's Delight, and once more a current proud resident, Myers supports her meandering writing journey as a bilingual psychotherapist in private practice. Myers holds degrees from the University of San Francisco and Santa Clara University. After graduating with Sociology and English writing degrees from USF, Myers headed to Dallas, TX to do legal aide work with refugees as a Jesuit volunteer. She then escaped the US to Sao Paulo, Brazil, for four years, volunteering in support of women and girls. Myers was fortunate enough to learn of social justice, human rights, and mysticism in her early spiritual formation, and she still has hope for the loving transformation of this world. Like her paternal grandfather, she loves birds and walking the hills. Unlike her grandfather, she loves salsa and Afro-Brazilian music, movement, and dance. Myers credits the wise, wild women of her Friday morning writing group with giving her the courage to reveal her writing to the public.

Kurt Newton *Distances*

"At the time I wrote this story, my daughters were very young. I remember we were all at the beach one day and I caught a glimpse of my wife looking at our daughters in a wistful way as they played in the sand, and I wondered if my wife had any regrets. The idea for *Distances* sprang from that moment. *Distances* explores the idea of a do over, a second chance at life. What would we change? And if we could change things, would that change be necessarily for the better?"

Kurt Newton's fiction has appeared in numerous publications including *Descansos: Words from the Wayside*; *Weird Tales: The 21st Century, Vol. 1*; *Year's Best Body Horror 2017*, and *Year's Best Transhuman SF 2017*. He is a lifelong resident of Connecticut.

James Penha *Tiger Hill's Thousand-Man Rock: Two Etymologies*

"A visit to the picturesque canal town of Suzhou, China, is incomplete without a stop at Tiger Hill where a poet can envision the competing legends one hears as to why the great plaza at the base of the hill is called Thousand Man Rock."

A native New Yorker, James Penha has lived for the past quarter-century in Indonesia. Nominated for Pushcart Prizes in fiction and poetry, his LGBTQ+ stories appear in the 2017 and 2018 anthologies of both the Saints & Sinners Literary Festival and the Seattle Erotic Arts Festival, while his dystopian poem *2020* is part of the 2017 *Not My President* anthology. His essay *It's Been a Long Time Coming* was featured in *The New York Times* "Modern Love" column in April 2016. Penha edits *TheNewVerse.News*, an online journal of current-events poetry.

Charlotte Porter *Foundling*

"My story, *Foundling*, explores an esthetic I call Ur-realism, a hyper reality with primordial roots in place. I like to ponder the role of responsibility in a world of happenstance, coincidence, and slips of the tongue. And, yes, my pets are strays."

Charlotte M. Porter, published poet and award-winning short fiction writer, lives in an old citrus hamlet in north central Florida. Enjoy her novella, *Agnes Person*, currently serialized by Visitant Lit.

Gabriella T. Rieger *Binate; Solastalgia*

"Globalization and environmental change have drastic effects on the world we once knew. New York City has undergone radical social and economic changes, which impact its infrastructure, architecture and social life. With a faded love in the backdrop, *Solastalgia* appreciates what is threatened but still here: tractors of midwestern farms, subways strained by Hurricane Sandy and rapid population growth, and restaurants despite real estate development.

"*Binate* was a letter to a friend. At the time I lived in the Negev Desert, in a city frequently plagued by rockets. For work, I traveled north to the center of the country. Once a week, I took the train all the way to Haifa, the port city of the North, where I studied psychological aspects of intergroup relations. During this time, my friend Yousef from Kuwait and Queens, emailed to ask me about Israel; he'd never been, but both his parents were born in Palestine, in the North."

Gabriella T. Rieger has a Master's degree in Creative Writing from Bar-Ilan University. She studied at the Bowery Poetry Club, the St. Marks Poetry Project, and Naropa's Summer Writing Program. Her work has appeared in the *Bowery Women Anthology*, *The Ilanot Review*, and *Yew*. A native New Yorker, the five boroughs are her eternal home.

Rikki Santer *Wardrobe Conditional*

"The poem was ignited in the intersection of my thinking about the conditional mood of verbs and then later that day witnessing that hawk's actions across the street. That night, *Wardrobe Conditional* woke me up in fragments and came through."

Rikki Santer's work has appeared in various publications including *Ms. Magazine*, *Poetry East*, *Margie*, *Slab*, *Crab Orchard Review*, *RHINO*, *Grimm*, *Slipstream*, *Midwest Review* and *The Main Street Rag*. Her fifth poetry collection, *Make Me That Happy*, was published recently by NightBallet Press.

Nancy Scott *1956*

"I met this Hungarian student when I was a student at Stanford in 1960. I came across the artist, Magda Ban, decades later, and that particular painting entitled *1956* was haunting."

Nancy Scott, managing editor of *U.S. 1 Worksheets* for more than a decade, is also the author of nine books of poetry, as well as a novella, *Marriage by Fire* (Big Table Publishing Company, 2018). The poems in *Running Down Broken Cement* (Main Street Rag, 2014) were inspired and informed by a long career as a social worker responding to allegations of child abuse and neglect and helping homeless families find permanent housing in the community. www.nancyscott.net.

Max Sparber *Grandmaster Clint Eastwood's Tour of Holy Places*

"*Grandmaster Clint Eastwood's Tour of Holy Places* probably came out of living in both New Orleans and Los Angeles for a while. New Orleans has a very strong, often mythic, sense of its own history. I used to hear tour groups going by my apartment all the time, telling stories of the history of the French Quarter, some of them true, some fanciful. In the meanwhile, as much as Hollywood is associated with the film industry and tries to capitalize on that, the place itself is almost willfully ignorant of its own history. I lived in a building that had once been inhabited by Bing Crosby, and where the Go-Go's had formed and rehearsed in the basement, and nobody knew this. I often found myself wandering around the neighborhood declaring places to be historic, and this felt a little like the Europeans mystics who wandered around Jerusalem, just declaring places to be holy. This somehow fomented in my head into this story."

Max Sparber is an author and journalist in Minneapolis. His writing has been published in *Strange Horizons* and as part of the anthology *People of the Book: A Decade of Jewish Science Fiction and Fantasy*.

Caroline Taylor *Creature of Habit*

"The genesis for *Creature of Habit* is the dilemma currently facing DACA immigrants. If they are deported to a country they've never known, where many of them lack fluency in the native language, how soon will they become victimized? I wondered what an illegal immigrant would do if faced with that prospect. Wouldn't they try to hide? If so, where would they go? This story is based on the idea that it might be possible to seek sanctuary in the home of somebody who is so much a 'creature of habit' they would never notice the person's presence—until the water bill comes due."

Caroline Taylor is the author of three mystery novels—*Loose Ends*, *Jewelry from a Grave*, and *What Are Friends For?*—one nonfiction book, *Publishing the Nonprofit Annual Report: Tips, Traps, and Tricks of the Trade*, and a short-story collection: *Enough! Thirty Stories of Fielding Life's Little Curve Balls*. Visit her at www.carolinestories.com

Jennifer Stuart *The Other Side; House for Girls*

"Border crossings evoke strong imagery and are natural lightning-rod moments in stories, since so much is often at stake. As an immigration attorney, I've heard more stories of US border crossings than I can remember. Yet, I'm continually amazed and fascinated at what people leave behind and endure when they cross the border. As I presented Florencia as a character in *The Other Side*, I also wanted to introduce the complexity of the risks and the decisions that led to this moment, which kicks off a novel.

Fictional stories of human trafficking often end with a rescue or escape, the physical separation of victims from their persecutors. But my real-life work with individual survivors of human trafficking never ended there. The survivors I worked with struggled to overcome the effects of victimization for years, and their fear never vanished completely when the trafficking ended, but rather very gradually, if at all. I wanted *House for Girls* to put a spotlight on the long-lasting effects of victimization, and to reveal shelter as the beginning, not the end, of a long healing process."

Jennifer Stuart is an attorney in Raleigh, North Carolina. She always wanted to be a writer, but she procrastinated for a long time by going to law school and practicing immigration law for more than a decade, among other ways. Her fiction has been published in *Brilliant Flash Fiction* as the second place winner in an international contest. The two works featured here are parts of a novel in progress about human trafficking.

Emily Vizzo *However Deep the Glass*

"I wrote *However Deep the Glass* as an exploration of the physicality of sadness; that, and the challenge of loving those parts of yourself that are hard to love but need you — even if the need relates only to the hope of an eventual healing. Suffering can be dogged; so too can healing."

Emily Vizzo is a writer working in California. Her work has appeared or will appear in *Ninth Letter, FIELD, North American Review, The Normal School, Blackbird, jubilat, Cincinnati Review,* and elsewhere. She was selected for *Best New Poets 2015,* and had an essay noted in *Best American Essays 2013.* Poems were nominated for Best of the Net in 2015, 2016, and 2017. She is active in the literary community, having volunteered with VIDA, Writers Resist LA, Drunken Boat, Hunger Mountain, and Poetic Youth. Her chapbook, *GIANTESS,* is forthcoming from YesYes Books in 2018.

Bernardine (Dine) Watson *Ritual*

"I began writing *Ritual* while reflecting on a faltering friendship. By the time I finished writing, I understood that my friend and I would always be connected."

Bernardine (Dine) Watson is a writer living in Washington, DC. For many years, she wrote social policy reports and articles for major non-profit groups, foundations, and news organizations, including the *Washington Post.* Dine began writing poetry seriously about a decade ago and has been published by the *Beltway Poetry Quarterly, These Fragile Lilacs Poetry Journal,* and the DC Humanities Council. She performs her poetry with More Than A Drum Percussion Ensemble, and teaches poetry writing to adolescent girls at Arts for Our Children, a nonprofit organization in Washington, DC.

Sarah Brown Weitzman *In Rooms*

Sarah Brown Weitzman, a past National Endowment for the Arts Fellow in Poetry, has had work in hundreds of journals and anthologies including *Rosebud, The New Ohio Review, Poet & Critic, The North American Review, Bellingham Review, Rattler, <id-American Review, The MacGuffin, Poet Lore, Spillway,* and *Miramar.* Pudding House published her chapbook, *The Forbidden.*

Sarah has chosen to let her poem speak for itself.

Michele Wojcicki *Art Director*

Michele Wojcicki is a graduate of Yale University. She has worked in design (graphics and textiles) since the late 1980s. Most of her career was spent in New York City; in 2006 she relocated to Arizona to be Art Director of a small textile company. In 2010 she founded her own agency (type4udesign.com). She is now semi-retired.

Ariadne Wolf *Getting Away Safe*

"I've been thinking hard this year to try to understand how to use my position as a Jewish woman to aid the Palestinian struggle, which has increasingly become a struggle not for territory, but for survival. My insistence upon the humanity of the Palestinian people and the legitimacy of their struggle dovetails with my search for support for my own liberation from the patriarchal norms I learned growing up. I was raised in a conservative Jewish synagogue that taught support for Israel alongside belief in the sexist tropes of the Torah, the Old Testament. Yet my parents' ideology taught me that I deserve equal treatment in public and private spheres, even though my parents themselves did not always practice this. That same open-minded and compassionate perspective convinces me that a safe and sane Middle East must recognize the rights of the Palestinians who became refugees on the same day Israel was granted independence. I truly believe we can coexist in harmony, that this is the only way forward for humanity; I also believe that real peace also requires real justice, and that cannot be achieved without real change, in our ideas and our beliefs, in our hearts and in our minds. Those people out there are not the problem; *I* am the problem, and those like me, who were complacent in the face of horror done in our name. To be on the side of justice, I must seek redemption for my years of complacency. Essays like this one are my way of trying to accomplish that."

Ariadne Wolf's emphasis tends toward magical realism, feminist fantasy, and mythological reinterpretation combined with a gritty look at life events condemned to the margins of the Western imagination. Ariadne is currently at work on her first book, a speculative memoir entitled *But It Will Hurt*. The memoir explores memory, insanity, ancestral trauma, and the role of fantasy in recovery and survival. In this world, girls are mermaids, mothers are witches, fathers are sympathetic demonic wannabe angels, and normalcy is turned on its head. Wolf will spend her summer in writing residencies at Wellstone in the Redwoods, Alderworks, and Sunpress. Her work has appeared in *Helen*, *Din*, *Plot Number Two*, the anthology *11.9: The Fall of American Democracy*, and elsewhere.

Also Available from Darkhouse Books:
The first book in the *RIFF* series

Descansos
Words From the Wayside

Paperback available via your local bookstore or Amazon.
Ebook available on Kindle, Nook, and Kobo.

Also Available from Darkhouse Books:

Duck Lessons
by James M. LeCuyer

Paperback available via your local bookstore or Amazon.
Ebook available on Kindle, Nook, and Kobo.

Also Available from Darkhouse Books:

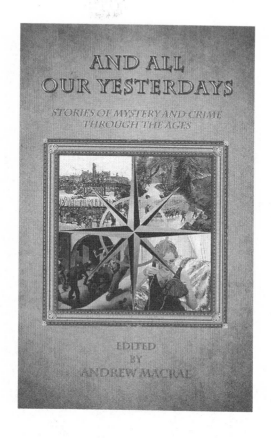

And All Our Yesterdays
Stories of Mystery and Crime Through the Ages

Paperback available via your local bookstore or Amazon.
Ebook available on Kindle, Nook, and Kobo.

Also Available from Darkhouse Books:

Stories From the Near Future

Paperback available via your local bookstore or Amazon.
Ebook available on Kindle, Nook, and Kobo.